THE MISADVENTURES OF BUDDY JONES

A NOVEL

THE MISADVENTURES OF BUDDY JONES

A NOVEL

DAVID MARGOLIS

Uranus Publishing Company | St. Louis, MO

Uranus Publishing Company LLC
St. Louis, MO

Publisher's Note: This is a work of fiction. Any real people or places are used in a purely fictional manner.

Manufactured in the United States of America
Set in Avenir Next and Adobe Garamond Pro
Interior designed by Blank Slate Communications
Cover Design by Blank Slate Communications

ISBN: 978-0-9912154-5-4

To my children, Robyn and Jon

Jim said that bees won't sting idiots, but I didn't
believe that, because I tried them lots of times
myself and they wouldn't sting me.
—Mark Twain, *The Adventures of Huckleberry Finn*

ONE

THAT FIRST MORNING, I sure had a rude awakening. Our twelve-pound mongrel was licking the stubble on my face. Pepper does that when she has to pee real bad. Little did she know she wasn't included on this crazy-assed trip. Dogs never know nothing till the last minute. As I sat up and swung my legs over the bed, the first rays of Missouri sunshine hit me smack in the eyeballs. I squinted through the tiny window above my bed and could just make out the rusted jalopies in the junkyard behind our trailer. I put the leash on Pepper, who by this time was yapping and pawing at the door, which I finally got open with an assist from my shoulder. While she sniffed the weeds and gravel, looking for a prime spot to do her business, I couldn't help but notice that the February sunrise in Middleberg was plumb beautiful that day, owing to the fact that the coal-fired electric plant had belched a whole bunch of black smoke the evening before. My live-in friend Penny was still asleep, so I dropped Pepper off with our landlord, Stu Lumpkin, who was kind enough to take care of the little mutt until we got back.

Penny and I were about to take off to St. Petersburg, Florida with a stop in Atlanta. For the past five years, I'd been disabled with a mule-stubborn back, bad knees, and a clogged heart, so we made our way south for a few weeks each winter, but this trip turned out to be special. You see, my ex, Connie, had called me a few days prior, while I was washing my truck. And believe me, she never called. She told me that our daughter, April, was going to announce something important, and April wanted me to be there in person when she told me. I hadn't seen my only kid since she was eight years old. That's when Connie and I split, and she and April moved to Atlanta.

Anyhow, I let Connie know that me and Penny would be happy to come by and see April on our way to Florida. I left out Connie on the *happy to see* part because I didn't really wanna see *her*, but I didn't say that. I'm glad I didn't call her an insane bitch over the phone even though that's what she was and still is. Why April couldn't've called me and told me herself, I don't know. She didn't have my cell phone number, but she could have got it from Connie. I wasn't in attendance at April's wedding to Jimmy Hotchkiss in 1999 when she'd was only nineteen. Jimmy was on his way to jail so the wedding was kind of rushed, and I didn't get much notice of it, but looking back, I should have been there for my only child. The marriage didn't last long. Jimmy killed a man while he was in the pokey, and the judge tacked on another 25 years to his sentence. April divorced him soon after that.

I hoped we could hitch the trailer to my 2010 Ford F-150, and not have to stay in a hotel, but Stu said he didn't want the trailer moved because it could fall apart on the highway. After living in it for the past three years with Penny, I could appreciate those sentiments. Every time one of them huge dump trucks hauled out down the road—a gravel quarry was pretty near us--the place shook like an earthquake. That got poor Pepper barking until I put her on my lap, or more likely Penny's lap, because the little runt liked her better. Stu had some nerve charging us even 80 dollars a month for that shack, but that's the cheapest place we could afford right then, plus he boarded Pepper for only the cost of her dog food which wasn't much.

The night before we left, Penny and I had one of them humdinger arguments. It all centered around me bringing my gun. Last year someone broke into our trailer park and robbed some people. After that, I went out and purchased an AR-15 at one of those gun shows that's real popular in the great state of Missouri. I hadn't owned a gun since my felony conviction several years back, but I felt kind of good about having a firearm near me at all times. I'm a big Second Amendment guy, always have been, and always will be. I mean we live in a dangerous part of the world. Not just with burglars, but I worry about foreign terrorists, and even worse, our own govermint coming to get me some day. Anyway, I told Penny that I'd like to have some protection this time around, but she couldn't see the need to bring a semiautomatic like that. Finally, after a lot of shouting and carrying on, mostly by Penny I might add, I left it at home. I had to live in a vehicle with this woman for two days, and when I couldn't get the cruise control to work, or the fuzz buster to operate properly, I needed to be on speaking terms with her. I'm sorry to say that this didn't last for the whole trip, but I'm getting ahead of myself.

If you haven't figured it out by now, I'm not a booster of the govermint. Every day except Sunday, Uncle Sam delivers a crap-load of mail that you never need or want: coupons for half-off on Rice Krispies, or Raisin Bran, or tofu, catalogues for lawn furniture and flower pots, and stuff from Victoria's Secret. Okay, sometimes I look at the Victoria's Secret catalogue, but not to buy anything that would look good on Penny. The models in there aren't much older that twenty-one or two, and Penny's pretty mature in the wrong places and even in the right places if you get my drift. And then there's all them bills with *past due* on them. I know to pay them, and I don't need them reminding me.

The only good thing that I get from Uncle Sam is the direct deposit of my Social Security payment into my bank account. Good old Bank of America has a branch on the main street of Middleberg, along with a saloon, a Walgreens, a grocery store, a restaurant, a laundromat, and a bunch of vacant buildings. Come to think of it, they left out one word in the bank title. It should be *Bank of Rich America*. I know they're not for the little guy, but then again what bank is these days? Nope, no more George Baileys around, but then I ain't never seen an angel neither.

At my age, technology has pretty much passed me by. Let me be honest. I don't know a fuck about setting up a GPS location. All I know is it helps me get to where I'm going. I do have a cell phone to text and read emails--one of them cheap Korean models--but I'm pretty much lost if the thing freezes up, or crashes, or won't take my password. When I was a kid, you didn't need a goddamned computer or fancy phone to entertain yourself. You could read the funnies or the sports page from a newspaper that was delivered by a paperboy pulling a rusted red wagon. And there were milkmen who brought milk to your doorstep. I don't remember all those percentages like 2% or 1%. And guess what? All us kids survived on regular goddamned cow's milk.

Penny did the packing and organizing because I never had the patience for that kind of thing. I needed only a couple of tee shirts and a pair of blue jeans, but Penny had my only suit cleaned seeing as we were to visit Connie and April, and Connie's husband who I'd never met. I don't wear fancy clothes because we're pretty casual at the church where I attend, and even at that, I don't attend as often as I should. That's not saying I'm not a believer in Jesus Christ, it's just that I like to get to the bar early and get a good seat before NFL football begins. I'm usually good for three games on a Sunday. That pretty much eliminates church in the fall, and as I said before, we aren't in town for part of the winter.

I like to do all the driving. It's kind of a macho thing with me. There's some road hogs out there on the highway, but with my truck, they think twice before messing with me. I like to drive fast, with my fuzz buster plastered to the front window. Some might call it tailgating, but I like to get behind some rich bastard driving a Lexus or a Mercedes, and just drive up his ass, if you know what I mean. Before that, I had an old Chevy Malibu with one hundred and fifty thousand miles on it. But what the heck, I went into more debt when I bought it. I mean I was never going to get out of the hole without owing somebody something. I've always said, *live life while you can with a vehicle that you can't afford*. Penny put up the money for the down payment which I didn't have at the time. I had my *Trump-Pence* sticker on the rear bumper along with an old *Nobama* one, at least I don't have any rebel flags on the corners of the tailgate. Penny told me that I'd be looking for trouble if I did that and she was probably right, but I would've loved to see the looks on those hotsy-totsy horseshit hypocrites when I breezed past them with the *stars and bars* flying flat out. Now I hope all that's behind me, and the fact that I drive sober has helped with that.

When we crossed the Mississippi River into Illinois, I became a little nervous. I was glad I had a full tank of gas, because you don't want to stop in East St. Louis, if you can help it. Most of the black folk that live there are on food stamps. I mean if they didn't get handouts they'd have to go and get a job. No, I'm not a racist, that's just the plain truth. Sure, I was on food stamps myself when I'd been out of work, but that was different.

We trucked on to Marion where they have that big maximum-security prison. I had a second cousin, Milt Gowdy, who was sent there. When he got out about ten years later, old Milt wasn't the same man I remembered. I saw him over at my uncle's house one time. He never said much, just stared ahead and squeezed a tennis ball between his left and right fists, with his jaw kind of clenched. He mostly kept silent except for using the f-word. Soon after, he moved to Texas, and killed a man in a robbery. I got to admit, we have more than our share of criminals and ex-criminals in the family.

After passing through Metropolis IL, Superman's home town, Penny started to nag me about needing to use the restroom even though the gas gauge showed three-eighths of a tank. If she hadn't been guzzling that Big Gulp from the 7-Eleven that she bought while I was filling up in Middleberg, we'd have made it further, and fuck, the truck only gets fifteen miles to the gallon. I pulled into one of them fancy stations just off the Interstate. You know, the ones with about ten aisles of candy, nuts, and beef jerky. There were sweat shirts on sale with the logo of the University of Illinois football team that haven't won their conference in over 30 years. After I filled up, I went in and got a Snickers bar and a cup of coffee while Penny relieved herself.

Just then, I saw two women wearing some headgear, and my antennae shot up like a red ant after a crumb. I'm behind these two in line and I figure they're from Somalia or maybe down in Yemen the Lemon. I'm not shy when it comes to strangers, particularly foreign strangers, but I tried to keep myself from saying something that would've embarrassed Penny who was now standing next to me with another big soda and a package of chips. She's not so thin herself. She's pre-diabetic with a bad hip, but she thinks that goddamned Web MD gives her some license to be an expert in medicine. Nowhere on any website is a bag of barbecue potato chips recommended for your health, but she don't nag herself when it comes to her own cravings.

The women came back toward us after paying their bill. I started talking real loud about President Trump, and how he's going to have a travel ban in place to keep us safe from the radical Islams. I figured this would shake them up plenty good. If they can't dress like us, then in my book, they don't belong here. Then I noticed that they had crosses hanging from their necks. Penny, who used to be a Catholic, said "Good morning sisters."

"Have a blessed day," they said. Go figure. But hey, it's easy for any red-blooded American to jump to the wrong conclusion.

TWO

WE MADE IT THROUGH Illinois despite all of the police vehicles hiding in the culverts. It's my belief that they don't like pickup trucks in that state. Christ, the fuzz buster was buzzing like a chain saw trapped in a woodpile. We crossed the Ohio River into the western edge of Kentucky. At that point the river is as wide as the Mississippi. First thing we saw in Kentucky was a billboard for Jim Beam bourbon--Missouri's not known for its production of whiskey, just for the drinking of it. I started to smile as I listened to Toby Keith's *Courtesy of the Red, White and Blue* on the country music station that Penny located. Soon I'm singing at the top of my lungs, *we'll put a boot in your ass, it's the American way.*

We stopped at a Waffle House for lunch, just outside of Paducah, Kentucky. You can tell you're entering the south by the number of Waffle Houses along the highway. I'll eat waffles anytime, with an extra order of link sausages piled high on my plate, damn the cholesterol. There weren't any free booths, so Penny and I sat at the counter. I was a lot bulkier then and I had to take a deep breath to squeeze my size 44 waist between the counter and the stool. I'm one of them hombres that likes to wear his jeans kinda low with my belly hanging out over the belt buckle.

The waitress came over. She was a bit past her prime, but I immediately fixated on her chest. Most males will attest to the fact that when you see some big knockers, your eyes just find their way there, kind of like radar. I was also looking sideways at Penny to see if she saw me staring, but she was busy studying the menu. When we first got together, I used to whistle or say *wow* at a good-looking female, but I soon learned that Penny doesn't like that, so I don't make any comments while I'm gawking. I do know this. As you get older, the time spent admiring tits goes down. That's part of the aging process that doctors never mention. Nowadays, I probably spend as much time in a restaurant looking for the pathway to a toilet as I do about any woman's body parts. It turned out she wasn't going to be our waitress, she just gave us our menus. Then some skinny little gal showed up, just as perky as all get out, with that sugary southern accent.

"Y'all know what you want to order?"

"I sure do sweetie. I'll take the All-Star Special with waffles, eggs, and extra sausage, and bring me a large cup of coffee as soon as you can. Oh, and I'll have a toasted English muffin if you have one."

It turned out she was addressing Penny. The *y'all* didn't include me. She looked over at me and smiled, but there was a kind of a scolding look in her eyes. She was probably thinking what a rude dumbass I was, and she might have been right, but she doesn't know how slow Penny is in the ordering department. She studies the menu like she might find the gluten free oatmeal there, or some other sissy thing such as yogurt or a spinach salad, but nine times out of ten, she doesn't order it. Finally, she decided on the blueberry waffles and a Diet Coke. I repeated my order but left out the sweetie part. She wasn't going to be my *sweetie* with that attitude.

We're sitting at the counter, sipping the coffee and waiting for our food, when a big black fella plunks down beside us in the one open stool next to me. Now right off the bat, I'm wary of this dude. No, not what you might think. I repeat what I said before. *No prejudice in old Buddy Jones' bones.* But this gent was wider than a bulldozer, with thighs like tree trunks, bigger around than most people's waists, not mine, but most people's. He had this big round face with a salt and pepper goatee. His nose was broad with nostrils like woodpecker holes in a black cherry tree.

At this point, busty came over, and it's pretty clear that this guy was a local. They started to talking, and I can't help listening while my eyes wandered back to her cleavage. I'd got nothing to say to Penny right then, so I just kept quiet. Penny and I'd been together long enough that if I got something to say to her, I'd already said it. You ever notice a couple when they're courting? They're laughing, smiling, and talking, not like the people who've lived with each other for a while. Those folks just sit there, kind of glum. Seems that the food they're eating is more interesting to them than each other. They'd heard all the jokes from their partner more than once, and they probably weren't too funny the first time around.

This guy kept yakking and rubbing his thigh against my pants. Fortunately, he didn't smell bad. That's one thing I don't like. I've used the Mennen Speed Stick for over fifty years. It's great for men who tend to stink pretty bad, and I kinda put myself in that category, plus I sweat a lot. If I don't take a shower that day, I just put on more. Anyhow, you can't believe what they're talking about—history, goddamned history. It turns out that this gent was a Civil War buff. He's on his way to Chattanooga to visit some old battlefield.

To tell the truth, I don't know much about the Civil War. I learned just enough to know that the South didn't win. Nowadays, it's not politically correct to feel bad about that, but down in Middleberg, some of them fellas--friends of mine from the Red Parrot Saloon--are still kind of pulling for the South, like the Chicago Cubs before they won the World Series. Randy Belcher, the leader of the group, told me that Lincoln overstepped his bounds, and each state had a right to keep slavery if they wanted to, and it would have died out on its own. He said the slaves weren't ready to be freed. I'm willing to treat every man like an equal as long as he isn't trying to take food off my table, or use my tax dollars for welfare, or take my girlfriend away. I regret thinking about it now, but there were some days when they could've taken Penny away, as long as she came back to wash my clothes and cook me a meal.

Suddenly, the big guy turns to me and says, "Can you please pass the sugar sir?" I reached over Penny to locate a glass container filled with sugar.

"You don't see much of 'em no more," I said. "Seems like they mostly use them packets nowadays." I slid it over to him.

"I like a lot of sugar in my coffee, one little packet won't do the job, no sir. Sometimes that's all they give you."

"Yeah, you're right on that."

"Hey, I hope you didn't mind me talking about all that history stuff?"

"Nope. You sound like you're a real expert on the Civil War."

"Well not really, it's just a hobby. How 'bout yourself?"

"Not too much, I warn't the best student in high school." I spent twelve years at it and only got to the tenth grade. If I wasn't sleeping, I sat at the back of the class and made all sorts of animal noises, fake farts and some real ones. I flicked rubber bands and shot spit balls at the other kids, particularly some of the better students, to get a laugh from the guys in the back with me. I was the kind of student—*student* might be overstating my presence there--that the teachers pretty much hated. But I never saw my Daddy, or my Mom for that matter, ever pick up a book to read, except maybe the Bible from time to time, when things got bad around the house. Nobody told me learning history would get me anywhere where I wanted to go in life, but to tell the truth, that didn't come up too much, *the where I wanted to go in life* thing.

"I wasn't much of a student until I was a junior in high school," he said. "We took a bus tour to the battlefields around Atlanta. I sorta got hooked on it after that."

Just then, the waitress arrived with our meal. I dug into the sausages. I like mine nice and rubbery. When you cut into them, the grease should squirt out like a leak in a high-pressure hose. Penny knew to pass the ketchup, and I smothered them little critters under a big slug of Heinz's finest. Then I attended to the sunny side-up eggs, jiggling on the plate next to the stack of waffles. I separated the waffles from the rest of the food and dumped a load of maple syrup on them. This takes a bit of practice, so you don't get the syrup mixed in with the ketchup and the egg yolk. Along with these important operations, I was busy passing the salt and pepper back and forth with Penny. Suddenly, Big Boy piped up again.

"My name's Floyd, Floyd Washington."

"Washington eh, no relation to George, I guess."

"No sirree," he chuckled. "You ever meet a white man with that name?" He talked in that gravelly Louie Armstrong voice, kind of like a loud whisper, like something don't work quite right in his voice box. He pushed it up from his gut.

"Cain't say I have," I answered. I turned back to my food. With the help of Penny's toast, I sopped up some of the yolk where the eggs had been. She doesn't like it when I take food off her plate, but I'd wolfed down my muffin, and the egg yolk was heading toward the maple syrup pretty fast.

"You live around here?" Floyd asked.

"Nope."

"Where you from?"

"Missourah." That's what us natives call Missouri. Not the people that live in St. Louis, but the rest of us.

"St. Louie?" Nobody calls it St. Louie neither.

"No south, in Middleberg."

"Never heard of it."

"Well you wouldn't. It's a pretty small place." Christ, I was trying to finish my friggin breakfast and this man was crowding me off my stool with them telephone posts for legs. The last thing I need to hear is his bullshit. I pulled out my credit card and waved it, trying to get the waitress to come over and take it.

"Hey, maybe I want a refill on my soda," Penny said.

Well thanks, Penny. Maybe we'll get to Atlanta by Christmas.

"So what line of work are you in?" Floyd asked.

"Don't work no more. The old ticker gave out a few years back."

"Yeah, I've had some heart trouble too. Had some stents placed. Doc told me to lay off the high fat, but here I am at the Waffle House eating bad things."

"I reckon I shouldn't be here neither."

"I didn't catch your name."

"Buddy."

I looked over to Penny hoping that she was done with her Coke so we could go, but now she'd pulled out a crossword puzzle from the St. Louis Post Dispatch that she'd brought on the trip. She didn't want to leave, and she didn't care to talk to me, so I'm stuck gabbing to a big black bear that I don't want to gab to.

"Buddy Jones." I stuck out my hand and he shook it. Even his hand was overweight, like a chocolate éclair.

"Well Buddy. Where ya off to?"

"We're on the way to Floreeda." I dunno why, but I like to say Floreeda. "Before that, we'll spend some time in Atlanta."

"Well whaddya know? I grew up in Atlanta. Moved to Paducah when I was in my mid-twenties."

"Oh."

"Tomorrow, I'll be going in that direction myself, to visit the grave of my great-great-grandfather, Ebenezer. He was a slave to a Confederate lieutenant at the Battle of Chickamauga. He ran away to Chattanooga during the battle and joined the Northern army. He was in the 44th US Colored Infantry and fought in the Battle of Nashville when the Union whipped the Confederate General, John Bell Hood."

"You don't say."

"He lived in Chattanooga till he died, worked as a blacksmith all his life. He's buried in an old black cemetery. I found it five years ago."

"Yeah, I heard you talkin' to the waitress 'bout that." *Shit, I don't need to hear it again.*

"I found his name in a registry of Confederate soldiers. Being a slave, he didn't have a last name, but I found an Ebenezer Washington as a private in the 44th. I'm pretty sure it's one and the same person. When he got freed, he took the surname of Washington. A lot of the slaves did that."

"Did what?" I was trying to open a little package of grape jelly to smear on the last piece of Penny's toast. That's hard to do without reading glasses.

"Took the last name of Washington. Some slaves took the last names of their masters, but I guess Ebenezer didn't want that, seeing as he'd run away. He'd have been 175 years old this week, according to my estimate."

"So, is she also a Civil War buff?"

"Who?"

"The waitress."

"Gloria?"

"Yeah." Now I know that the buxom gal's name is Gloria.

"I don't think so. She's worked here four or five years. She listens to my stories and doesn't seem to get bored, or so she tells me." He grunted a bunch of times which I came to know was his way of laughing. "You know that slaves weren't allowed to do any actual fighting. They worked as cooks or stable men or stacked the cannon balls for the artillery. Ol' Ebenezer might have helped his master with his horses. And they had one other important job." He waited for me to ask what it was, but I don't say anything. No sense giving him any encouragement. "They did most of the burying of the Confederate dead."

"Oh yeah?"

"But you know, they fought like hell when they joined the Union army. When General George Thomas saw the carnage of the black infantries lying on the battlefield at Nashville, he told his staff, "The question is settled, the Negroes will fight."

Just then Gloria come up, all smiles. I can see she liked big Floyd. "Punkin', can I get you anything else? We just put on a fresh cup of coffee."

"Sure thing, I'll take another cup before I shove off."

"By the way, how's Helen doing?" she asked.

"She's coming along just fine, but that new hip is still pretty painful. She'll be laid up at home for a few more weeks, so I'll be making this trip myself." Floyd looked over at me. "Gloria, this is Buddy Jones from Missouri and his wife, I didn't catch her name."

"My name's Penny. We're not married."

"Good to meet you, Gloria," I said real nice-like. "You guys do a great job. The waffles were A-1 and the eggs were cooked just right." I handed her the credit card, it's in Penny's name. After my last bankruptcy, I can't get a card.

"Well, thanks. We always appreciate a satisfied customer," answered Gloria. Penny threw me a dirty look. For the first time, she'd noticed that my gaze was a little lower than Gloria's face.

"We got to be shoving off, don't we Penny? We got a long trip in front of us."

THREE

THE HEART ATTACK hit me five years back. At first it felt like indigestion. I had eaten a big old T-bone the night before. You know, the sixteen-ounce size, smothered in mushrooms with a big mound of fried onion rings. Dickie's Roadhouse Grill in Middleberg is a pretty good place to eat if you haven't been there. I popped a few Alker-Seltzers. That was all I had. During the night the pain got worse, and I thought maybe I had pleurisy. I woke up Frankie, my lady friend at the time, to go out and get me some Vicks VapoRub, but she refused. Instead, she took me to the hospital. But while I was in there, she went back to her husband. I got no idea why.

In the emergency room, they put me into one of those sissy gowns with my ass hanging out. Then they hooked me up to an EKG machine. I guess the ER doctor didn't like what he saw so he called in Doc Haqq who'd I'd never met before. I don't much like doctors and have avoided them most of my life. The next thing I knew, they had me on the operating table. Doc Haqq put three stents in, and I went home two days later. The nurses told me if I'd waited any longer at home, I might have died. Doc said that the aspirin in the Alker-Seltzer saved my life, but it was just luck that I took it. I mostly keep it around for hangovers that I get from time to time.

When I first met Doc Haqq, I knew he was foreign. Down in Middleberg, we don't have any white doctors. We mostly get them from other countries. I found out later that his first name was Mohamed, so I guess he must be a Muslim although I never asked him. He's from Pakistan. You know, where they have sharia law and all that. They'll cut off a man's hand for stealing, and his balls for illegal fornicating. Christ, I would've have lost my arms and the crown jewels a long time ago if that was the law here. I've got to admit, Doc Haqq is a great doctor and a pretty nice son of a bitch. I give him more credit for saving my life than the Alker-Seltzer.

The hospital bill was a whopper, and I had to declare bankruptcy for the second time. I had no health insurance because Billy MacConkey was too cheap to offer it to his employees at the grocery store. There wasn't Obamacare then, but dang it, that's more govermint control over your pocketbook. When I got them bills from the hospital, I just ignored them until they sued me. Hey, hardly anyone in Middleberg paid their hospital bill in those days. I mean half the people were unemployed after the lead smelter shut down and Chrysler moved the minivan assembly line to Canada. After I got my disability, I was entitled to Medicare which worked out pretty good. Now I can go to any doctor without having to worry.

The bank took my house away, and my Uncle Waldo was nice enough to let me sleep on his living room couch for almost six months. I met Penny filling my prescriptions at Walgreens. She hadn't been with a man for quite some time. Her two daughters lived in Arizona and she was pretty lonely living in that old trailer, and let's face it, she wasn't Miss America. I told her off-color jokes while my prescriptions were getting filled. She found them real funny. Not long after that, I moved in with her. Over the years, I've had quite a way with the opposite sex when I put my mind to it.

Before we left on the trip, Doc told me that some of my liver tests were off. I was growing a small pair of tits and the you-know-what was softer that I would like it to be on the occasions where I'm called on to perform you-know-what. He said that could be a sign of liver disease and that wasn't good. I mean they don't call it a liver for nothing. It's not called a dier, if I could make up a word. I swore off the Jack Daniel's Tennessee Whiskey—you can't call it bourbon unless it's made in Kentucky—before we started out. I was drinking mostly beer and I'd cut down on that too. Penny harped on me that beer was just as bad as whiskey. She read about that on goddamned WebMD.

I cut back on my cigarettes too. I was down to a half a pack a day. It seems there's less and less smokers in the world and that's a shame, because by and large we're honest people who pay all that tax to the govermint for those little sticks. Shit, even some bars are smoke-free these days. Come on, how can you have a beer without a long drag filling your lungs? For some reason, actors in the movies still smoke. I guess those candy-assed liberal producers still think it's sexy to have a cigarette dangling from some left-wing faggot's mouth.

Penny and I don't have much savings, in fact, we only have eight hundred dollars for a rainy day. I don't spend money on myself except for my fishing gear and an HDTV that I bought last year with Penny's help. I own about 25 rods and tons of lures. And the funny thing, I don't like to fish all that much. When I'm out in the middle of a quiet lake on a hot day, I'd get a hankering for six or eight cold frosty Budweiser's. When Doc told me to cut back on the hooch, then the fishing wasn't so great like it was before.

Penny forgets that there's payments on the truck, rent on the trailer, and propane for the gas heater every month. She'll end up buying those Precious Moments and other knick-knacks that she doesn't need. You know, stupid statues of smiley dogs, a turtle with a party hat, and silly-assed cupcakes. You pay 40 bucks for some little boy proposing to a little girl. Now that doesn't make sense to me, spending hard earned cash on shit like that. And she spoils her grandkids rotten at Christmas, it seems like the less we have, the more Penny spends. She gets together with her rich sisters, and she doesn't want to look cheap, so she buys all them expensive gifts for her nieces and nephews. They probably never look at the crap once they take it out the box, except maybe the PlayStation stuff. Kids really like that, particularly boys.

I would've liked to go back to work at the grocery store, but after the heart went on the blink, I just wasn't able to lift all those cases of peanut butter and ketchup any more. If I was good with numbers, I could have maybe worked the checkout counter, but Billy MacConkey, the owner, told me to forget it after he asked me if I knew my multiplication tables which I didn't, at least not after six. But what did that have to do with operating the cash register?

FOUR

WE GOT BACK in the truck. I rummaged in the back seat for some peanuts, I just love salted peanuts. Ever eat an unsalted peanut? They got no taste. Mind as well eat a piece of raw celery or a stale carrot. Screw Doc Haqq's low salt diet, I'm on vacation.

I turned the key to start the truck. Nothing happened. I pumped the gas, I don't know why, but most everyone does that when their car don't start. I turned the key a bunch more times, click, click, click. The truck was dead as a fucking door nail. I looked at Penny and shrugged my shoulders.

"Let me try," she said, like I'm turning the key wrong. I got out and she settled behind the wheel. It didn't do any better with her. I guess she didn't know how stupid she looked, but that's a woman for ya.

"Didn't we just put a new battery in?" she asked.

"Yeah, 'bout three weeks ago. That's why when the battery light came on last week, I didn't do nuthin about it. I figured it was a faulty light."

"You saw a light come on and you didn't do nothing about it?" She was getting her snoot in a snit. I knew right then that I'd made a mistake telling her about the light.

"Oh shit, those lights come on all the time. They usually don't mean nuthin. You know that."

"Jesus Christ, Buddy. *I don't know that.*"

"Well I do, and I'm the driver here." As far as I'm concerned that ends the conversation.

"Where's our triple A card?" She asked.

"Triple A card?"

"The card, stupid, so we can call someone, and have the truck jump-started."

"I threw away the bill last year. We never needed it. In Middleberg I just call Phil over at the Shell station. We don't have 75 bucks a year for that, and by the way, don't call me *stupid*." Now she's really hot.

"You're right, you're not stupid. You're just a damned asshole!" There's nothing more dislikable in a woman as when she starts to swear for no reason. I got out, slammed the door, and headed back into the restaurant. Floyd was still there, chatting it up with Gloria. *Shit, don't these people work?* I'm not in a good mood after all what happened, and I don't want to deal with someone like Floyd. But who the fuck else do I know in Paducah?

"Wouldn't you know it? My truck's dead."

"What's wrong with it?" he asked. *If I knew what was wrong with it, I wouldn't be coming back in here to tell him about it, would I?*

"Dead as a doornail. It won't start."

"Battery?"

"I just got a new one put in a few weeks ago."

"Oh, then it must be the alternator. Did a warning light come on over the past few days?"

"Nope, no warnin' at all."

"Well, let me call Elmer's Auto Repair. Someone'll come out to get you jump-started."

"Maybe they gave me a faulty battery."

"Could be."

Penny came in and Gloria gave us both a free cup of coffee. Penny tried to be polite, but she never looked at me, so I knew she was still mad.

"I've got to be going, Buddy," Floyd announced after he got off the phone. "Elmer said he'd send someone out in about fifteen minutes. Here's my card if you need to get in touch with me. I own an exterminator company here in town."

"A bug killer eh?" *Shit, the only pest control I needed right then was someone to take care of Penny.*

I went outside and waited for the tow truck by myself. I didn't wanna hear no more from her. About 45 minutes later, some pimply squirt from the auto place showed up. He looked too young to be a babysitter never mind an auto mechanic. Penny came over as I was explaining the problem.

"It's probably the alternator. I'll give you a jump-start. You say the battery was just put in?"

"Yep." *Shit kid, weren't you listening?*

After he got the truck started, he said. "Turn on your lights." I turned them on.

"Yeah, the lights are flickering, got to be the alternator. I wouldn't drive that car anywhere until we put in a new one."

"When can you do that?" Penny butted in. I don't know why she can't let me handle it.

"Probably not 'till Wednesday. We're pretty busy even if we get the part by tomorrow."

"I guess we're stuck here 'til then," Penny said.

"There's the Dew Drop Inn just down the road from the repair shop. You get a free breakfast." The little prick had all the answers. Penny and I followed him in the truck to the auto place, then he drove us over to the motel.

The fella at the desk was one of them overweight Mexicans with a crew cut. He'd got them little ears without any earlobes.

"How many nights, sir?"

"Just one night," I responded.

"Two," piped up Penny, "the man said it would take two days to fix it." *Goddamn it. Can't she let me handle it.*

He looked at Penny and started talking to her as if I'd disappeared. "A king or two queen beds ma'am?"

"Two queens will be fine." No surprise there. "And a non-smoking room, please."

"We're a non-smoking hotel, ma'am." He pronounced ma'am like maum. "There's a free breakfast starting at 6:30. How many card keys do you need?"

"Two," answered Penny.

"We only need one," I said. "Is the Wi-Fi free?"

"We don't really need it Buddy. We didn't bring a laptop and our phones are on 4G." He handed her two room cards, and we hauled our suitcases up to the second floor. The room had a faint smell of tobacco smoke. Don't kid yerself, people smoke in those rooms. I plunked down on the bed and began scrolling the TV looking for ESPN. I found a demolition derby and watched it for a while. Then I fell asleep.

When I woke up, Penny was gone but that wasn't unusual. There was a women's softball tournament on the TV, so I switched to Fox News. Let me come clean right off the bat, and if you're a liberal you might not like what I have to say, but I don't much care for the lefty news that you see on TV such as CNN or freeloading PBS that takes a handout from our govermint. My favorite was Bill O'Reilly who I thought was a pretty smart SOB. Now he's off the air for sexual harassment which hasn't been proved, but if I worked among all that cheesecake, by that I mean the commentators with the long legs, I'd be doing all the harassing I could do.

Finally, Penny showed up with another Big Gulp. She'd given her kidneys one hell of a workout since we left Middleberg. She wasn't quite so mad any more. I could tell because she started talking about a little knick-knack place she'd visited. She showed me an embroidered pot holder that she'd bought, Tibetan children riding a yak. Great, we have fourteen others, but I guess no Tibetans or yaks for that matter. I'm in enough hot water to scold her about the way she spends money, but then I go get real stupid.

"You know Penny, I wish you'd jes let me handle things. I mean this is kinda man-stuff." No response. "These service people wanna hear from the man in charge of the household, you know, the alpha dog. Otherwise they're gonna overcharge us." I looked over at her. She was lying on her back on the other bed. Her eyes were closed and the wrinkles in her forehead looked like a dry dishrag.

"I've got a headache. Can't you just shut up for once in your life?"

"Wait jes one minute, that's no way to talk to your superiors." Honest, I meant that as a joke. She sat up and her lips took on the shape of a snarl. A man wants them nice and soft, not like a pit bull that's about to put its teeth in your ass.

"Buddy, you're the dumbest fuckin' moron that I've ever met in my life. I can't talk to you right now." A woman is never very attractive when she uses the f-word.

FIVE

I'VE LEARNED THAT no amount of arguing is going to get Penny out of her mood, and I was getting hungry. I put on my coat and rummaged around for my wallet. After I rummaged for a while, she announced from the bed, "It's in the top drawer of the dresser where you put it when you came in." How'd she know that? I put the wallet in my back pocket and went out the door. I passed the same bugger at the desk. He's got that fake grin on his face that they taught him in his training program. I guess they didn't ask him for his Mexican birth certificate when they hired him.

"May I help you sir?"

"Know where a decent restaurant is?"

"Somewhere nice to take your lady friend?" The fake grin got wider.

"No, she has a headache."

"There's a nice salsa restaurant a few blocks from here."

"I just want a steak and a shot of whiskey."

"Pete's Bar and Grill is just across the street, amigo." *I'm not your amigo or anybody's amigo.*

I headed across the road and enter Pete's. It was dark in the restaurant, like out of the seventies or eighties. A haze of smoke hung over the bar. I pulled out a cigarette and plunked down on the nearest stool. The bartender came by, and I ordered a double Wild Turkey and a steak. I had told Doc Haqq that I would lay off the whiskey, but now that the trip was all screwed up thanks to Penny's mood, I was determined to settle my nerves with a smoke, a shot of whiskey, and a good piece of American beef.

I noticed a guy sitting two seats over from me. I was thankful that there was an empty stool between us. He was wearing a black leather jacket and an Old Glory doo rag wrapped around his head. I know from experience that these bikers are touchy, particularly when they've got some hooch in them, so I kept my distance. I had enough go wrong for one day.

"I've never seen you in here before," he said and smiled.

"Jes passin' through, we started in St. Louis."

"I biked through there one time on the way to Sturgis, up in South Dakota. Used to be in the Hell's Angels, now I sorta freelance." *A biker that freelances?*

"Yep, used to ride meself, the Bandidos. I rode with Bad Balls Paczjakowski for five years." I can bullshit with the best of them.

"Bandidos eh?" The man's voice started to rise. "Let me show you something." He rolled up his sleeve. There was a six-inch scar on his arm, just above a skeleton wearing a motorcycle helmet. "I got this here in a knife fight with the Bandidos down in Texas. A few of your motherfuckin buddies came at us. We cut those fuckers apart. I took one for the team when some no-good motherfucker tried to carve a turkey on this here arm. If you're friends of Little Swiss, Pokey, Ramadoodle Jim or any of them other motherfuckers, you better get the hell out of here before I filet your soul." Then he laughed in this high-pitched crazy sort of a way, reminded me of a movie I once saw where zombies took over the world.

"Nosirree, never met or know any of 'em," I said. "Never got anywhere near Texas. Actually, my gang warn't really in the Bandidos, more like a farm team. As a matter of fact, last year a guy in our group told me that we were never part of the Bandidos. Bad Balls just made it up. As a matter of fact, we were known more for our work with kids on motorcycle safety than stirring up trouble, especially with you boys." Even to me that sounded like horseshit, but it seemed to settle him a bit. He hunkered down on his food and guzzled another beer. The bartender came by, bent over me, and whispered.

"Don't worry about him. Marvin's harmless as long as he takes his pills. His mother comes by about nine o'clock and picks him up."

This got me to wondering. If he had taken his medicine, why was he drinking? But then again, why was I drinking? I ordered another whiskey and dug into my steak. It wasn't bad, but to tell the truth, it's hard to mess up a steak. I munched on a few French fries which I smothered in ketchup. I tend to put ketchup on most things I eat, except waffles. I like ketchup, always have and always will. And I don't know if I said this already, I like Heinz Ketchup with a '57' on the bottle, not the knock-offs.

I was just about finished and fishing in my wallet for the credit card when Marvin came lunging towards me with his steak knife. He screamed. "Bad Balls Paczjakowski was a killer. I remember that motherfucker!"

I almost shit my pants, but fortunately, he's pretty drunk by this time. He fell off his stool and nicked himself near the skeleton's left foot. He banged his head on the floor and kind of laid there twitching, like road kill after being run over by a semi. The bartender and a few waitresses came over and helped him up. His arm was bleeding, and he had a strawberry on his forehead.

"Call his Mama," declared the bartender matter-of-factly. It seemed like this had happened before. They sat him on a chair in the restaurant with a towel around his arm. Soon Marvin's mother showed up. She was a grey-haired woman up in her seventies, well-dressed and all that. Her other son was probably a doctor or an accountant. They helped Marvin out of the restaurant. Things got quiet again.

I was kind of shaking, heck, who wouldn't be. I ordered another whiskey, and soon I was pretty much wasted. I was just about to leave, trying to think of an excuse to explain my drinking to Penny, when all of a sudden, I heard a woman's voice.

"Buddy, is that you?" It was comin' from the restaurant proper. "Remember me, Gloria, the waitress at the Waffle House. Come on over and have a drink with us." In the haze of smoke, I seen her get up and come over to me. She was wearing a tight sweater with her titties lurking inside of it.

"Well hi there, honey."

"Where's Penny?"

"She's got a headache."

"You guys've had a pretty rough day, I guess."

"You come here often?" I couldn't quit staring at her.

"Well, there aren't that many eating places in a little town like this. Come over and meet my girlfriends."

"Sure, let me go pee first."

I wanted to stay but nature wouldn't let me. I paid my bill at the bar and asked where the restroom was. Now that's a stupid word, *restroom*. It's pretty certain in my mind that nobody ever goes there to take a rest. My suggestion would be *pissroom*. That wouldn't explain all the activities in there, but it'd cover pretty near ninety percent. I did my business and washed my hands. One of them air dryers was in there. It was an old one and there was no power to it, just when I'm in a hurry to get back out there. Whatever happened to an old-fashioned paper towel? I wiped my hands on my jeans and rushed out looking for Gloria. She was sitting by herself in a dark corner of the place. My heart started to race.

"What happened to your friends?" I asked.

"They left. They've got to work tomorrow. They're waitresses like me."

"How about your husband?"

"Who says I have a husband?"

"I just thought a beautiful woman such as yerself would have a husband."

"I'm divorced."

"If you were my wife, I'd never divorce you."

"Why don't you buy me a drink, and I'll tell you the whole story."

"Sure thing." I got another Wild Turkey and she ordered an Old Fashioned.

"He left me about ten years ago. We were living in Vegas then. I worked at one of the clubs as a you-know-what."

"What?"

"A stripper."

"Well I can see where you could be good at that." She saw me fixated on what's inside her sweater.

"You're very observant, but what you're looking at isn't real."

"Lookin' at what?" I said sly-like.

"Oh, come on, that's what they're there for." She laughed. "They cost me plenty. I needed them in Vegas after the real ones started to sag."

"Well, that would explain 'em."

"My husband was a professional gambler. He left me for some twenty-year-old. They got hooked on Quaaludes, then heroin. I moved back to Paducah about six years ago. Once you're over 40, the Vegas jobs don't pay much. I moved in with Hank Thatcher last year."

"How come he ain't here?"

"I'm not sure. Monday's his bowling night. Sometimes he visits his kids after that. He might come by to pick me up, I don't know. Sometimes he can be a real prick."

"How will you get home if he don't come by?"

"I'll take an Uber."

"Not much of a boyfriend who lets you take an Uber."

"I guess not. Since we moved in together, all Hank talks about is his ex-wife and children, and his bodybuilding routine." At this point she started to tear up, and if it's one thing I can't stand, it's a woman who's teared up. I could see the mascara starting to run down from her eyes. But the more I drank, the more beautiful she looked. We sat there, drinking in silence, while she continued to blubber. Suddenly, I lunged toward her to put my arm around her. She pulled away kind of abruptly. I fell forward, and my head bounced off her left boob. Then she blurted out, "Isn't that

Penny?" Sure enough, I raised my head and there was Penny coming toward us. She got within about three feet of us and looked down at me. I was no longer in physical contact with Gloria, but I knew it was too late.

"You're a son-of-a-bitch," she said. She turned on her heel and walked out.

"I thought you told me she was in bed with a headache?" asked Gloria. I shrugged my shoulders.

"Well you're kind of a dumbshit, you know that, an old dumbshit. You're weren't going to get to first base with me, not even out of the batter's box. Now you've pissed off your wife."

"Girlfriend, she's not my wife."

"Okay girlfriend. You've pissed off your girlfriend."

"Oh, I dunno that Penny don't deserve some of this. She's headstrong and don't listen to the reasoning of a man."

"You've got to be kidding? At the Waffle House, she told me that you drove with that light on for a week without checking it out. Don't you take any responsibility for that?" She's no longer all tearful and sweet. I see the bitch coming out, and now I'm not surprised her husband left her.

"I guess I don't. It could happen to anybody and I don't need a lecture from you." I'm getting a little tired of *Big Tits.* Correct that, *Fake Big Tits.*

"I guess I'll call a cab. I've had too much to drink as it is." Now her voice had the coldness of a Budweiser in an ice chest. She pulled out her cell phone and started tapping on the Uber app. Just then, Hank showed up.

"Hi Hank, I'm over here," she called out. He was a ruggedly built fella wearing a sleeveless tee shirt. The tattoos on his arms were fighting with his muscles for space.

"This your new boyfriend Gloria?" He grinned, and his top teeth showed like a crocodile.

"Not on your life. This is Buddy, Buddy Dumbshit Jones."

"Well hi Buddy Dumbshit, good to know you." Now I'm getting rankled. No one makes fun of Harold Irwin Jones Jr.

"Buddy drove all the way from St. Louis with his battery light on and didn't think to get it checked. Then he made a pass at me a few minutes ago."

"Well then, I guess they don't call him *dumbshit* for nothing."

"I'd appreciate you not callin' me that Mr. Thatcher, and by the way, your girlfriend here called you a prick. I stood up, the guy was about six inches taller than me. I took a swing at him and missed. Sometimes if you go after a bully, they'll back off and leave you alone. That wasn't the case here. He grabbed me my by the collar and ran me into the wall. I could feel the bones in my neck and back line themselves up in different directions.

"Okay, take it easy, I'm just kiddin'. She never called you any bad names. I'm an old man and I've had too much to drink tonight."

"Well listen to me, you old cocksucker. If I ever catch you near Gloria again, I'll take your dick and tie a rope to it and swing you around that ceiling fan." He pointed to a fan overhead. He pushed me against the wall again, his fist pressed against my windpipe. I started feeling dizzy and I couldn't catch my breath.

"Leave him alone, Hank, that's enough." The pain moved from my back around into my chest. Then I must've blacked out. The next thing I remember, a paramedic was standing over me.

"You okay sir?"

"Yeah, I feel better now. Just a little pain in my chest, I guess."

"We better take you over to the hospital and get you checked out."

"Now wait a minute. My girlfriend's waitin' for me at the motel. I've got to get back to her."

"I'm right here Buddy." I looked up and there was Penny standing over me. She had a concerned look on her face. "Gloria called me after you blacked out. You'd better go to the hospital. You know your heart ain't so good."

Well Goddamnit. *I know my heart ain't so good.* I don't need any more of her lectures, but I don't say anything. It was only a short ride to the hospital in the ambulance. Paducah's a pretty small town.

SIX

THE EMERGENCY ROOM was like most of them. The smell of antiseptic mixing with the smells of stale pizza and body odor. They wheeled me into a big room and hooked me up to the EKG monitor. Soon I heard the beep, beep, beep so I knew that my ticker was ticking. The nurse came in, a short fellow with tiny slits for eyes. He was bald and looked like he could be a karate instructor.

"You'll feel a little stick." I pretty much knew the routine. Soon he had the IV running and of course I had to pee. He brought over a jug with a long handle. By then my pants were off, so it wasn't difficult to get it between my legs. As the bottle started to fill up, I got this scared feeling that it might overflow, but I guess they make these things big enough to accommodate even the biggest piss. I brought it out to hand it back, but by then he was gone. I was left holding the jug, kind of fearful it might spill. Finally, Kung Fu came back with the doctor right behind him. He was a dark-skinned man with an accent. *Goddamnit, it's the United Nations in here.*

"Hello, I'm Dr. Goyal? How are you feeling?"

"I'm okay now, Doc. I just got a little dizzy over at Pete's.'

The guy looked a lot like Dr. Haqq, but then I guess all those Indians look the same.

"Yeah, Darrin just told me that."

"Who's Darrin?"

"Your nurse, Darrin White Cloud. He's a feather and I'm a dot." I wasn't sure what he was talking about.

"Your EKG's okay, but the blood work's a little off. Your liver function is abnormal and your blood sugar's a tad high."

"I ate and drank a lot over at Pete's."

"Maybe so, but I think you should stay with us, at least overnight."

"Oh, I don't think that'll be necessary, Doc." Just then Penny and Gloria came in. They seem to have bonded out in the waiting room, almost like they have one asshole in common, me.

"How're you feeling, Buddy?" asked Penny.

"A lot better. Her boyfriend roughed me up." I pointed to Gloria.

"I'm sorry about all that. Let's chalk it up to a misunderstanding, just stupid men being stupid men." Gloria replied. *And what about stupid women?*

"We'll put him on a monitor and check out his heart beats until the enzymes come back," said the doctor.

"Really Doc, I think I could go back to the motel, I'm feelin' pretty good." I saw Penny looking pissed again.

"Let's do what the doctor recommends," said Penny. "Then we'll head for home to see Dr. Haqq." That's not going to fly, but I wasn't going to argue with her right then.

Up in my room, I couldn't sleep. I listened to the beep, beep, beep. I worried that the ticker would stop and if that happened, I'd be dead. Finally, I dozed off. Sometime later, there was a loud alarm. The nurse came running in. She was a young girl, almost too young to be a full-fledged nurse. I must've looked scared.

"Your EKG leads fell off, Mr. Jones. It's nothing to worry about."

"Yeah, that happened after they put in my heart stents." I tried to sound matter-of-fact-like.

The next morning a different doctor showed up, a woman. "Hi Mr. Jones, I'm Sally Johansen, your doctor today. How was your night?" This Dr. Sally Johansen was something to look at, honey blond and tall, with glossy lipstick. I wanted to say *Hi Sally, I'm Buddy, let's go out for a beer tonight and get to know each other.* Of course, I didn't say anything. There was a time when all the doctors were men, old white-haired white men, like Marcus Welby on TV.

"I need to examine you, if that's okay." Now this made me a little nervous, a woman poking and prodding at me, even a hot babe like Dr. Johansen. I can't tell you why, I just didn't want a woman's hands on me. Well I do, but not like that. I started to worry. Maybe she'd need to check out my prostrate or something like that. As it turned out, she just listened to my heart and my breathing. She got real close and I smelled her perfume. Dr. Haqq has bad breath, maybe it's all that hot food that he eats. She took off the stethoscope. "Everything checks out. We can send you home today, but you'll need to follow-up with your doctor. He might want you to have a stress test. Where are you from?"

"South of St Louis."

Just then, Penny walked in. "Your wife can do the driving," the doctor said.

"I'm his friend," she corrected. I don't like Penny getting anywhere near the steering wheel if I'm a passenger. I've been driving all my life and I know what I'm doing behind the wheel. The same can't be said for Penny. She goes real slow. When the speed limit's 70, that means you can go at least 75, maybe 80. The few times I let her drive, she just poked along. It just drives a fella crazy the way she stayed behind those eighteen wheelers. I mean you got to pass them. Dr. Johansen saw the frown on my face.

"Well, I say that because you don't want to have a cardiac arrhythmia while driving a car."

Them big medical words usually don't mean anything good for you.

"You need to get your blood work repeated too."

"My doctor knows all about that stuff," I said. I don't want this female camel nosing around in a tent where she doesn't belong.

"Your blood alcohol was well beyond the range of intoxication. Good thing you didn't drive a car last night."

"That's why we're here," Penny piped up. "Our truck broke down yesterday. We're waiting to get it fixed. Buddy went to a bar and got into a fight," *Dang it, that's more than anyone needed to hear.*

"You'll need to drive him back home to see his doctor and get all this checked out." Okay, now I've heard that twice.

"Yes ma'am, we will," answered good old reliable follow-all-the-rules Penny. I kept silent. No point starting an argument in front of *long tall Sally*. Anyhow, she was already out of the room and on to the next patient. Doctors are always in a rush to get to the next critter on their list. I got dressed, and I asked Penny how we'd get back to the motel.

"Gloria's waiting for us in the lobby. We had breakfast this morning and she drove me to the hospital. She said she'd hang around if you got released. She's not due into work until noon."

"Geez, what's she all of a sudden? Your BFF?"

"She's a really nice girl who's helping me out?" *Helping you out, who's helping me out?*

"Well, we could take a cab, we're not broke," I said.

"No, not completely broke, just a little broke." I'm in no mood for Penny's jokes. We went down the elevator and there was Gloria. She hugged Penny liked she hadn't seen her for ten years. My BFF comment wasn't too far off the mark.

"How ya feeling Buddy?" Gloria asked.

"Better." I didn't feel like talking to her.

"I want to apologize again. I got drunk and made a fool of myself," she said.

"Is Hank sorry?" My neck was pretty sore from where he tried to tack my body to the restaurant wall.

"You'll have to ask him." I noticed by the tone of her voice that Hank wasn't too high on her list. "I'll only be working for a few hours today. Why don't y'all come over and have dinner tonight?"

"No, thanks. I think we'll just hang around the motel. We're both pretty tired." That was the first halfway smart thing I'd heard from Penny since we'd left home.

"I understand Penny, call me if you change your mind." Shit, the last thing I want to do is spend more time with Gloria and the gorilla.

"I sure will, you've been a real help," Penny said. A real help, was she? Almost got me killed and Penny calls her a *real help.*

SEVEN

I GOT IN BED as soon as we got back to our room. The mattress was lumpy and the pillows overstuffed, but I hadn't hardly slept a wink since we left Middleberg. Soon I was soundly snoring. Of course, that's a lie, a person can't hear his own self snoring. I just know from Penny and my other sleep partners that I snored a lot. All at once, Dr. Johansen appeared. She was completely naked, and she could no longer resist the urge to have sex with me. There was one condition. She needed to remove my balls with a scalpel that she was holding.

When I woke up, I was covered in sweat and the old ticker was pounding pretty damn fast. The room was dark. For a few seconds, I didn't know where I was. I put my hand on my crotch and everything was still there. I called out for Penny, no answer. I found the remote on the bedside table and turned on the TV. I tried to find some bowling or car racing, no luck. I turned to FOX News. President Trump was having a rally in Nashville. He mentioned Hillary Clinton and the crowd broke into a chant, "Lock her up! Lock her up!" That's amazing. People still want Clinton in jail. That's how bad her crimes were. I read on the internet that she and her husband were responsible for fifteen murders. And now I come to learn from Trump that Obama wiretapped his phone. They should lock up Barack Obama too, but they won't. I start to doze again. I heard the door open. I looked at the clock, seven p.m. Penny was back.

"How're you feeling? she asked.

"Okay. Where you been?"

"Out."

"Out?"

"Yeah out."

"Not with your new friend, I hope"

"And if I was, is it any of your business?"

"Yes, you're my business."

"I'm your business? Like some kinda property?"

"Yeah." Since she met Gloria she was becoming nastier by the minute.

"Well, I got news for you. Slavery ended with the Civil War," she said.

"Now *you're* some kinda history buff?"

Penny seemed tired. She took off her jacket and sat down on the one chair in the room. "You want me to get you something to eat?"

"I asked you where you were. I'm entitled to a straight answer."

"I was over at Gloria's for dinner."

"God damnit, I was right. Where was meathead? Was he there too?"

"No, he was having dinner with his kids. Gloria's leaving him."

"Well he's one lucky guy."

"Christ Buddy, you're just impossible to talk to."

"Well God damnit. I just got out of the hospital and where were you all day? I'm beginnin' to think that you don't give a shit about me."

"Well at least you're *thinking*. That's a welcome change." She laughed, not a nice laugh but a mean laugh. Then I don't know what got over me. I jumped up and pinned her against the wall, kind of like Hank's move. She started to struggle, and when I looked into her eyes, I could see some fear. Suddenly, I started feeling dizzy from the exertion. I sat back on the bed.

"You're insane Buddy, fucking insane," she yelled. "You know the one good thing I did in my life?"

"I cain't believe it. You did *one* good thing in your life?"

"Do you know what it was? Do you?"

"I don't, and I don't fuckin' care." I guess by this time, I was shouting too.

"It was not marrying you!"

"Thank God you didn't! I would've been corralled like a sick mare just like your first husband. No wonder he died." When a Jones gets mad, he gets real mad. That's just in our blood.

Penny put on her jacket. She held her mouth kind of twisted and her eyes just fixed on me, like a half-crazed ghost in *The Walking Dead*. She grabbed the suitcase and threw all my clothes on the floor. Then she gathered up her dirty underwear, jammed them into it, and zipped it up. A bra strap hung out one end. She wheeled the suitcase out the door and slammed it behind her.

I laid back in bed, kind of sad that I'd lost it with Penny, but I guess it wasn't the first time. I figured Penny wouldn't be back until sometime around midnight. I popped a nitro from a pill bottle on the night stand. Then I got up slowly so that the dizzy feeling wouldn't come back. I took a shower and cleaned all the adhesive tape from my arms, and the goop from the monitor pads on my chest. I got dressed and took the elevator downstairs. I ducked past the front desk, afraid to look.

I heard that sing-song tenor again. "Senor, how are you feeling?" Juan Valdez was back at work.

"Better."

"Will you be joining the senora for la cena?" He knew damn well I wouldn't be with her.

I kept going with my head down. Outside, a cold wind blew. It was starting to sleet. *Good thing we'll be out of this damn place tomorrow.* I wondered where Penny was, probably over at Gloria's. I found a Burger King and bought a Whopper with French fries and a large Coke. As I was picking up my order at the counter, I heard a high-pitched voice.

"Hey, mister, over here!" Wouldn't you know it, Marvin, the psycho was there. "Come on over and sit with me."

"No, it's okay, I don't want to bother you while you're eatin'."

"I'm not good enough for you, is that it?" It was easier to sit down with him.

"Feelin' better tonight?" I asked. He had on a plaid shirt and blue jeans. The doo rag was gone.

"Yeah, some. I'd been off my medication for a few days. Some of the pills make me sleepy so I stop taking them from time to time. I'm a paranoid schizophrenic, you know what that is?"

"Kinda."

"Basically, I'm off my rocker. You know some of the most prestigious artists in the world have had my disease. Look at Van Gogh, one of the greatest painters the world has ever seen. One day he became so agitated he cut off an ear."

"Never heard of him. In fact, I dunno the name of any painter except the fella who painted the soup can. Andy sumpin or other."

"Andy Warhol."

"Yeah that's it. One of those goddamned soup cans went for well over a million bucks."

"Actually, it went for two million at an auction in New York City. Now they're worth even more than that."

"How do you know so much about this stuff?"

"Oh, I'm a dissertation short of my PhD in fine arts. I can show you some of my paintings if you want, and mother could make us some tea. I dropped out of NYU went I was 26, after my first bout of the crazies. I just wear that biker outfit to impress people."

"You sure did impress me."

"I have a picture hanging in the Museum of Modern Art in Manhattan. If you don't believe me, just google my name, Marvin Schultz." I got on my phone, and sure enough I found him. They mentioned his painting, *Urinal with a Bouquet of Flowers*, that's hanging in some art museum.

"Schultz, eh? The only Schultz I ever heard of was Sergeant Schultz from Hogan's Heroes."

"Who's he?"

"Oh, come on, from the television show. They still play the reruns. You know, about a Nazi prisoner of war camp. Still makes me laugh even though I've seen each episode a dozen times."

"That stuff about Nazis gives me nightmares. My Mom had gypsy blood in her. The Nazis exterminated gypsies as well as the Jews. I don't watch that stuff." There's no point trying to talk to this guy about anything. I don't say anything while I'm putting ketchup on my fries.

"You ever see Bad Balls anymore? I hid under the covers all night thinking about him."

"Don't worry, I was bullshittin' about Bad Balls."

"How do I know you're telling the truth?"

"He ain't in Google like you."

"Okay, I'll take your word for it, I guess."

"How's your arm?"

"It's okay, they put in a few stitches at the urgent care center. I told them not to mess with Henry."

"Henry?" He rolled up his sleeve to show me the skeleton with the helmet.

"Henry's my best friend. He's been with me through thick and thin for fifteen years. You might not believe this, but he's a better artist than me. If you come by tonight, I'll show you his paintings too. Mom likes it when I bring a friend by other than Henry."

"Well I guess he must be at your house a lot."

"Well sure, he lives with us."

"Sorry, I've got to be goin'. I'll be hittin' the road tomorrow after my truck gits fixed."

"Okay, good luck for the rest of your trip."

"Thanks. I won't tell Bad Balls where you live."

EIGHT

I WALKED BACK to the motel. By this time there was snow coming down. An ugly-faced gal was at the desk. She gave me a nod. I didn't nod back. I don't have to be nice to people if I'm paying the freight.

I took the elevator up to our room and slid the card in the lock a few times until I finally got it to open. What ever happened to an old fashioned goddamned key? Now they've got them pieces of plastic. Nine times out of ten, I slide in the wrong side or upside down, or I pull it out too quick and that little red light goes on to tell me to try again. Then I get angry and start rattling the door handle back and forth which of course don't do any good. Sometimes, you even have to go down to the front desk and get a new keycard if the old card was near your cell phone and don't work any more.

Penny wasn't in the room. I wasn't surprised. It always took her some time to come back after a blowout like that. I knew I should take some of the blame if only she'd let me. I told myself, *no more getting mad at the bitch.*

I watched some reruns of *Mork and Mindy*. I brushed my teeth, turned off the lights, and went to sleep. The next thing I knew, the sun was shining through a slit in the curtain, still no Penny. The other bed hadn't been slept in. Now I'm getting somewhat concerned. I looked out the window at the parking lot on the slim hope that Penny had gotten the truck and was downstairs eating breakfast. There was a few inches of snow on the ground. No truck. I tried to call her on my cell, it was dead. The charger was in the suitcase that Penny took with her. I got dressed and headed over to the Waffle House. Maybe she was there with her new buddy, Gloria. I like that--new buddy as opposed to me--old Buddy.

Neither one of them was there. Cindy, the perky one, was working the counter with a heavy-set woman named Mary. She was wearing a sleeveless top and had that giggly fat hanging low on the under part of her arms. They were real busy in there. There was a line of three or four parties waiting for tables. I snuck into a seat at the end of the counter. Cindy came over. "Where's Gloria?" I asked.

"I have no damn idea. She called in and said she was leaving town on some sort of emergency. Left us high and dry." I saw that her perkiness had been replaced with a kinda surliness.

"Did she say where she was goin'?"

"Nope, she didn't."

"Did she say anything about Penny?"

"Who's Penny?"

"My girlfriend, remember her?"

"No, she didn't say nuthin 'bout her."

Well, there was no point going all half-cocked. The truck probably wouldn't've been fixed yet anyway. I settled in to a plate of waffles with a double order of sausages. There was a young fella next to me with a Coca-Cola logo on his jacket. He had those ears that stuck out like some kind of bat and a few long hairs on his chin. From the smirk on his face and his stale jokes with Mary, I could tell he might be trouble. After I started on my second cup of coffee, the place started to clear out. Cindy came over.

"Sorry, I'd been so rude, but I've been working my butt off since 6 a.m. what with Gloria flying the coop. Do you think she went somewhere with your girlfriend?"

"Penny got up and left early this morning. She's probably down at Elmer's checkin' on the truck. I thought she might wanna have breakfast here. She's been hangin' out with Gloria this weekend, so I thought she might have come in here to say good-bye to her."

The guy next to me sniggered. "What's wrong, you lost your honey?" I didn't say anything. Just kept drinking my coffee. For most people, that would've been enough to keep him quiet, but not this jackass.

"That's the trouble with women these days," he said. "They dunno their place. There's too much of this women's rights crap. I know your problem. You ain't tough enough with the little lady."

"You some kind of an expert in this?" The ugly little bastard didn't look like much of an expert in anything.

"Well I know this. I'd know where my girlfriend was."

"Do you even have a girlfriend?"

"I did once."

"Once?"

"I kicked her out for cheating on me. I called her six times a day. She still managed to cheat on me."

"So, I guess she was somewhere you didn't know?"

"No, she was at home. A guy who fought in Iraq came over every day and got in bed with her, our bed. He was a buddy of mine in high school." He half-laughed. Maybe because he realized how stupid he sounded, or maybe because he was just stupid, period.

"Well I gotta be goin'," I said. God gave you only so many words to say while you're alive, and you can't waste them on misfits like him.

Elmer's was only a block away. The kid that jump-started us was behind the counter. He looked surprised to see me. "You having more problems with the truck?" he asked.

"Hey, don't be a stupid shit with the jokes. I'm here to pick it up. You got the new alternator put in?"

"Well sure, we did it first thing this morning."

"Then it's ready."

"Your wife picked it up about two hours ago."

"I guess she went out for breakfast." I looked at my watch. It was almost eleven o'clock.

"Gloria called Elmer yesterday and asked him to put a rush on it."

"What the fuck has Gloria got to do with this?"

"She came in with your wife to get the truck. You know she's just a really nice person. Not hard to look at neither, if you know what I mean." He made a few squiggles with his two hands, exaggerating that first squiggle.

"They're fake," I said. I started back to the hotel. Up to then, I was still figuring that Penny and Gloria were out shopping or eating or doing something that women do. When I got back to the hotel, Big Mex was checking in a guest, but he gave me a nod with his head. After the customer left, he said in a sad voice like he knew it was bad news. "Your wife was by a while ago, senor. She told me she try to text you five times, but you don answer."

"My phone was dead. I left the charger in the truck."

"She left this note for you." He pulled out a small envelope and handed it to me. I tore it open and started to read the card that she must've bought that morning. I'm not a very good reader, so Penny had written it in block letters.

DEAR BUDDY

WHEN YOU READ THIS LETTER I WILL BE ON MY WAY TO MIDDLEBERG IN THE TRUCK. I AM SORRY TO BE WRITING THIS BUT YOU MUST HEAR THE TRUTH. FROM YOUR ACTIONS OVER THE PAST FEW DAYS AND WAY BEFORE THAT, I HAVE COME TO BELIEVE THAT YOU ARE A MEAN STUBBORN BASTARD AND I NO LONGER WANT TO LIVE WITH YOU. WHEN I GET HOME I WILL TAKE ALL OF YOUR BELONGS AND PUT THEM IN YOUR STORAGE UNIT WITH YOUR FISHING GEAR AND YOU MODEL TRAINS. YOU CAN PICK THEM UP WHEN YOU RELOCATE TO ANOTHER RESIDENCE. I WILL KEEP THE TRUCK WHICH IS IN MY NAME IN CASE YOU FORGOT. I WILL BE LIVING IN THE TRAILER UNTIL I FIND A BETTER PLACE TO LIVE. AFTER I MOVE OUT YOU CAN GET IN TOUCH WITH STU IF YOU STILL PLAN TO LIVE THERE. GLORIA HAS DECIDED TO LEAVE HANK AND SHE WILL BE COMING WITH ME. I HOPE I NEVER SEE YOU AGAIN!

FUCK YOU!!

PENNY

PS. I WILL KEEP PEPPER UNLESS YOU WANT TO FEED HER, WALK HER, AND TAKE HER TO THE

VET (NONE OF WHICH YOU HAVE EVER DONE). OTHERWISE SHE WILL LIVE WITH ME.

Well there you have it, straight up. She was gone. I knew she'd never written that nasty letter if it wasn't for Gloria. That's not to say I couldn't've sweet talked her back if I'd wished to, but I didn't. That's the trouble with women. You say some things to them, things that you don't even mean half the time, and they go off the deep end. Looking back, I'm grateful to her for helping me buy the truck, but it wasn't rightfully hers.

I walked over to an Office Depot and bought a new charger for my phone. Then I went up to the hotel room. I pulled out my wallet to take stock of its contents. I had an old MasterCard that was cancelled, a VISA card that was in Penny's name, a twenty-dollar bill, a ten-dollar bill, and three one-dollar bills. I had a driver's license, my expired AAA auto card, and my Medicare card. I had a small photo of Penny and me in Florida right after we met. That was it, except for two quarters in my pocket. I knew that wasn't going to get me very far. I'm not that stupid. I lay down on the bed, kinda hoping Penny would change her mind and call me. She didn't. Then I took a nap. That's what I do when I don't know what to do.

NINE

I WAS CHRISTENED Harold Irwin Jones Jr., but my half-brother Dexter called me Buddy, and the name just stuck, and who would want to be called Harold or Irwin anyway? Harold Irwin Jones Sr. didn't like it neither. Some of Dad's old friends from high school called him Homo, but he wasn't one of those, at least I don't think he was. It was kind of a joke, although he did have a slender build and his voice was a tenor. But hey, he sired me, so I guess he wasn't, except nowadays that doesn't mean anything. I read about some guy who came out of the closet after having seven kids. That's the trouble with these times, you can't be sure about any one, and that's what scares me. Daddy died at 45, fell off a roof and crushed his skull on a concrete driveway, so I never got around to ask him, but he'd left us well before that, and most likely he wouldn't've have told me anyway.

My mother had two sisters, Henrietta and Winnie, a kid-brother Waldo, and five husbands which is more than normal for one woman, the husbands that is, not the kin. The first one was Monty Pacelli. Mom and her sisters met Monty and his pals at a drive-in movie theatre in Owl Hollow, a town just west of Middleberg. Dexter was already in the oven when they got hitched, and Mom quit high school when her pregnancy started to show. That's one of the downsides with being pro-life, which I am, because sometimes it allows a fella like Dexter to sneak into this world, and I don't use *sneak* without good reason. Monty and Mom lived in the basement of my grandparents' house. Dexter moved in too, after he got born. My grandfather, Homer Dixon, owned a small roofing business which made him one of the richer men in Middleberg. It didn't take long for the fighting to begin between husband and wife and soon it got physical. One day, Granddaddy got in between them, and Monty broke the old man's jaw with a right cross to his kisser. After that, Monty moved to the south side of Chicago where he got hooked up with the Mafia. Mom said he was only small potatoes in the Mob. When I was a kid, I wasn't sure what that meant, but I didn't like potatoes, so it didn't sound too good for him to be one of them, even if he was a small one.

Daddy was the second husband in line. He and Mom had known each other since grade school. Mom didn't like Daddy too much even back then, or so she told me later, but Granddaddy Homer and Grandma Bess were good friends with Daddy's parents, being that they attended the same Baptist church. Mom told me that Homer and Bess were keen for her to date Daddy, who by then had dropped Homo for his real name, Harold. After they got married, they moved to a small rented bungalow in Middleberg. Mom was happy to leave her parent's basement, and I think the rest of the Dixons were happy to see her and Dexter leave. She liked to stay up till one or two in the morning, drinking and smoking and playing music on her gramophone. There was plenty of hanky panky with Daddy in the basement before they got married, at least that's what Dexter told me many years later. Come to think of it, he was only four years old, so I'm not sure how he knew that.

Middleberg in those days was mostly white, and it still is, except for a few black families that lived near the train tracks and worked as day laborers in the watermelon fields and the hog farms nearby. Missouri's always been a big producer of watermelons and pigs. In the fifties and sixties, Middleberg was known for its lead mining when lead was used in gasoline, paint, and pipes. There was a lead smelter in the center of town for over a hundred years. Those were good paying jobs, and Daddy started work there when he dropped out of high school. His father was a foreman at the plant as was his daddy before him. A few years ago, the plant closed after they found high lead levels in the kids that lived near the smelter. The homes around the plant including Daddy's childhood home were bulldozed. They say that lead can damage the brain for your whole life. I always wondered if it didn't affect Daddy in that way, and maybe even me, though we lived a little way away. The govermint could have chipped in to clean the area up and keep the smelter open, but it didn't. It just made regulations.

I can attest to the fact that many of the people in Middleberg were hardworking, but my Daddy wasn't one of them. A few years after he started work at the smelter, he was laid off. Granddaddy Homer gave him a job putting roofs on houses, but Daddy felt that hammering shingles in the heat of the day was below his calling, so he quit. For a short while, he worked as a door to door Fuller brush salesman, but it seems he wasn't cut out for that either. Something about too much walking. He tried to sell life insurance but got fired.

Mom told me it had to do with Daddy going to a Ku Klux Klan meeting which didn't sit well with the owner of the agency who turned out to be a Jew. Mom said he could never hold a job that required any brains or any energy which I believe pretty much ruled out most things. Looking back, I guess she didn't have much good to say about him in any department of life.

Mom was a hairdresser and manicurist and worked out of our home. Her work was not steady and that left a lot of time for her and Daddy to drink, smoke cigarettes, and argue. He would yell at Mom for the littlest thing particularly when he had some hooch in him. Then they'd go at it. Mom could be a hellcat in a fight, with those long fingernails of hers. She'd scratch him up pretty good. By the time I was ten or twelve, whiskey had become the beverage of choice at the Jones household. It wasn't unusual for two or three empty Jack Daniels bottles to be in the trash bin each week, waiting for the garbage man to pick them up. Daddy would sit in his underwear at the kitchen table with a sad look on his face, staring at the help wanted ads in the newspaper. I guess today he'd be diagnosed with depression. He never seemed to have time for us kids except to scold us or threaten us with a whupping, which he often did, the whupping that is. I can still recall the sour look on his grey face as he removed the belt from his trousers. There must have been some good times with Daddy, but I can't remember any of them right now.

One morning they had a pretty big dust up, by morning I mean around four a.m. They'd been cussing and yelling at each other all through the night. When Daddy finally left, he slammed the door as hard as he could. The rotted slats on the frame house rattled, and Mom's precious china teapot toppled off the hutch in the kitchen. I could hear it crash on the floor from my room. Now how could a boy a fourteen-year-old stay asleep with all that racket? The next day, I noticed Mom had a red circle under her eye which over a few days turned a dark purple. I reckoned he must have hit her with a lot of force. I never saw the damage that she put on him because he never came back.

For a while, Daddy lived down in the Ozarks and got himself involved with meth production which was just getting going as a business. Nowadays, those labs are as common as the local 7-Eleven in that part of the state. He served five years in jail for manufacturing and distributing methamphetamines. After he got out, he moved to Jefferson City. If you haven't paid attention in school, it's the capital of the great state of Missouri. He'd come to Middleberg a few times a year and write Mom a check to help us out. Mom said it was less than peanuts, but he claimed he could only get part-time work mowing lawns and washing dishes, being that he was an ex-con. In the cooler months, he would do a little of the hated roofing if he really needed the money. That's when he had the accident that caused his death. There was a rumor that he was drunk at the time, and I wouldn't dispute that.

The last time I saw Daddy was at his mother's funeral. I was about eighteen at the time. If I had known it was the last time I'd see him, I'd have talked to him more and asked more questions in regard to how he was doing. Maybe we could have had one of them father and son chats while we were out on a boat doing some fishing. I might have asked him if he loved me. Even to this day, I wonder about that, like a lot of other people who've had fathers, which I guess is most everyone. I've carried his name for my whole life and never really known much about him. I would count those men lucky who had a chance to spend time with their Dad.

TEN

I REMEMBER THE SUMMER PICNICS with Grandma Bess and Grandpa Homer on the bluffs overlooking the Mississippi River. We'd bring a blanket, and Dexter and I would eat chicken and mayonnaise sandwiches with potato salad. In those days, I liked mayonnaise almost as much as I liked ketchup. Sometimes, I'd slather both of them on the same piece of pork loin that all us kids liked to eat. Grandma Bess would bring her famous chocolate cake. Since she died, I never ate a cake so good, not even close. Her pecan pie was nothing to sneeze at, particularly when it was loaded up with a whole bunch of whipping cream.

Grandma Bess and I always got along really great. She only lived about two blocks from us and I'd go over there after school. Grandma was a big reader and she always had a book in her hand. Sometimes she'd read heavy stuff like *To Kill a Mockingbird* and *Gone with the Wind*, but mostly she liked those Agatha Christie mysteries as well as tons of romance novels. She would read to me when I'd stay over at her house on weekends. She must have had every book that Dr. Seuss ever wrote. I always wondered why a doctor would spend his time writing funny kids' books, when all the doctors I ever knew would crack their faces if they even smiled. Then I found out a few years ago that he wasn't even a doctor. Looking back, it seemed liked it was the only place where there was some peace and quiet. The little studying that I ever did was done there.

Dexter was four years older than me. He was real smart. I don't think I ever met a smarter human than him. I mean if he had applied himself, he could have been a doctor or a lawyer or even an architect if you get my drift. He was good at drawing and he'd draw portraits of dogs, and landscapes. He even won third prize in a statewide competition. It was a water color of the Mississippi River with barges and tugboats and trees and stuff like that. I looked up to him, and tried to copy him, but I didn't have his brains. The only occasions that I ever had a big roll of money in my pocket was because of Dexter. Sadly, the big roll usually became a small roll and then no roll at all. Some of that was my fault and some of it wasn't. Some of it was on account of Dexter's shenanigans.

Dexter started playing hooky when he was about thirteen. His specialty was forging Mom's handwriting. She had this custom-made note paper that was made at a local stationery store, before it was put out of business by an Office Max, which was later taken over by an Office Depot. Dexter would steal them from the kitchen drawer where Mom kept them, and he'd write excuse notes to the teacher that looked just like Mom had written them. Sometimes he'd be out one or two days with a sore throat, other times with the runs. Once he had the mumps for a whole week. He'd get up early like he was going to school. Then he'd just take the day off.

If the Cardinals were playing a day game, he'd hitch a ride into the city and go to Sportsman's Park where the Cardinals used to play and the Browns too, before they moved to Baltimore and became the Orioles. One time, ol' Dex brought along a Cardinal uniform that Granddaddy Homer had bought for him for his birthday. He jammed it into his book bag which that day didn't contain any books. He got dressed in a public bathroom near the park and told the gate attendant that he was filling in for one of the regular batboys that was sick. He showed up in the dugout and claimed he was a nephew of Branch Rickey, the general manager of the team. He talked about Mr. Rickey like he'd had dinner with him every Sunday or something like that. He got some of the batting practice balls autographed by the star players and sold 'em in Middleberg for ten bucks a piece. Dexter had some balls.

One day, the teacher called Mom in for a conference. She wanted to know if Dexter had been to a doctor seeing as he'd missed so many days of school. Then she pulled out all the sick notes that she thought Mom had written. Mom went ballistic when she got home, and when Daddy found out, he had Dexter pull down his britches and practically wore the polish off his belt beating it against his bare behind.

When Dexter was in the tenth grade, he quit school and moved to Chicago to live with Monty. Monty used his connections with the *Outfit*, the name of the Mob that ran Chicago, to get Dexter a job as a gofer. He spent his time getting coffee and salami sandwiches or picking up laundry for the muckety-mucks in the Mafia.

Dexter would come back to Middleberg almost every Christmas. He'd bring all sorts of gifts for me and Mom and Grandma Bess who was a widow by that time, Homer having died of a busted appendix. One time he gave me a crisp hundred-dollar bill, and I remember spending it on a brand-new bike with them hand brakes that were popular then. Other years, if we were short on cash, Mom would have me spend the money on clothing for school and shit like that. I was plumb amazed that Dexter could make all that money living in the back of a saloon. He told me that it was important that I finish high school and not quit like he did, but it seemed like he'd done real well without all that schooling.

Sometime after Daddy checked out, Mom decided to move up to St. Louis where her older sister, Henrietta lived. She was a manicurist too, and was making pretty good money, or so she said. I remember Grandma Bess begging us not to go. She told Mom that we could move in with her until Mom got a better paying job. She even offered Mom half ownership in her house if she would just stay in Middleberg, at least until I finished high school. Grandma Bess had saved some money for me to attend a community college and maybe be a teacher or an engineer. I think she might have been overrating my school smarts seeing as I had already flunked the third grade, but that's what grandmas are for-- to make their grandkids think they're special. Maybe that's the most important thing they can do for a kid. I think I would've finished high school if I'd stayed with Grandma, but then again, maybe I wouldn't've.

I didn't really want to move. I was a catcher on our PONY league baseball team and I thought I had a good chance of making junior varsity at Middleberg High. Dexter bought me a big brown catcher's mitt, with Yogi Berra's signature. Yogi was a Hall of Famer, and he was raised in St. Louis. I was pretty good at catching foul balls, and I hit a home run the last game of the season. Okay, it was a grounder down the first base line and the right fielder twisted his ankle running over to get it. I circled the bases before the center fielder came over and threw the ball into the infield. I guess I thought I was better than I actually was, but what's wrong with that? Damn, I figured I could make the Cardinals or maybe the Cubs in a few years, but I guess every kid thinks that about their abilities.

I had my first girlfriend too, Norma Jean Fiddler. Her Dad owned the GM dealership in town and them people were pretty damn rich. Grandma said that her folks were uppity, but I think Norma Jean really liked me. I could always make the girls laugh and still can. Her old man would drive us to the movies in a big red Cadillac. The trunk was so big you could put a washer and dryer in there and still have room. That's why no one needed an SUV or a truck in those days. Everything could fit in a trunk. Anyhow, we'd sit in the back of the theater and make out. Norma Jean would let me feel her up pretty good. She was a good kisser too. I had big plans for our sex life once I got my driver's license, but that was before we moved away. Norma Jean still lives down there. She's had six children, and she's a grandma now herself. It's amazing how time just seems to fly by.

Mom was real headstrong about leaving. She wouldn't listen to good advice on just about anything. Bad advice was different. She was all ears for that. Looking back, I think I followed in her footsteps in that department, at least for some things. I reckon she wanted to live it up in the big city. The only place to hang out in Middleberg was The Red Parrot Saloon. It those days, it closed down around ten p.m., even on the weekends. I believe you get the drift. It was a dull place for a woman such as herself, that was still in her prime.

We rented an apartment in a suburb just north of the city limits. At that time, it was mostly white, but after the blacks moved in, it went downhill. Most of the stores that I remembered have closed, including the nail salon where Mom worked. I started school there in the ninth grade. In the beginning, things went pretty well. Mom and I would eat dinner by ourselves, then she'd walk me up the street for an ice cream. Her new job, with tips and all, made her twice as much as she was making in Middleberg. We went to church pretty regularly. That may sound strange to some, but Mom came from a Scotch Irish clan, and it wasn't unusual for them to drink hard on a Saturday night and attend church on a Sunday. Us Jones' and Dixon's too, never seem to feel too bad after a night of heavy boozing. Unlike some folks, a few aspirins and a screwdriver after we get up in the morning, and we're good to go for the rest of the day.

It wasn't long before Mom got to thinking about getting married again. It seemed like she never wanted to live without a man in the house. I dunno to this day why. All in all, marriage is a lot of luck. But you also have to be a person that's good at marriage, and Mom wasn't good at it. Looking back, none of my kin were good at it. Christ, her older sister Henrietta was married three times, and Waldo had two wives. Their younger sister, Winnie, converted to the Catholic religion and became a nun. She might have been the smartest of the bunch. Things went great during the dating period, but as soon as the new man moved in, she'd start fighting with him. First, just smartass comments between them, then the cursing, and then they'd get physical. In a stubborn sort of way, I think Mom kinda enjoyed the rough and tumble.

Mom's third husband was a garbage collector for the city. She met Ernie Wagner in a bar. Mom was a decent looking woman, and when she put on some makeup and a tight turtle neck sweater, she could turn heads until she was in her late forties. I've spent a lot of my adult life in bars, and the people who attend there on a regular basis are not people that make great husbands. To be perfectly honest, I include myself in that category along with Ernie.

Ernie was big man, with a big balding head, and a nose that had been broken more than once. He had beady dark eyes so that you never knew what was going on in his brain. His biceps were like Popeye's from years of lifting trash cans. Being a garbage man in those days wasn't easy. There weren't any of them fork-lift like contraptions on the trucks. Nowadays, a trash collector can sit on his ass and drive a truck and never get his hands dirty.

After Mom got hitched, we moved out of the apartment and into Ernie's house. It was a little red brick box with grey stone around the front door that's common in St. Louis. I remember him walking around in a sleeveless undershirt. That's a man thing, to show off his muscles. Just like a woman with some goods on the top or the bottom likes to wear a tank top and short shorts. Today, all that politically correct stuff about sexual harassment just makes me puke. Hey, look at them Greek statues. There's lots of naked men and women with exposed sex organs, even if some of the arms are missing. Some things don't change and never will. Ernie liked to watch television with his arms up over his head. Maybe he thought Mom would be attracted to all the hair in his armpits. Christ, it looked like a blue jay's nest in there. He usually took a shower after he got home from work. I'll say that much for him.

Ernie took me and Mom to a bunch of Cardinal games that first year they were married. At that time, baseball made some sense. A bleacher seat was only a few bucks. There were eight clubs in the American and eight in the National. The teams that finished first played in the World Series and the games were during the day when a kid could skip school to watch them. Today, there's teams from places that don't know much about baseball, like Seattle, and Colorado, and Canada. Most of the players come from Cuba or the Dominican Republic and half the team is named Gonzales or Rodriguez. There's a bunch of different divisions that don't make no sense. With the playoffs and all, there's snow on the ground before they're done, all to line the pockets of them billionaire owners and players.

About two years after they got hitched, Mom started nagging and sniping at Ernie, and he started hanging around with his old gang. He began to ignore me like I was a piece of furniture or a stale ham sandwich. All the good things we'd done like playing catch or shooting a basketball just stopped. When I asked him to do stuff, he'd just grunt and tell me that he had more important things to tend to.

His pals weren't like them gangbangers that you have today, just a bunch of roughnecks that liked to mix it up. They were big men like himself. They'd go to bars and pick fights--at least that's what Mom told me after they divorced. At first, he went out with his buddies just one night per week, but pretty soon, he was gone most evenings. If he wasn't at the bar, he was at the bowling alley. St. Louis was a hot bed for bowling in those years. Mom even tried to bowl with him in a mixed league, but this only lasted a short while. Pretty soon, Ernie was staying out the whole night and not coming home. One night, Mom went to his favorite bar—the one where she'd first met him—and caught him with an old girlfriend. That night, Mom and I packed up and left.

ELEVEN

MOM LOCATED A DUPLEX near Forest Park. This is a real nice park in the center of town, if you've never lived in St. Louis or never visited. The building was owned by an old Jew, Abe Horowitz. I never knew much about the Jews, but what I'd heard wasn't too good. After Daddy got fired from the insurance agency by his Jewish boss, he bitched that they were dishonest swindlers, and it wasn't a good idea to do business with them. Ever heard the expression, *I jewed him down?* It means you got a better deal that you should've got. Daddy used that a lot. He once told me that a Jew would step over a dying man in a bread line to get something to eat. I guess he was talking about the depression. He said the Jews couldn't be decent people if they didn't accept Jesus Christ like us God-fearing Christians did. I guess he included himself in that group, although I never seen Daddy in a church. Mom never said nothing about that, one way or another. She did complain that Horowitz was a cheap son-of-a-bitch, but she was ornery toward a lot of people.

Mom got very depressed after she left Ernie. This mental disorder ran in both sides of my family, and I've been subject to it on more than one occasion. I could hear her crying at night after she split with Ernie. I think that's when she plumb lost interest in me. She'd get home from the nail salon about seven or eight o'clock in the evening and microwave one of them Swanson fast food dinners or heat up some wieners and beans. I don't ever remember her cooking an actual meal like Grandma did. She started to drink by herself every evening. In those days, she got a real hankering for Beefeater gin with a splash of tonic water. On weekends, she'd sleep most of the day.

After a while, some of her co-workers at the beauty salon convinced Mom to go out with them on Friday nights. Soon, she'd hooked up with some man friends again. They'd pick her up on early Saturday evening, and she wouldn't come home until the wee hours of the morning. Today they might be called *friends with benefits*, but to be honest, I don't know what she did with them. She never slept with them at our place. On those nights, she'd bring home a pepperoni pizza for me. This was before Pizza Hut and Dominoes started delivering. She'd get an extra big one, and I'd eat the leftovers for breakfast the next day. Sometimes, Aunt Henrietta would have me over for a Sunday dinner, but she had three kids of her own and couldn't spare much time for me. She'd just got done with her third husband too. I spent a lot of my time in front of the TV watching game shows and reruns. My favorite show was *My Three Sons*, about a friendly widowed man who raised his three sons by himself.

By this time, I was on my second visit to the tenth grade. As I said before, I wasn't a very good reader. I don't ever remember reading a book that wasn't attached to school work and I didn't read too many of them. If I wasn't watching the boob tube, I'd throw a tennis ball against the steps of our duplex and pretend I was pitching in the Major Leagues. Old Horowitz drove by one day and yelled at me. He told me that all that thumping of the ball was bothering the other tenants.

I liked gym and I was a pretty good drawer, not as good as Dexter, but not bad. I had no interest in subjects like Science or History. Mom never talked about what was happening in the world. She didn't seem to care about anything other than bitching about work. I don't recall her showing up at any of the parent-teacher meetings, but maybe that was for the best. They wouldn't've had much good to say about me anyway.

About that time, I got in with a bunch of rowdy kids. I guess we were bullies, but I don't think I thought much on it at the time. We'd pick on the fat and ugly and awkward kids, call them names and push them around. There were some colored kids in the high school and we had some dustups with them and used the *n-word*. That's when I heard the word *motherfucker* for the first time. One time, a big dude came at us with a knife and put a gash in the chest of one of the guys in our gang. He was in the hospital for two weeks and nearly died. After that, we kinda laid off the black kids.

Our ring leader was a kid named Roger Hanks. He was a big son of a bitch with buck teeth and squinty-like eyes. The rest of us looked up to him, I dunno why. He was the type of kid that was real funny as long as he wasn't picking on you. He liked to call the Jew-kids names like *Kike* and *Shini*, particularly the kids that wore the beanies on their heads. Someone once told me that Muslims believe Jesus was a prophet. I'd have to check it out further before I'd believe that. We didn't have any Muslims in our high school that I remember, and nobody owned up to being gay.

Our gang would get together on Friday and Saturday evenings. We'd ask one of the older brothers or just strangers to buy us beer. One evening, Roger showed up with a can of paint and told us he was fixing to cause a Jew problem. I don't recall if I liked his idea, but we all went along with it. We painted swastikas on some of the Jews' homes in the area and on a synagogue. I was surprised when we painted one on my own building. Roger said the building was owned by a Jew. I don't think he knew that Mom and I lived there, but I kept my mouth shut. I had no reckoning that the whole thing would cause such a ruckus. Looking back, the whole thing was pretty stupid.

The following Monday, the police talked to everyone at the school. One of the kids in the gang cracked and spilled the beans. All of us were hauled into the police station and charged with disturbing the peace and vandalism. No one went to jail, but it stayed on our records. We got expelled from school which was no skin off my nose because I was flunking anyway. When Horowitz found out that I was one of the kids that did it, he raised the riot act with Mom and told us we had to leave. Mom was furious at me. She predicted that one day I'd be in jail. To be honest, I never heard Mom say anything good about me.

We rented another apartment in a western suburb, far away from the blacks and the Jews. She decided to join AA and she was sober for a while. It wasn't long before she met her fourth husband who was a humdinger. Mom met him at a single's bar, a few blocks from our new place. He was a laborer in the Streets Department, one of those guys that picked paper off the boulevards and cut the grass with the big mowers. He had a dark complexion and wore his hair slicked back like The Fonz. He wore a blue jean vest over his bare chest which was popular then. He had a real good physique, and I guess that's what must've attracted Mom. It wasn't for his brains. He always boasted that he had some Cherokee blood in him. I never hung around long enough to see them get married.

TWELVE

WHEN I WOKE UP, it was midafternoon. At that point, I began to believe that Penny wasn't coming back. Screw Penny. I decided to go back to the Waffle House for a bacon patty melt and a side order of hashbrowns smothered in onions. There's nothing that gets a man thinking straighter than when his belly's full. As I hunted on the dresser for my reading glasses, I noticed a business card sitting partially under the hotel telephone. No one ever uses them anymore, now that every dick has a cell phone. After I located my readers, I looked at the card. *Floyd Washington: Exterminator,* and the next line below it, *Floyd's the best, for every pest.* His mobile phone and work number were there too. Floyd seemed like a decent kind of a guy, and he was fixing to go to Chattanooga which was closer to Atlanta than Paducah. It made me uncomfortable to travel with a black man, but what choice did I have? If I couldn't get back to Middleberg, I might as well continue on to Chattanooga. Maybe I could hitch a ride to Atlanta after that. I decided to eat first. And wouldn't you know it? As I was working on my Coke refill, big Floyd came through the door. This seemed like a message from the Almighty.

"Hey Floyd, how ya doin'?"

"Barney? You still here?"

"Buddy."

"Yeah, Buddy. I thought you and Penny would be on the road by now, probably near Nashville."

"Shit no, it hasn't worked out that way. Come sit down here with me." Big Floyd got his big body into the booth and put his order in for a ham and cheese omelet. Mary and Cindy were gone for the day, and a foreign gal named Natasha took our order.

"The truck's not fixed yet?" he asked.

"No, they got it fixed. At least I guess they did?"

"What do you mean, *you guess they did*? Haven't you been to Elmer's to check on it?

"Penny picked the truck up. I hain't had a chance to talk with her about it."

"You haven't had a chance to talk with her about what?" Then I saw this look come over his face. His nostrils flared, and I could see the hair in them. "She left you high and dry?"

"Yup. She's headed back to Missourah with her new BFF."

"Not Gloria Slaughter?" That's the first I heard her last name.

"How'd you know?"

"Oh, they'd been having trouble, her and Hank, for a long while. She and Penny seemed to hit it off pretty good when you were waiting for the truck to get towed. You know, yack yack, yack. I just put two and two together."

"Yep, they've been gone since early this mornin'."

"So, what happened between you and Penny?"

"Oh, she got cross with me. I thought she acted out of place for a woman when I was tryin' to git the truck fixed.

Then she thought I was makin' a pass at Gloria at Pete's Restaurant. Then we argued after I got released from the hospital, and we got a little physical-like. She left me a note to inform me that she and I are done for good."

"Oh." I liked that about Floyd. He warn't one to ask stupid questions after I done all that explaining to him.

"So whadda you gonna do?"

"I've been axin' the same question myself."

"And?"

"Well, I'll be goin' on to visit my daughter in Atlanta."

"I could give you a lift part way. I'm heading in that direction."

"Yeah, you told me that."

"My brother and his family are getting together to celebrate ol' Ebenezer Washington's one hundred and seventy-fifth birthday at his gravesite. I didn't know where it was until just a few years ago."

"Yeah, you already told me."

"After that, if anyone's interested, we'll have lunch and tour the Chickamauga battlefield. I like to renew old acquaintances with the park rangers."

"Where they from?"

"Who?"

"Your kin."

"Atlanta, I'm the only one that ever left. I was the black sheep in the family." He grunt-laughed. "You get that joke, black sheep?" He grunted again.

"Yeah, I got it, pretty funny." I tried to smile.

"My brother's a doctor in Atlanta, a urologist. From Chattanooga, it's only about two hours to Atlanta, if you don't use a mule. It might be good to have some company for the ride, to keep me awake." Another rumble from the deep.

"Well that would really really be nice of you, but I could take a bus." I never considered taking a bus, but I didn't want to sound like I was begging.

"I'll be leaving first thing in the morning."

"Well you know you're a real prince of a guy to help me out."

"I've been called a lot of names, white boy, but never a prince." I figured that was another joke. I laughed too even though I never wanna be called *white boy*.

"I'll have to buy a new suitcase and maybe get some new underwear. Then I'll be ready to go."

"She took your underwear too?"

"Well no, but I'm not one to do wash, and they're well… kind a sweaty."

"Oh, don't worry 'bout that. Give 'em to me and I'll wash them tonight." Now any man who'd wash my underwear *is* a real prince. I wished I could've remembered that thought for the entire trip.

He took me back to the hotel and I gathered up my dirty clothes. I checked the underwear for hash marks but there weren't any. He drove me to JCPenney's, and I bought myself a new purple suitcase made in China. I was thankful that Penny hadn't cancelled the credit card. Maybe she felt bad about the letter she'd wrote.

THIRTEEN

THE NEXT MORNING, I went down to the lobby for the free breakfast before Floyd showed his face. This was my last chance to try the food at the Dew Drop Inn. The first morning I'd been in the hospital, and the second, down at the Waffle House looking for fucked-up fucking Penny. Most motels in those small towns have a free breakfast and the Dew Drop was no different. I wished they'd just forget the breakfast and take the money off your bill.

I hunted for the coffee. It was in a can with a black spigot and a chain around it to tell you if it was decaffeinated or not. Why would anyone drink coffee without a kick? Might as well drink a bottle of warm milk. Most jokers need that shot of caffeine to keep them going at their shit jobs all day. There's this itty-bitty paper cup next to the coffee. It looks like something to dispense medicine, it's so small. Then I realize it's a coffee cup. I guess they don't want you to take too much of their free coffee. After I saw that the pancakes were all stuck together, I stuck a spoon in the oatmeal. It bounced off it like it was goddamned concrete. I gave up on it and popped a bagel in one of those rotating toasters. I never saw a bagel so thin, a bagel on a hunger strike. That's one thing I learned from the Jews, bagels. I found the cream cheese in a little plastic container about the size of a thimble. I wolfed down a few strips of soggy bacon and another tiny cup of coffee before I headed to the front desk to pay my bill. My Mexican buddy was back on duty. I wasn't in the mood for him.

"How was your stay, sir?" he asked with this fake smile on his face, as plastic as my credit card that he's swiping. Why do I have to put up with some wetback who's taking a job from a red-blooded American? I only got so much patience.

"How do you think it was?"

"I have no idea. Tell me, amigo." *More Goddamned Spanish from this jumping bean.*

"Yeah, you're right, you have no goddamn idea. My girlfriend left me. I lost my truck. I spent one night in the hospital, and I pretty near puked up your lousy free breakfast." He looked at me with that phony grin like I'm giving him a four-star rating.

"I'm sorry for all your trouble. Did Penny get back okay?"

"How would I know?" *Maybe I'm hoping she didn't get back okay. Maybe she got in an accident and broke a leg and totaled the truck.*

"Just asking, that's all. Do you want a copy of your bill, or an email with a customer survey to fill out?"

"You're goddamned right I wanna fill out a survey. What's your name?"

"Carlos." He pointed to his name tag that said CARLOS.

"And your last?"

"We don't give out our last names, sir. It's against company policy."

"I'd like your last name, so I can email the management and tell them what a prick you are. They need to git you back to the laundry."

"Sir, I'm sorry your experience has not been up to your high standards. I would be happy to bring the manager out." His face was fixed in that stupid smile. I was just about ready to knock out a few teeth in that smile. If you've been paying attention, you'll appreciate that I've got a pretty short fuse at times. Suddenly, I felt a squeeze of pressure in the chest. Shit, if I was ten years younger, I'd have that taco-eater on his ass.

"Just give me the receipt. Forget the survey, your manager won't read it anyway."

When I got to the exit doors, I saw Floyd's van parked in the driveway. A light snow was falling. I was hoping we might travel in something more comfortable. My back was still sore from the trip to JCPenney's to get the suitcase. The springs were shot and the passenger seat felt like your ass was on a concrete block. And who'd want to travel in a vehicle with a picture of a dead cockroach on each side panel?

"You ready, bro?" he asked.

"I guess."

"Sorry about the van, I had to leave the Oldsmobile at home. Helen might need a car, and with her new hip she can't get in and out of this thing." I tried to smile. He opened the back of the van and I threw my new suitcase in with his stuff. I saw my underwear stacked neatly in a cardboard box. "Carlos at work today? He asked.

"Yep. Let me tell you about that son of a—"

"Carlos goes to the same church as me."

"Church-going, huh?"

"That guy's the reincarnation of Jesus Christ."

"Yeah, no kidding." I had to laugh at that one.

"No seriously. He and his wife are fostering four kids and they have three of their own. He was honored as Paducah Citizen of the Year in 2015. The mayor gave him a key to the city. He's kind of a celebrity in this town." *I'm sposed to believe that bullshit?*

"How long will it take to get to Chattanooga?" I asked.

"Oh, three and a half hours, maybe four. The weather could slow us down. By the way, did Penny get back to Missouri okay?"

"I hain't heard from her so I wouldn't know."

"She's a nice gal. I hope you two get back together."

"Floyd let's make a deal. Let's not talk about Penny no more."

"Sure enough, whatever you say, Buddy." He put the van in first gear. It was one of those stick shifts in the floor. There's a grinding sound like someone put a sack of gravel in the gearbox.

"I sure hope this clutch makes it a while longer," he laughed. That doesn't seem so funny to me. We got on the Interstate. The snow started to come down a little heavier. He moved over to the slow lane. "The tire treads are a little worn so I gotta be extra careful." He turned on one of them hip hop stations.

"Who's singin'?

"Kanye West."

"Aren't you a little on the old side for that?"

"I dunno, bro." I'm not his *bro*. I wish he'd quit calling me that. "Some of the lyrics are kinda poetic. My son, Floyd Jr., plays his stuff all the time. But you're right, I'm more of a Chuck Berry guy." I start listening, nothing but *pussy* and the *f-word* a dozen times. Something about living in the ghetto.

"You buy into all that ghetto stuff, Floyd?"

"What do you mean, *ghetto stuff*?

"I mean all those punks hangin' around the corner, gettin in trouble with the cops. You know, them lazy bums that should be out workin', not living on food stamps." *It wasn't the first or the last time I said something stupid, but dadgumit, I'm telling the truth.* I started to backpedal. "I don't mean you, Floyd. You're a hard workin' God-fearing man."

"You ever been to a ghetto?"

"Well I seen it on TV lots of times. And you know, in the movies, too."

"Well, until you walk in those shoes, maybe you just don't know shit." The rasp in his voice got a little louder.

"Well you don't live there neither."

"How do you know where I come from? You don't know jack about me."

"I guess I don't." The guy's going out of his way to help me out and I just can't keep my mouth shut.

After a few minutes, Floyd piped up. "Ever heard of the Bluff in Atlanta?

"Nope."

"That's where we lived until I was fourteen. Then we moved to a safer part of town. That place was filled with motherfuckers. The gangs were just getting started then. You kept yo' ass out of their way if you didn't want to get robbed or raped or knifed or killed. I had the good fortune to have a Mama who kept me clear of all that."

"So, I'm right, there's a lot of bad dudes out there."

"Sure, there are. I don't like them any better than you do, but most of the folk in the ghetto are hardworking poor people who just want to be left alone. You can't lump us all together. You wouldn't like me to call all yo' people a bunch of rednecks, now wouldya?" *Yeah, blame everything on us white folk.* Floyd kept quiet for a while but a muscle in his jaw started to spasm.

"After high school, I attended a black college, Tuskegee University, on a football scholarship. I played defensive tackle, but I was hoping to be a history professor. I was never dumb enough to think I could make it in the NFL."

"Yeah, you've got them big thighs, tough to block. I played some football myself in high school." Not really, but I could have made the team if I'd tried out.

"I tore up my knee and lost my scholarship my junior year. I'd have needed four or five more years to get a PhD, and I'd run out of money. Anyway, in those days, who'd hire a black guy to teach history?"

"How'd you get in the pest killing business?"

"Oh, it's not much of a story. My wife Helen's from Paducah. I met her at college. She's taught English in the Paducah public schools for almost twenty-five years. I went to work for a white guy. Give him credit for hiring me. I know he lost more than a few customers after I started working there, but I brought in some minority business so it all worked out. When he retired, I bought the company from him. I earn a pretty good living off of it, and my son'll run the business when I retire."

We crossed over the border into Tennessee. Big Floyd rumbled. "I'm going to pull over in Clarksville, I got to pee and we need some gas."

"I'm with you there." I said. Black or white, that prostrate gland can grow pretty ugly in all of us men. Gets you peeing nine or ten times in a day, and you get wakened up from your sleep at all goddamned hours. You learn to keep a clear track to the bathroom at night, so's you won't trip and fall on a stray shoe or get tangled up in your lady friend's undergarments. When you do find the toilet, it takes five minutes to get the goddamned thing to work.

FOURTEEN

AFTER CLARKSVILLE, the snow stopped and we tooled along pretty good. Soon we were on the other side of Nashville approaching Murfreesboro. We settled on an oldies station and we were singing along to Chucky Berry's *Johnny B. Goode* when suddenly Floyd slowed down, and I saw flashing lights behind us. Christ, we couldn't have been going more than 55 in that shit can.

"What's up Floyd? You warn't speedin' were you?"

"No, I don't think so." We pulled over to the shoulder. The highway patrol officer approached us, the glare of them red bulbs blinking behind him. He was a big man with a Smokey-the-Bear hat that the lawmen like to wear in the south. Floyd rolled down the window.

"What's the problem, officer?" I noticed there was a quiver in his voice.

"When you braked a few miles ago, I noticed one of your tail lights was out on this here van, sir." He doesn't say *sir* politely, but mocks Floyd with his tone. I looked at his name tag, KRUCKENBERG, nothing like a Polack for meanness and dumbness. "It's illegal in Tennessee to drive with a defective brake light. Let's see your driver's license."

Floyd fumbled for his wallet and his hands were shaking. "I believe my wallet's in the glove compartment, sir."

"Well that's a problem ain't it? I'll need you out of the car and your hands on the roof."

"I checked my vehicle pretty carefully when I left. Everything seemed to be working okay." Floyd was meek as a puppy.

"Why cain't he just step on the brake, and we can see if the brake light is out?" I said.

"Hey bud. If I said the light was out, it was goddamn out. You keep your mouth shut unless I ask you something. Both of you, out of the vehicle. I want to see some identification from your passenger as well."

Floyd and I did like he said. We hung with our hands on the roof as cars whizzed past. You never realize how fast those vehicles are travelling on a highway until you're out of a car and stranded on the shoulder. The officer patted us down and took my driver's license. He got in on the passenger side and used a screw driver and a hammer to open the glove compartment. Then he headed back to his car. We stood there shivering on the shoulder of the highway while he ran our stuff through his computer. You could see the frown on his face through the front window of the cop car. Then we heard sirens shrieking. Two more cop cars pulled up behind the first one. Soon there were three or four officers coming at us with guns in their hands.

"Holy shit, Floyd. What did ya do?"

"Nuthin. What did *you* do?"

"Nuthin, at least not for twenty years."

Just then I felt the steel of a gun in my rib cage and the patrolman barked. "Are you Jones?"

"Yes sir."

"We've got a three-state alert for a Harold I. Jones. You're under arrest."

"You must've mistook me for a different Harold Jones, sir. I mean Jones is a pretty common name. Whad I do, sir?"

"Don't get smart with me, asshole." He stuck the gun in a little bit deeper. "You know goddamned well what you did. Armed robbery in regard to four banks in Kentucky, Tennessee and Georgia."

Kruckenberg looked at Floyd. "And you're under arrest for harboring a fugitive. I knew you were up to something when I pulled you over." He sniggered through his yellow-stained teeth. He put cuffs on us and pushed me and Floyd into the squad car. Soon we were behind bars in Squirrel Summit, Tennessee. There was a few drunks and a gay pimp in the cell with us. We hadn't said anything since we got in the car.

"Jeez Buddy, that really you? All those robberies?"

"Fuck no, Floyd. It's got to be some sort of mistake. If you'd had your brake lights workin' this wouldn't have happened."

"Are you kidding? That's just what they do."

"Do what?"

"Pull us over."

"Pull who over? I don't get it, Floyd."

"You know, driving while black. Stop us for no reason. That's a favorite excuse. Your brake lights are out. How'd he know that? I never braked for miles. There's hardly any traffic."

"Just to harass you?"

"You that stupid, white boy?" A guy in the cell hollered out.

"Yeah, a stupid white mon is in here wid us." *I needed to take crap from some Jamaican fruitcake.*

After a few hours, the sheriff came by our cell. I could tell he was the man in charge because he had four stars on both of his lapels, like some sort of big shot Norman Schwarzkopf. You ever notice that they give these local sheriffs all those stars for a police force of about five guys?

"Who's Mr. Harold I. Jones here?"

"Sir, that'd be me sir." Never hurts to use a liberal sprinkling of *sir* when you're in contact with the law.

"Looks like we made a mistake. Your name and birthday exactly matched a Harold I. Jones wanted for armed robbery. It's only when we matched your social security number that we figured out that you weren't the guy we're looking for."

"And who's Floyd Washington?"

"That's me, sir."

"We're dropping the charges of harboring a fugitive." He gave Floyd and me back our wallets and the keys to the van. "After you pay your fine for the malfunctioning brake light and not wearing a seat belt, you're free to go. We broke the lock on your glove compartment door when we searched your van, so we're going to subtract twenty-five bucks from your fine. That's a total of 195 dollars."

"Can't we test the brake lights outside to see if they're workin', sir? If they are, you can't fine my friend here, sir." He glared at me with a face like a jagged rock, but he didn't say anything.

"Do you take a credit card, Misteh Sheriff?" Floyd sounded like Uncle Tom's aunt.

"Yeah. Pay up at the exit desk." And he walked away.

"What about the seat belts?" I whispered to Floyd. "I'm pretty sure we had them on. Goddamnit! We need a goddamn lawyer."

"You're dumber than a moron, Buddy. Let's just get our asses out of here or he'll find something else wrong with us, and we'll be here a week. You mark my words."

"Hey, we're in the U.S. of A. We have rights in this country. Let's fight this thing." Floyd got his credit card out of his wallet. It's no use talking to someone who's not listening. When we got to the van, I asked Floyd to pump the brakes while I stood behind it. The lights were working just fine.

FIFTEEN

IT WAS WAY PAST DARK and we were still fifty miles from Chattanooga. I suggested we stop at a Subway along the road, and we split a twelve-inch turkey sub. The meat was so thin you could have used it for a window pane. Hey, I was trying to eat healthy like Dr. Haqq told me. The turkey didn't stay with me too long, and Floyd complained he was still hungry. At the next exit we stopped again. I got a big bag of salty peanuts and an ice cream cone with hot chocolate topping. Floyd bought two hot dogs that were rolling like little logs on those grills that you see at every rest stop. He filled the bun with fried onions and guzzled a super-sized Coke. I had to smell his belches when we got back in the van. If his legs weren't so thick and heavy, I would've said that both of them were hollow.

We found a motel off the freeway, the Sleep EZ Inn. There was a neon sign in front that advertised a room for thirty bucks a night. Maybe it was one of those daytime places for couples that want to procreate the species without their spouses knowing it, if you get my drift. There were only a few cars in the lot this time of night. Floyd went in to get us a room. He came out about one minute later. "The man inside says he's all filled up for the night."

"Whaddya talkin' about?"

"I'm just tellin' you what the man said."

"That's some kinda bullshit." I decided to check it out myself. There was an old guy sitting on an old stool behind the desk. He looked like he hadn't combed his hair for a couple of weeks. It was standing up in the back of his head like one of them cockapoo birds that you see on the National Geographic Channel.

"You gotta room for me and a friend?"

"Yep, man or a woman?"

"A man."

"I'll just warn you once. We don't allow none of that sodomy in this hotel."

"It's not what you think. He's jes my friend and we're sharing a room."

"That's what all of them say," and he cackled, like he thinks it's pretty funny.

"Who owns this place?"

"You're looking at him, yessiree!" He laughed again. That's when I start worrying about a person's mental sanitary. Just then Floyd walked in. "Didn't I tell you, we don't have no room for you."

"This here's my friend, that's going to stay with me. You just told me there was a room for us." I wasn't going to let this crackpot get the best of me. Buddy Jones don't take that garbage from anyone, especially an old fart that's off his rocker.

"I said for you, not for *him and you*."

"Now wait one Goddamned minute. You ever heard of civil rights?" I never thought I'd be speaking up for a black man.

"You ever heard of the Civil War? We would've won if we'd killed Lincoln sooner and if General Stonewall Jackson hadn't been shot at the battle of Chancellorsville. He was the greatest general that the South ever produced, and a God-fearin' man too. He wouldn't let any buggering men into his hotel neither." Then he started this shrieking again. I started toward him with the thought of making a pizza pie out of his face. Then I felt a tug on my shirt which stopped me in my tracks. It was Floyd.

"Let's go Buddy. We don't want to stay in this flea bag."

"Fuck, Floyd. I'll beat the shit out of this old rooster." The one guy that's got a weaker heart than me. But maybe Floyd was right. Maybe the guy worked out five times a week.

We stopped at a Holiday Inn Express along Broad St., the main drag in Chattanooga. There was a chunky black girl roaming around behind the check-in desk. She told us she didn't think there was anything available that time of night, but Floyd told her to check anyway. While she's on the computer, he started *jivin'* and *shivin'* and *shimmyin'* with a bunch of *sho'nuff* this and *sho'nuff* that. Soon she was chuckling and laughing with some *oh yeahs* thrown in. She flashed her pearly white teeth, and she wore that big thick red lipstick. I could see Floyd was having a good time with her. I just kept quiet and let Floyd do the talking. My big mouth hadn't got me too far on this trip. He got us the best room in the house for 99 bucks.

We had a suite with two queen beds. Thank God for that. There wasn't any way I was getting in the sack with Floyd for reasons I don't need to go into. Floyd plunked down on the far bed. The springs creaked in pain knowing they'd have to support the big fella for the next eight hours. I'd never slept in a room with a black man, but I soon found something out. He snored louder than any man or woman that I've known so far in my life, even louder than Penny, but don't ever tell her I said that.

In the morning, ol' Floyd headed into the john with a big hardcover book that he'd been reading, *The History of the Civil War* by Shelby Foote. This thing must've weighed over five pounds. Floyd said it was the third book of three that Mr. Foote wrote on the Civil War. He was reading it for the second time. I never knew anyone to read that big a book on the toilet, or anywhere else for that matter. He told me it read like a novel, but I had trouble believing that.

I turned on the TV. I like to watch Fox & Friends when I wake up. There was some Senate committee investigating Trump for something with the Russians, more fake news in my book. The lefties are always harassing him, and he can't get any work done with all the witch hunts. I turned up the TV louder. I don't want to hear all the noise that goes into moving your bowels, particularly from a person like Floyd.

Then I heard water running, and I reckoned he was in the shower. I got out my phone to check the Greyhound bus schedule. There was nothing leaving for Atlanta until five o'clock that evening. Soon Floyd came out with the steam from the bathroom following along with him. He had a towel wrapped around him. The towel was pretty small in relationship to his big behind. It barely covered his private parts. He rummaged for his undershorts in his luggage. Finally, he pulled out a pair the size of a tablecloth. There were red hearts on them with little arrows shooting through each one of them.

"Got these for Valentine's Day from Helen years ago," he chuckle-grunted. "I know they look kind of goofy, but whenever I'm away from Helen I like to take them with me. Kind of reminds me of her, if you know what I mean." I nodded my head. I fixed my eyes on the television while he got dressed. Like most men, I don't like to look at another man's private parts unless of course you like that kinda thing which I don't. Floyd didn't seem to worry about stuff like that.

"I was reading about General Nathan Bedford Forrest in my book."

"Don't know him Floyd. The only two generals I ever knew about was Grant and Lee. Like I said before, history ain't my thing."

"He fought on your side."

"How'd you know what side I was on? I warn't even born then."

"I just know. I bet you have a Confederate flag on the back of your truck."

"You're wrong there, Floyd. I don't own one."

"You know, he started out in the Civil War as a private and ended up a General."

"Who?'

"Nathan Bedford Forrest."

"I guess that don't happen nowadays."

"No, it sure doesn't. He supposedly was the only Confederate general that Grant feared. He killed 30 men himself and had twenty-nine horses shot from under him."

"No shit. That's a lot of horses."

"In the Battle of Fort Pillow, he and his men killed three hundred black Union soldiers and some white soldiers too.

Some claimed that he massacred them as they were trying to surrender but it was never proved."

"Didn't you tell me your great-granddaddy fought with the South and then the North?"

"Yes and no, he was a slave at Chickamauga helping his master. That's a lot different than actually fighting for the South. He ran away to the Union lines during the battle."

"Well Jesus, that's not very patriotic."

"What's not?"

"Desertin' during the battle, jes when the lieutenant needed him."

"You expected him to remain a slave when he could be free?"

"But, what if he treated him nice and all that? Wouldn't he owe that man?"

"Owe him for what? Owe him to keep him as a slave? You work for nothing and they sell your sons and rape your daughters." I could see I wasn't going to convince him of anything.

"How's the shower?" I asked.

"Oh, not too bad, at least the water's hot. Be careful you don't slip and break a leg in there. It's kind of slippery. These cheap showers they put in nowadays aren't built for big men like us."

Floyd was right. I almost killed myself getting out to look for the body wash that I forgot to bring in there with me. Then there was them tiny little bottles of shampoo and conditioner. The print's really small on the labels, and I wasn't able to tell one from another without my readers. What do they want me to do? Bring eyeglasses into the shower with me? When I got out, Floyd was reading his book again. The

TV was off. He's a real bookworm. Not like too many people I ever knew. He was dressed in a white shirt and sport jacket.

"Why're you so spiffed up?"

"I like to look my best when I'm visiting a grave. It shows respect for the dead. By the way, how ya getting to Atlanta?"

"There's a bus that leaves at five o'clock."

"Whadda you gonna do 'til then?"

"I dunno, just walk down Broad St. Maybe sit on a bench and look at the Tennessee River."

"Why don't you come with me? We'll be at the grave for about ten minutes, then we'll all go out for a bite to eat."

"I dunno, Floyd. Dead people aren't my thing."

"There's a great barbecue place near the cemetery. We went there the first time we were here, when ol' Ebenezer was one hundred and seventy. Then if we got time, we can tour the Chickamauga battle site."

"Okay, if I won't be a bother to you." Shit, I haven't got nowhere else to go, and his rich brother would pick up the tab for all of us.

"My family loves the whites. Some of our best friends are white." Floyd laughed like somehow that was funny.

"Where we going to eat breakfast?" I asked.

"I was thinking the same thing myself," answered Floyd. Now that's one thing Floyd and I got in common, thinking where we're gonna eat.

"Don't we git the free breakfast? I thought your lady friend included that in the package?"

"She did, but I'd rather go to a Waffle House or a Bob Evans. Get something that can line my belly for a while."

"Okay, the Bob Evans. Maybe I've got my fill of the Waffle House for a while."

Floyd ordered *The Farmer's Choice Breakfast:* two eggs, three hot cakes, two slices of French toast, and a side order of bacon. After he'd chowed down all that, he got some hot rolls with his third cup of coffee. I got the *Big Egg Breakfast*: three eggs sunny side up, four sausages and three strips of bacon, hash browns, and freshly baked bread. Then I ordered some blueberry hotcakes with a dab of whipped cream while Floyd was eatin' his rolls. To hell with Doc Haqq, I'm on vacation.

SIXTEEN

AFTER BREAKFAST, Floyd pulled out his smart phone and checked Google Maps to find the cemetery. He parked the van near a small field overgrown with a bunch of thistles and crab grass. I followed him as he hiked through the cemetery. We came to one that said EBENEZER WASHINGTON. No date of birth or nothing like that, I could barely make out his name. I guess you're really dead when your gravestone's so old that your name's been worn away.

There was a cold wind blowing, and the sky was overcast. Luckily, I still had my heavy coat. I tugged the collar up to my ears. Floyd spent several minutes just staring at the grave marker, like he was thinking deep about something. I didn't want to interrupt, but my fanny was starting to chill, and my feet were going numb. I don't have too good a circulation in them according to the Doc. Finally, Floyd started to talking almost like I wasn't there.

"Imagine what it must have been like to be a slave. Just think, you're not really considered an actual person, more like a horse, or a donkey, or a pig." He chuckled but it wasn't that he found anything funny. Floyd sometimes made those noises when he was plumb serious too. "If your master considers you his equal, then it would be against his religious teachings to rape, beat, or kill you, but making the black man subhuman, I guess eased his conscience. Kind of the same as what Hitler did to the Jews."

We didn't talk for a while. I was going to tell him that we'd been there a lot longer than ten minutes, but I kept my mouth shut. You could hear the gusts whistling through the bare trees, but the sleet had let up.

Just when I was about to head back to the van by myself, here come two black people very well dressed, in fact better dressed than most whites I knew. The man was tall and lean, younger than Floyd, and a lighter color. He looked like Harry Belafonte in his prime. He was wearing a fancy suit with a zigzag pattern on it. I think they call it herring bone. He'd got on nice shiny black shoes that people don't wear in Middleberg. His wife was one good-looking bitch, straight black hair and straight white teeth.

"Hey Booker, how long have you been here?" The man talked like a white gent. None of that jive in his voice.

"Oh, about ten minutes." Floyd gave them each a big hug. "Olive, so glad you could come." The wife stood stiffly while Floyd was bear-hugging her, like he might mess up her hairdo.

"I just had to bring her along to show her the grave," said Richard. She smiled weakly like she could have done without seeing ol' Ebenezer's grave.

"This here's my friend Buddy, Buddy Jones. Buddy, this is my brother Richard Washington, MD." He added the MD with a special tone to show how proud he was of him. "Buddy's from up north, near St. Louie."

"Good to meet you, Doc. Your brother was kind enough

to drive me from Paducah after my truck broke down." I shook his hand, no callouses or grease on his fingers. No need for a bigshot like that to cut his own lawn or fix his car himself.

"This is my wife, Olive."

"Hello." No *Howyadoin'* Buddy or *Hi there* Buddy, just a *hello* that could freeze a dragon's breath in hell.

"Floyd tells me this is the second time y'all have visited the grave." I tried to sound interested.

"Yes, there's quite a history here. For many years, all we knew was his name. My big brother here did all the work finding his grave. He's quite a history buff. I'm just a urologist."

"A urologist huh? I visit one up in St Louis once a year. Got trouble with the prostrate like most men my age."

"Prostate," interrupted Olive. Well fuck, she's got to put me down. If I wanna call it the *prostrate*, that's my business.

"How'd you get into *that* profession?"

"Oh, it's a long story." Richard smiled, seemed like a nice sort of fella.

"I always wondered about what a urologist talks about when he gets home for dinner? Some guy who took Viagra and had an erection that lasted more than four hours?" I gave it a hee-haw. No one else laughed.

"Floyd researched the archives at the National Military Parks in Chattanooga and Chickamauga. It turned out that Ebenezer settled here after the war. It was my brother's idea that we get together on his quartoseptcentennial."

"Quarto what?"

"His one hundred and seventy-fifth birthday," Richard laughed. He found *that* real funny I guess. "Sorry Helen couldn't make it, Floyd. How's the hip coming?"

"Oh, slow progress but she's getting there," answered Floyd.

"And Floyd Jr?"

"Doin' well, doin' well. He's fitting into the business pretty good. He wanted to come but someone needed to mind the store. He seems to have all that drug stuff and drinking behind him. He's going to church regularly too."

"That's good to hear, bro. Maurice should be here soon. I gave him instructions how to get here. His plane landed from LaGuardia half hour ago."

"Maurice?" I asked.

"Yeah Maurice, my son." Just then I saw a young man coming across the field with a cocky swagger that I didn't like right off the bat. He'd got on torn blue jeans in the knees and a faded jacket to match. He was wearing sunglasses even though there wasn't any sun. He had them corn rows on top of his head, with braids down his back.

"Who's this dude?" he asked.

"Mr. Buddy Jones, a friend of your uncle's," Richard said. He looked embarrassed to introduce me to his son who had *fuck-up* written all over him.

"I didn't know any white boys were invited to Ebenezer's birthday party." Maurice laughed. He didn't bother to shake my outstretched hand.

"Now that's no way to talk! What'd we ever teach you?" Olive barked.

"Maurice is a hip hop and rap recording artist. He's just moved to New York City." Floyd tried to smooth things over.

"Hey Floyd, did you hear my record on Real 96.1?"

"Can't say I have," answered Floyd.

"It's called 'Beating the White Man's Ass'. It's exploding on the charts." He started to chant, "*There's a mother fucker white man down the street, the kind of a man that likes to cheat, poor black folk that have to eat. He drives a big old caddy and carries some heat, and he likes to kill niggers from thirty feet.*"

No one said nuthin. If I was about twenty years younger, I'da whupped this kid, made his face look like chocolate pudding with strawberry sauce. Richard looked whiter than a ghost and that's hard for a black fella to do, even a light-skinned man. Olive looked straight ahead, you could see the pain in her eyes. *"One day the old man ran out of luck, we tied his wrists and feet to the back of a truck, we pulled down his pants and started to …."*

Floyd cut in. He was desperate to change the subject. "How's your wife doin', Maurice?"

"Doin' okay. She's almost done with her master's degree." Now what's an educated woman see in a little bastard like him? Just then, another chilly blast of wind came up.

"I made some lunch reservations at Willie's Smoke House," said Richard.

"Remember Willie?" said Floyd. "He wore that big white cowboy hat, quite a character. Buddy, you'll get a kick outta Willie. He's got a bunch of--"

"Floyd, can you say a few words for Ebenezer and then we'll go," interrupted Richard. The icy rain started again.

"Sure enough," Floyd answered. He took out a piece of paper. It was a memo sheet from his work. I could see the motto: *Floyd's the best for every pest on the back*. He started in.

"We gather here to honor our dear departed great-grandfather, Ebenezer Washington, on his one hundred and seventy-fifth birthday, and to remember that we'd still be slaves if it weren't for him and all the black and white men who fought and died so that we could be free. I know he'd be happy that we had a black president for eight wonderful years. Barack Obama will go down in history along with Lincoln and our namesake George Washington, as one of the greatest presidents of all time."

Hey, now that Mr. Obama's gone, we got a man that was born right here in the US of A., Donald Trump, a man for everybody. A man that will fix this mess we're in. Of course, I don't say anything.

"Let us pray for the soul of Ebenezer and all the Washingtons that have come after. Granddad Ebenezer, and our dear parents, Mamie and Jimmy Washington, and our dear departed brother, Roosevelt and his departed wife Theresa. I'm sorry that my wife Helen couldn't be here today along with our…." Jeez, how manAnoopy more SOBs did we have to hear about? It's freezing cold out here. What happened to the summer barbecue with hot dogs, and ribs, and watermelons, and tee shirts for every year that they got together? Finally, Floyd stopped talking. We trudged back to our cars and drove over to Willie's Smoke House.

SEVENTEEN

FLOYD FOLLOWED RICHARD'S big black Mercedes to the restaurant. We sat down at a large table in the corner, all except Olive, who headed to the women's toilet. Suddenly, the good old-fashioned aroma of barbecue hit me in the face. I forgot all about that big breakfast we'd ate that morning. My stomach was ready for more victuals. I stared over at Floyd. He was already checking out the menu. I saw that he was fixing to eat something big, maybe some smoked ribs smothered in Willie's Special Barbecue Sauce. He looked up and gave me a wink and a little grin. It was just about noon and we were a little early for the lunch crowd. There was a mix of white and black in there. That's one thing just about everyone has in common, the love of smoked meat, except of course them lefty vegetarians. Christ, they can't be happy eating tofu and carrots, but they want to believe they are. They're on their way to the grave just like all of us. Okay, maybe it'll take a few years longer, but how much fun will they have eating like frigging rabbits. Stuff like Swiss chard. I knowd about it because Connie liked to eat it. We got lots of food in America. We don't need to eat no crap from Switzerland.

Olive came back from relieving herself or whatever she was doing in the can. She was wearing a tight black dress that showed her curves. She looked over at me as I'm lookin' over her, and she don't like that look on my face. I don't how that *look* looks to a woman, maybe it's because a man's jaw drops, and he doesn't blink. Whatever it was, it wasn't a look that she particularly cared to see from me. She sat down and pulled up the menu near her face.

Just then, the waiter came up, a heavy-set guy with dark skin and a full beard cut short. He was wearing a turban. "My name is Anoop. I'll be your vaiter. You all know vat you vant?"

"Well, tell me about your ribs," said Floyd. I kinda laughed. What does Alibaba know about good ol' southern barbeeQ.

"Let me tell you truth. The best ribs in Chattanooga!" He pronounced it *Chaattanoooga* like he was singing a song.

"Where's Willie?" Richard asked.

"Our family took over the business last July." Goddamnit, a bunch of immigrants making food they ain't never ate in their life.

"Where ya come from?" I asked.

"The Bunjab, B as in Beter, U N J A B." He spelled it out.

"Where's it at?"

"It's in India," piped up Olive. *Well, who the hell asked her?*

"My uncle and my father ran a Sikh restaurant in a little town near Chandigarh. They served mostly vegetarian meals but some mutton and chicken too. The town was boor and couldn't support both of them. Therefore, my uncle moved to the States, a great land of opportunity." He had this big smile on his face and his arms opened wide. "I came to join the business ven I vas eighteen years old. My uncle vorked as a vaiter in Nashville for ten years. He saved up enough money to open an Indian restaurant here in Chattanooga. It's called Sahib's. I vould highly recommend it to you. Last year, he bought this blace from Villie. Villie's retired in Florida. Ve also own the batent on his secret sauce."

"Would you go with the St. Louis ribs or the baby back?" asked Floyd.

"I recommend the baby back, best in town."

"Do you think a half slab will do it for me?" Floyd doesn't give a shit about what people look like or talk like. He just wanted that plate of food in front of him. I'll give him credit for that.

"Vell sir, a big fellow such as you should have a whole slab. You look like a man who needs more than a half-slab to fill your insides." He laughed, and Floyd laughed too. "And for you Madam, vat can I do for you?" He looked over at Olive.

"How's the plain Caesar salad without chicken?" How in the hell does she expect the Caesar salad to be? This was a rib place, *a Goddamn Indian rib place,* but still a rib place.

"Ve have best salads in Chattanooga, I not kid you."

Maurice was wearin' headphones and tapping out beats on the table. Annoying as hell, but at least he'd kept that foul mouth of his shut. Richard ordered a half slab for him and one for himself, almost like his son wasn't there.

"And vat can I get for you sir?"

"How's the pulled pork?" I asked.

"Ve have best bork sandvich in all of Tennessee, you can take that to de bank."

"How do you guys know anything about pork? You ain't sposed to eat it."

"Sikhs can eat bork. It's Muslims and Jews who can't," answered Anoop.

"You get a bagel at McDonalds, don't you?" Olive chimed in. "No Jews are baking them there. Are Mexicans the only ones preparing the food at Taco Bell?"

Maurice suddenly burst out. "Hey man, you some kind of bigot? This guy here is trying to make a living." Anoop had disappeared to put in our order.

"No. I don't think Buddy meant it that way, right, Buddy?" said Floyd.

"No sir, I didn't. I just thought none of them camel jockeys ate pork. Hey, that's a joke," I laughed. There was silence. Maurice had put his ear phones back on. I don't reckon he heard me. The food came pretty fast. I got to admit, the pork was pretty good, not like what you get in some places, but not all bad. Meantime, they're going on about Great Auntie this and Uncle Tyrone that.

"Too bad DeWayne couldn't make it," said Richard.

"Who's DeWayne?" I asked.

"Our nephew, Roosevelt's son. He's the only other relative that has a connection to old Ebenezer."

"Guess what?" said Olive. "He got married a few weeks ago. He's invited all of us to celebrate with him and his new wife this weekend. No wedding, but they're hosting a dinner at a restaurant downtown."

"He wanted your number, Floyd. Did he call?" asked Richard.

"Yeah, I got a message a few days ago. I've been too busy to call him back. Haven't seen much of him since Roosevelt died."

"What happened to him?" I asked.

"Died in a car accident with his wife. He was only forty-two," Floyd answered.

"Floyd, you could drive down and stay with us. Then we'll all go to the party," added Olive. I saw her smile for the first time.

"Let me check with Helen and Floyd Jr. to make sure the business is running okay. You know, I haven't been to Atlanta for quite a while. I could catch up with some of my old high school buddies while I'm there." I sure could use a ride all the way but for once I kept my mouth shut. Floyd got on his cell phone with Helen and put it on speaker. They repeated all the family gossip that they had just talked about. Helen thought they could manage a few more days.

"Okay it's settled," said Floyd. "I'll take you into Atlanta, Buddy. It's not a long drive."

"Geez, that's really good of you Floyd." Shucks, I was starting to think that Floyd maybe liked me.

EIGHTEEN

WE LEFT THE RESTAURANT and drove until we came to a two-lane road. We saw a little sign that said *Welcome to Georgia*. It looked just like Middleberg. Lots of old frame houses, some with rusted cars and other junk in their yards. Other than some strip malls and fast food restaurants, it didn't seem like anything had been built in the last forty years. We passed a bunch of buildings and a sign that said Fort Oglethorpe, Georgia.

"What's all this, Floyd?"

"It's an old army barracks. Regular folks rent them now. It housed several thousand German prisoners in World War I. It's where the WACs trained in World War II."

"The WACs?"

"Yeah, Women's Army Corp. In World War II they were file clerks and telephone operators, stuff like that. Some people were against them being in the war, called them lesbians and prostitutes, but they freed up men for combat missions."

"Shit, now they're flyin' fighter jets and joinin' the Marines. I cain't agree with that. Them's men jobs. You get a long deployment in Afghanistan or Iraq, and men will be men."

"You ever in the military, Buddy?"

"Nope. I was 4-F from a hernia. You know a little bulge above my groin. By the time I got it fixed, Vietnam was over. I would've loved to have killed them Gooks."

"I guess that's why we lost that war."

"I don't get your drift, Floyd."

"That's a joke, Buddy."

"Oh, I guess I forgot to laugh."

"I was too young to get drafted," said Floyd. "Maybe I should have enlisted. The army could have paid for my college. It's something I sometimes regret." We drove up to the Chickamauga Visitor's Center. Floyd's van was the only vehicle in the visitor's parking lot.

"No one's here," I said.

"It seems like people just aren't interested in the Civil War anymore. It's mostly retired people that show up here now. You gotta have a car or a horse to see the place. You know this was the second bloodiest battle next to Gettysburg?"

"No shit. I never even heard of Chickamauga until you told me 'bout it. I just ain't interested in history."

"You got a Confederate flag, don't you?"

"I have a decal, no flag. I put it over the toilet in the trailer just for a joke. It's all about state's rights and gettin' the federal govermint off our backs more than it is about winning any war." Floyd looked like he was going to say something, but he just kept quiet.

"Hey, how long we gonna be here?" I asked.

"Oh, just a bit."

"I don't wanna spend the rest of the day huntin' dead soldiers."

"I just want to say hello seeing as I won't be passing

through here anytime soon."

Floyd got out of the van and we went in. At the main desk there was a woman in a park service uniform with a big gold badge. She seemed to recognize Floyd and gave him a hug. A tall guy came out of his office. He was wearing the same uniform. He shook hands with Floyd real friendly-like.

"Buddy, this is Chuck Stevenson. This guy knows more about the Civil War and Chickamauga then the next ten people in the world. This is my friend here, Buddy Jones."

"Good to meet you Buddy." He stuck out his hand. "You a Civil War buff like Floyd here?"

"Not really."

"I'm giving Buddy a ride down to Atlanta. I stopped at my great-grandfather's grave this morning. I just had to drop in and say hello."

"Glad you fellows came by. Can I show you around the place, Buddy?"

"I bet Buddy would love to see the exhibits," answered Floyd.

We came to an exhibit of some big field guns on wheels. I'd never seen stuff like that close up. Chuck explained. "These are the Napoleon twelve-pound cannons, the most popular gun used by the Union Army. It took six horses to pull the gun and the caisson that held the ammunition. Each horse ate fourteen pounds of hay and twelve pounds of corn each day, even when the guns were just sitting idle. Imagine, supplying that amount of food, as well as rations for the soldiers."

Chuck showed us the rifle collection. "This is the Spencer repeating rifle. It'd just been developed at the time of the Civil War. The gun could fire fourteen rounds per minute. The older models could only fire three."

"So, you could kill more people in a shorter period of time, huh?"

"Yes Buddy, it made a huge difference in the number of bullets you could fire into your enemy. As a matter of fact, the Union Army was concerned with the cost of all those bullets. The gun was only used by selected regiments. Colonel John Wilder and his brigade had to purchase the guns themselves. They used them to great effect against the Confederates here at Chickamauga."

We lollygagged through some more exhibits until Floyd said we'd best be on our way. But nothing Floyd did was quick. He chitchatted some more with Chuck and the others before we headed toward the exit.

"Jeez Floyd, maybe if I'd seen some of this in high school, I might've paid more attention."

"Let me give you a tour of the battlefield." I had to open my big mouth, but Floyd was as happy as a goose taking a shit. We climbed back into the van and turned into a narrow lane. The sign said *Lafayette Road.*

"This is what they were fighting for, this road. It leads back to Chattanooga. General Bragg, the Confederate commander, planned to destroy the Union force and control the entry into Chattanooga. Then he'd be able to retake the city for the Confederacy. The town was a major rail center and a prize for both armies." He stopped the van. "This is where the battle was fought."

"In them trees?"

"Yep, the whole battlefield was mostly forest. The soldiers couldn't see more than a few yards ahead. They just slugged it out in bloody combat. Let me tell you what Col. Wilder said many years after the battle. He pulled out Foote's big Civil

War book and began to read: Th*e two armies came together like two wild beasts and each fought as long as it could stand up in a knock-down and drag-out encounter. If there had been any high order of generalship displayed, the disasters to both armies might have been less.*"

"It's hard to believe that there was ever a battle here," I said.

"Yeah, it's all grown back to its natural state. In those days, this was pig farming country. They just let the pigs loose to eat what they could. After the battle, the swine had a fine meal eating the dead horses and some of the soldiers too."

Floyd drove toward a peaceful stream with tall trees on each side of it. You could hear a woodpecker in the distance. "This is it," said Floyd, "the Chickamauga Creek." It wasn't very wide, but the sides were pretty steep.

"It must have been tough to get the horses to pull those heavy guns up and down them banks," I said.

Floyd nodded his head. "The Cherokees named it *River of Death* long before the battle ever took place here." After a few minutes staring at the water, we started back to the van.

"This might be a stupid question, Floyd, but who won the battle?"

"The Confederates. They broke through the Union lines on the third day of fighting and chased the Blues up Lafayette Road. Most of the Union army made it back to Chattanooga so it wasn't a total victory. General Bragg surrounded the city for a few months but wasn't able to take it. He was eventually beaten by a new Union general, Ulysses Grant. Let me show you Wilder's monument and where his infantry made use of those Spencer rifles."

"Sure." What choice did I have?

NINETEEN

AFTER I GOT EXPELLED from school, I decided I'd had enough of Mom and her husbands. I moved in with Aunt Henrietta who was Mom's sister if you forgot. Two of her kids had moved out by that time, and she had an extra room. I have to give her credit for helping her kids through college while divorcing three deadbeat husbands. The two girls became teachers and my cousin Steve is a lawyer in St. Louis. He helped me with my bankruptcies later on.

I took a job at Steak 'n Shake as a dishwasher. For those of you who never heard of it, Steak 'n Shake is a restaurant chain in the middle part of the United States that serves *steakburgers* which are really hamburgers. The chili is also pretty good. After a while, I moved up from dishwasher to cook and soon I was the head hamburger flipper. I was getting paid about five dollars an hour which I reckoned was pretty good. Nowadays, *hamburger flipper* is shorthand for a lousy job, but in those days, it had more prestige, I think.

I got to admit, I was pretty damn handsome by the time I was eighteen or nineteen. I had a big thick head of sandy-colored hair which reached down over my ears. I have some old pictures of me, and I kinda look like I'm wearing a hat.

Anyone who was alive in the seventies will remember that hair style. Later on, I grew them long sideburns that was popular then, too.

I used to go to the gym and lift weights and I developed quite a build. At that time, nobody went to a gym to run on a treadmill, and the elliptoid things hadn't been invented. There weren't many girls that came in there which was a good thing, because without them, us guys paid more attention to what we were doing. If you go to a gym these days—I don't go often as you've probably surmised--you see a lot of gals talking and laughing, looking each other over and checking out the guys. They never seem to get to lifting any weights. Then there's some women that get real muscular, like they want to look like men. Sometimes Penny would go to the gym when she was on one of her health kicks, but I know she wasn't one of the women that the guys were gawking at, otherwise I wouldn't've let her go there.

I worked at Steak 'n Shake for about four years. After that, I got a job in construction working for a concrete company. That was hard work, but it paid a lot better than the burger business. I said goodbye to Aunt Henrietta and moved into an apartment with a guy named John Pudulsky, a carpenter that I met at a job site. He had a square jaw and a square brush cut that looked like someone had mowed a lawn on the top of his head. He was missing a front tooth, and he looked a bit stupid if you didn't know him. Some people make jokes about people like him, and I've told my share of them, but John was a lot smarter than the average Polack, plus, he was half Irish. He'd finished high school and was working construction to save enough money for college. He used to read books in the apartment, real books, not comic books.

My pals and I hung out in bars drinking beer and finding the girls who were there to be found. I made sure to wear a tight-fitting undershirt like Ernie had worn, even in the winter. That was about the only useful thing that Ernie ever taught me. Those were the days before AIDS, and the girls were all on the pill, and there was plenty of sex to go round. If you've read this far in the book, you might know I don't boast too much, but I've had my fair share of sex with the fair sex.

John didn't mess with the bars or the women. My fuck-buddies would cause a racket in the apartment at night and sometimes in the morning, all that moaning and groaning and bed creaking and the occasional screamer. I know that would've kept me awake. The next morning, John would have a pot of coffee brewing. He would chat it up with me and my date about the Cardinals or some high-class novel he was reading. Some of the girls seemed to like him too. After they left, I'd tell John he could date any one of them. Shit, I wasn't married to any of them, but John said he was saving himself for the right gal.

Sure enough, one day he told me that he was going with a girl from his Catholic church named Connie O'Toole. John had known her since he was in diapers. She'd had a serious boyfriend that'd ditched her and joined the Marines. She'd moped around the house for a long time after that. Later on, I found out that she'd been in the hospital for depression. Anyhow, after some nagging by her parents, she'd agreed to date big John. He and Connie had sworn a pact that they were saving themselves until the day they got married. It wasn't long before she started to come around the apartment. I got to admit--as much as I hate to admit it--she was cute with a little turned up nose and she had bright blue eyes with long eyelashes. She always wore big bulky sweaters and sweat pants. John told me she was the bookish type. She went to college at Washington University which John said was a college for really smart people, but when John pulled out Will Durant's eleven volume *History of Civilization*, I saw that she'd yawned when he went on about all the wars that the Greeks had fought. One time, I caught her looking me over while he was reading from Milton's *Paradise Lost*. Her face sorta flushed, and she pulled down that heavy wool sweater as if to cover up things that were already covered up.

I always used to joke and act stupid in front of girls. I can be a pretty funny guy when I'm interested in someone or something. Connie seemed to enjoy my jokes, even some of the dirty ones. I don't why, but I got to walking round the apartment with my shirt off when Connie was there. Sometimes I'd get up real close to her as if I was interested in something she was reading. John didn't seem to notice. In fact, one day he asked me, "Buddy, how can I get to first base with Connie?"

"First base? I thought you two were swearing off sex until the day you got hitched?"

"Oh, sure we are, but I'd like to think we are, you know, compatible in that department before the wedding day. You know, first base before we round all the bases."

"Like a bunt single?"

"Something like that."

"Well first off, you got to put away them dull books. I mean they might be great readin' but it kinda stifles the hormones."

"The hormones?"

"Yeah, the horny hormones. I consider myself an expert in that department." And I do to this day, not counting Gloria which was a special circumstance owing to the fact that I was drunk. "You know, like findin' a romantic movie on the TV, puttin' your arm around her, then nibblin' on her ear." I went over to him and gave him a demonstration.

"Jeez, Buddy, I know what you mean, I'm not stupid." He didn't cotton to me nibbling on his ear.

"Then with the arm you got around her, you slowly, and this is important, slowly, slowly move your hand down so it's restin' on her boob. If she don't object to that, you're home free and you can move down further to where the money is."

"The money, what money?" At that point in time, I knew he was a virgin even though he told me he wasn't.

"The pussy man, the pussy that don't meow. That's where the money is." Did I have to spell it out for him? A few weeks later, I asked him how things were coming along. I'd been careful not to hang around when Connie was there. She still lived with her parents and the apartment was John's only shot.

"Oh, making progress."

"Like what?"

"Well, she liked the old movie we watched, *Casablanca* with Lauren Bacall and Humphrey Bogart."

"Yeah, that's a tear jerker, and what else?"

"What else?"

"The nibbling. The arm around the boob stuff."

"When I got my arm around her, she got up to make some popcorn."

"And what did you do when she sat down?"

"I didn't do anything. I guessed she wasn't that interested or she wouldn't have got up to make popcorn."

"Or you got cold feet?"

"Well, maybe I did, a little. Say could you help me?"

"Sure, what can I do?"

"I'm going on a religious retreat with the priest from our parish this weekend. I told Connie that you and she could maybe grab a bite to eat. I want you guys to get to know each other because you're my best friend and all that, but I really want you to put in a good word for me."

"Good word?"

"Like tell some stories about me. You know, we go to bars and all the girls go for me and all that. Like I'm experienced with women and all that."

"So, give her a hint that you ain't a virgin?"

"Yeah."

"Even though you are."

"How do you know that?"

"I just know. Look, I don't think that's goin' to help you. I told you the way to find the money."

"Well she's coming by tomorrow, then you two are going out for a pizza."

The next evening after I got home from work, I showered and put on the Old Spice cologne real heavy. I put on a pair of tight-fitting shorts, not the baggy tents down to my knees that the fellas wear nowadays. I got to admit, I had one hell of a six-pack when I was in my twenties. Anyway, there's a knock on the door and there stands Connie, and guess what? She's wearin' a shorter pair of shorts than the ones I had on.

"Hi Connie." I start to look her over.

"You look surprised."

"Surprised? Surprised at what?"

"Surprised that I'm not wearing a sweater and those sweat pants."

"Well, I guess … a little."

"Let me get to the point. All those evenings when I came over and you walked around half naked, you think I didn't notice?"

Now that kinda caught me off guard. This was my roommate's girlfriend and all that. The poor guy was on a retreat thinking of Connie. He was praying to God that she'd say yes when he popped the question. He was dreaming of the hymns that the choir would sing at their wedding, how they'd take communion with their families, and how they'd consummate their union only after they've said their vows in the eyes of God. All this, if only his friend Buddy would say a few good words about him to the woman he planned to marry.

The next thing I know she came up to me and gave me a French kiss and rubbed herself against me.

"Whadda ya want with an ignorant hillbilly like me?"

"I really like hillbillies, particularly the ones with all those muscles." She squeezed my arm.

"What about John?" I asked.

"Oh, the hell with John!"

"But you're savin' yourselves for each other in the eyes of God and all that?"

"That's what I've told him, but that's not what's happened. I've done it with three or four guys while I've been going out with John. I just wanted to keep my parents happy."

Well the next thing, we're in the bedroom going at it. She was one of those screamers. I thought the noise might be heard on the first floor and we were on the fourth.

Afterwards, we shared a cigarette. "I was sposed to tell you how good John was in bed and all that."

"Screw John."

"That's what you're sposed to do after you're married."

"Oh, you're so funny, Buddy. I just love your sense of humor." She laughed, and we did it again.

TWENTY

IT WASN'T LONG afterward that Connie and I rented an apartment together. Poor John was lower than a sow's belly when Connie told him she was breaking up with him to shack up with me. He called me a snake in the grass, and worse than the serpent in the Bible. Coming from him, that was about as bad a thing as he could say about anybody. I put all the blame on Connie which was pretty much true. I told him that she'd had the hots for me all along and never would've married him in a million years.

I didn't see John until years later when I ran into him at a Cardinals game. We were waiting in line to buy beer and hotdogs. He told me he was married with two kids and another one on the way. He declared that the best thing that ever happened to him was not marrying Connie, just as I was thinking that was the worst thing that ever happened to me, well one of the worst things.

For the first few months, she was a perpetual bitch in heat. She just couldn't get enough of my you-know-what. We tried more positions than what's in the *Kama Sutra*. That's one book I've read pretty thoroughly, or at least studied all the pictures. It didn't seem to matter that I couldn't've cared less about the poem she was reading, or the goddamned Bach organ festival, or the homily from Father Hugo that Sunday. Her main concern was Buddy in bed.

I lost my construction job in the recession of 1981. Connie was still enrolled at the university and working part time at a bookstore. We hardly had a nickel to our names. Fortunately, her parents were pretty well off. Her dad had a job as an inspector at the gas company, and her mom worked as a nurse's aide at a hospital. Okay, maybe they weren't rich, but they lived pretty cheaply in a small house with the mortgage paid off, and they'd saved some money, too. Mr. O'Toole was kind enough to pay our rent until I could find another job.

Now that I was unemployed, Connie suggested that I go to night school to get my GED. This was the first of her interfering in my life, but not the last. I went to the school for a few weeks but I soon quit. I just couldn't pay attention to stuff like algebra and chemistry, stuff that I wouldn't ever use or need. Maybe I should've stuck with it. I could've got a better job with that piece of paper, but that wouldn't have made me a smarter person. Like I said, I wasn't a good reader, anyway.

There weren't any construction jobs to be had, except maybe roofing, which I saw my Daddy do and he hated it. You ever been on a roof on a summer day in St. Louis? You could fry an egg up there and some bacon too, anyway, the immigrants pretty much had those jobs. Those wetbacks would work for almost nothing pounding shingles. Even the blacks didn't want that kinda work. I got so I started going to the bars during the day while Connie was at work, and she started to like me less when she came home to see me snoozing on the sofa passing beer farts. The A-shirt that I was wearing no longer seemed to charm her like it once had.

So you see, things were pretty much going off the rails just about the time when I noticed that Connie's stomach had grown a bit bigger and her nipples started to swell. Stupid me, I thought she'd been on birth control pills all along. Hell, every other pussy I'd been with was on them except Connie. It was only after she got pregnant that she told me it was against the Catholic religion. When she went to the doctor, she was already four months along. Son of a bitch! She hadn't had a period for four months! What did she think was going on, if it weren't a pie in her oven? The night she told me, she was all crying and carrying on, and how abortion was a sin, and how she wanted me to be a father to our child. She'd called her parents from the doctor's office. They were fixing for us to get married as soon as they could line up the priest and get a hall to rent.

Here I was, a guy just out to have fun and work as little as possible. Now I was going to have a wife and be a father. The next day I went over to the O'Tooles' with Connie. I was going to tell them that there wasn't any way I could go through with it, but you wouldn't have believed the happy faces of old man O'Toole, and that prune he called a wife. Their little girl was getting married with a bonus baby on the way. By God, the Lord himself had ordained our getting hitched. What could I do? Tell God he'd made a mistake? Even Mom was all excited about becoming a grandmother. I guess she was hoping to do better at that than she'd done as a mom.

We got married in the Catholic church by Father Hugo. Mom and Aunt Henrietta and my three cousins attended from my side of the family. Daddy had been dead for almost five years. Of course, Connie had a bunch of her friends there along with her parents, and some cousins and aunts and uncles. Afterwards, we went to the Machinist's Hall and had a buffet dinner of mostaccioli, white bread and ham with French's mustard, and some good old Budweiser. That's a favorite menu for Catholic weddings in St. Louis, I don't know about other cities. Connie was already showing her pregnancy in her wedding dress that she'd bought at JCPenney's for seventy-five dollars. Nobody said anything to me about a shotgun wedding, but you could hear a lot of whispering during the ceremony.

Dexter came down from Chicago to be my best man. I hadn't seen him since we'd moved to St. Louis. He was real prosperous-like, dressed in a fancy blue suit and a pale-yellow silk tie, with shoes that he said were made from alligator skins. He had that black curly hair, shiny like Dean Martin, maybe it was the Italian blood from his father, but he had the looks that the girls fell for. He was driving a Mercedes convertible, and he let Connie and I take it out for a spin. He told me he was a successful businessman, but he wouldn't exactly say what he did for a living. He told me that the hundred-dollar bills that he'd given me for Christmas weren't legit, and he laughed. You couldn't never be sure when he was telling the whole truth, or a half a truth, or a flat out lie. But I got to give him credit, he gave me and Connie a rocking chair that he'd made himself, or at least he said he did.

We didn't really have a honeymoon, but we went down to Middleberg to see Grandma Bess who was pretty frail by then from smoking all those cigarettes. She was still lighting the unfiltered Camels when we were there. When she died a few years later, I went back to attend her funeral. She was the one person I knew who loved me.

TWENTY-ONE

FIVE MONTHS LATER, April was born. With the weight of that burden on my shoulders, I became serious about finding a job. I landed one in a grocery store as a bagger at Schnucks. Now if you've never lived in St. Louis, you'd think I'm making that name up, but it was started by Mr. Schnuck many years ago. There's a bunch of them around St. Louis and even across the Mississippi in Illinois. The job didn't pay much, but it was indoors, in air conditioning, and was a whole lot easier than spreading goddamned concrete or hammering shingles. To make ends meet, we moved into a tiny room in the basement of the O'Toole home next to the water heater. Little April slept at the foot of the bed in a bassinet. Mom said it reminded her of the time that her and Monty had lived in the basement of her folks' house with Dexter. I'm sorry to say the results weren't much better.

Well, I'm not going to bullshit about what a great father I was. I mean in those days, fathers didn't do much with changing diapers and all that. The good thing about living with Connie's parents was that her mom helped with the baby after Connie went back to school. The bad thing was that there was no privacy, and Connie had this thing about having sex if someone could hear her. As I stated before, she was one of those women who yelled pretty loud when she was having an orgasm, so to tell the truth, sex was few and far between. I would say that Connie pretty much froze up in that department, probably colder than the glacier that's supposed to be melting in Greenland.

Suddenly, she became annoyed that I wasn't sofisticatered like her or what she thought was sofisticatered. I mean, is reading *Huckleberry Finn*, or some half-assed poem by Walt Whitman, a sign that you know more than the next dumb shit? It's one of the things that's wrong with America, all those colleges that teach about Karl Marx and evolution. I'm no religious person, but I know that the Bible makes a hell of a lot more sense than some of that. It's a pile of crap that man came from apes. We're a lot more civilized than some goddamned baboon. Connie kept pestering me to read books from the library and go to the symphony, always nagging at me to get a job with more money so the three of us could move out of her parents' house. To sum it up, the bitch in heat turned into just a bitch, period.

When April was four years old, Connie graduated with her Social Worker's degree. She got a job working at Barnes hospital which was the biggest hospital in the area at that time, and still is. She started out at $30,000 a year which was enough so we could move into a place not far from her parents. By then, her mother had retired. She came over and baby-sat April while Connie was at work. I had moved up the ladder at the store to a shelf stocker. My hours shifted to working evenings and nights. What with Mrs. O'Toole tending to the baby, I had lots of free time in the afternoon before I went to work. Looking back on that, free time wasn't always the best thing for me. I started going back to my old haunts and took up with my old buddy Roger Hanks. By then, he was pushing drugs and breaking into rich people's homes to steal stereos and jewelry. I can honestly say that I wasn't dealing or stealing just then, but I enjoyed my weed and alcohol same as the next guy.

As a red-blooded American boy, I started to take up with some of the girls I'd known before I got hitched to Connie. I have to admit that on more than one occasion, I was not faithful to my wife. As I've demonstrated before, *put a set of tits on a barstool and a set of steins on the bar, and the flesh is weak.* This is something I'm not proud of, but when a man is not getting at home what he deserves, he naturally looks outside for satisfaction. I'm proud to say that I'm not one of those fellas that ever needed to resort to hookers. More than one gal suggested that I leave Connie and move in with her. I won't tell you about this real nice girl named Margie that was my girlfriend for over a year. I mean it won't make any difference to this story. Let's just say that I regret not shacking up with her. Maybe if I'd had, some of the difficulties I got into probably wouldn't have happened, but I can't be sure about anything in regard to such things.

It took a few years for Connie to find out that I was cheating on her. I was real clever about keeping my lady friends hid from her. But when she did find out, well that was a day that Connie went off the deep end. Her mom wasn't coming by every day anymore, because her dad had been in the hospital with depression—that ran in the family. One day, he threatened his supervisor with a gun over some overtime pay that he thought he should get. Luckily, he didn't use it, but after that, he couldn't work there anymore.

Connie's mom was afraid to leave him, fearing that he'd use the pistol on himself, so Connie hired a babysitter to come in two days a week after April got home from school. I wasn't available those days because of my bowling league. Gosh, I remember how cute April was at that age. She was talking a blue streak by then, and she used to crack me up all the time.

Connie came home early one day, it seemed that she had a headache. She'd complain of some ailment or another most of the time, always going to the doctor. Unfortunately, that was the day that I'd missed bowling due to a sore shoulder. The babysitter, Jamie, and I decided to smoke some pot while April went out to the playground behind the apartment. She'd only been coming in for about a month, but I could tell she really liked me, maybe a teenage crush on an older man. After we were done with the pot, we snorted some coke that I'd stashed in the storage bin in the basement of the apartment complex. We got pretty high and one thing led to another. Pretty soon I had Jamie stark naked and was banging her on the living room rug just as Connie walked in the door. Connie went completely berserk, and poor Jamie had to skedaddle out of the place half-naked. The bitch threatened to prosecute me for having sex with a minor. How'd I know she was only sixteen? That night, Connie overdosed for the first time. She ended up in the same ward that her dad had just left.

When she got out, I promised to stay faithful to Connie forever, but that didn't last mainly due to Connie's horrible temper and crazy moods. There were a few years of marital dustups with me moving out and moving back in. Finally, Connie filed for divorce. She got full custody of April which was okay with me, because unlike today's wimp husbands who might as well be called Mom Two, I wasn't disposed to have April come live with me. I had to pay child support even though Connie was making way more than me, which seemed unfair. I'd come by and maybe buy April an ice cream, help her ride her two-wheeler, and take her to the park, things like that. The two of us really had fun together. She was always laughing and showing me how she could do cartwheels and swing on the jungle gyms.

Without Connie's salary—I was only making two hundred and fifty dollars a week at the grocery store—I decided to move back to Middleberg where it was cheaper to live. I had hooked up again with Margie, but she didn't want to live in a shithole town like Middleberg. I can't say I much blame her for that. I got a job there as a bagger at MacConkey's Grocery. Billy MacConkey was a good friend of Uncle Waldo's, and I'd had experience working at Schnucks all those years.

One day, I got a letter from Connie telling me that she'd found a job in Atlanta. She gave me an address where I could visit her and April. She sounded all nice and friendly-like in the letter, but I wasn't fooled. A few days later, another letter arrived, from the Missouri Department of Social Services. I was told that my salary at the grocery store would be garnisheed because I'd failed to pay child support on time. The bitch had gotten a lawyer to squeeze every fucking nickel from my soul.

TWENTY-TWO

I'D ONLY BEEN IN MIDDLEBERG for six months when Dexter came down from Chicago for a visit. I always enjoyed seeing Dexter. Now he was driving a big black Cadillac Fleetwood with plush leather seats and leather steering wheel. He had on a white linen suit with a tee shirt underneath. After eating a big dinner at Uncle Waldo's, pork tenderloins, home grown sweet corn, and key lime pie, Dexter suggested that he and I retire to the Red Parrot for some nightcaps.

Dexter remembered some of the gang down there from grade school. He bought everyone three or four rounds of drinks, and we stayed until closing time which by then had been extended to midnight. Sitting with Dexter over a fifth of Jack Daniels, I cursed Connie and Uncle Sam, and then Connie again for taking all my money. I use the f-word fairly liberally when I've had too much to drink. Dexter heard me out. Then he offered me a job working with him in Chicago. I later found out that he'd talked to Mom a few days prior, and she'd asked him if he could find me a job with his outfit in Chicago seeing as he'd done so well there. I don't think Mom exactly knew what profession Dexter was in. He promised that if I took a job with his company, they wouldn't take any money for Uncle Sam or child support. I'd get paid off the books which I later found out meant cash. It also meant that Connie wouldn't know my whereabouts which was fine with me, but I couldn't see April, which kinda broke my heart. But what could I do?

When we left, he gave the waitress a brand-new hundred-dollar bill as a tip. She repeated *thank you* about a dozen times and gave him a kiss on the lips along with her phone number. Maybe she thought she owed him more than just refilling our peanut bowl, or maybe she just liked a man with money which was hard to find in Middleberg. After we left the saloon, I asked Dexter if it was counterfeit. He just laughed. The next morning, we stopped at MacConkey's, so I could tell Billy to shove his job up his rear end, then we headed up Interstate 55 toward Chicago.

"Ever been to the Windy City, Buddy?" Dexter asked as we got on the open road.

"Nope, never."

"I hope you'll like it cuz I got big plans for you in our business."

"What kinda business Dex, you never told me what line of work you're in."

"Construction."

"Construction eh, what kinda construction?"

"Oh, you'll soon find out."

It took us about four and a half hours to get there. Dexter said he was extra cautious about speeding on the highway. He didn't want to attract the attention of the cops. I found out soon enough that the Cadillac was a stolen vehicle with fake registration papers. We pulled up in front of a small brick home on Hermitage Ave. in south Chicago. One of those houses that was long and thin, with several stairs in front leading up to a porch.

Dexter's dad, Monty, came out to greet us. He looked a lot older than I remembered him, probably because he was. He had long grey hair to his shoulders and a scraggly beard to match. He was stooped over and needed a walker with tennis balls attached to the front. His hand shook pretty bad when he put it out to shake mine.

"Well well, if it ain't Buddy Jones. Good to see you. How's your mom?"

"She's doing okay."

"How many husbands is it now?"

"She just divorced number four."

"And to think, I was number one in a long line of princes." I had to laugh at that.

"How you doin'?" I asked.

"Oh, not so good since I got outta Joliet. Got caught drivin' a stolen van with some Mexican ladies, fresh from the border. I thought they was just havin' a night on the town. How'd I know they was sex slaves?"

"How long were you there?"

"Where?"

"In Joliet."

"Oh, I got five years for runnin' a prostitution ring, got paroled after three. They don't like old men like me in there, too many medical problems. I cain't piss and I cain't shit. I got trouble with my balance. Doctor told me that too much booze affected my brain. You goin' to be helpin' Dexter here in the business?"

"I guess so, but construction ain't really my thing no more."

"Construction? That's what you call it, Dexter?" Monty laughed.

"Yeah. He's replacing Little Joey."

"Did he quit?" I asked.

"No, he got real sick. He'll never be able to work again."

The next day, Dexter and I headed toward Halstead Street. He parked the car in the parking lot of a meat packing plant. "You doin' some work on the hog pens?" I asked.

"Nope. We don't work here. I got this from a friend." He pointed to the *Acme Packers* sticker on the windshield. "I don't like to park the car too near our place."

We walked three blocks until we came to a rundown building. We took an old freight elevator to the basement. Dexter took out his key, and we entered a long windowless room. It looked like a print shop that might churn out advertising flyers or maybe the local newspaper. There was a large offset press, a platemaking station, and a paper cutter. There were stacks of ink canisters mostly green and black. An olive-skinned man came out from behind the printer.

"This is Sal," said Dexter, slapping a hand on his back. "He's in charge of the inside operations. Sal, this is my half-brother Buddy from Missouri."

"The *show-me-state*, eh?"

"Yep."

"You're going to be helping Sal here in the operation."

"I thought you were in construction?"

"See that paper over there?" answered Dexter. "That there is construction paper," and he grinned.

"We counterfeit money here, Buddy," said Sal matter-of-fact-like. "Mostly hundreds, they're the easiest to transport, but sometimes we'll do twenties depending on the client.

You'll help me run the presses and unload the supplies off the trucks. Stuff like that."

"Whadda you do, Dex?"

"I used to have Sal's job. Now I'm in distribution."

"So, you run things here?"

"Nah," laughed Dexter. "The real big boss, the capofamiglia, is Pinkie Pignatato. Every once in a while, he and his lieutenants come around to check on us. Don't ever give that man no lip, you understand?" Just thinking of The *Godfather* made me sweat. "Buzzer Buzzoni is in charge of the counterfeiting operation. We mostly sell the counterfeit bills to South America and Africa. They pay twenty cents on the dollar. After we get paid, Big Buzzer gives us our share of the profits. We're allowed to skim some of the counterfeit runs for ourselves, one or two thousand apiece."

"So the hundred that you tipped at the Red Parrot might have been..."

"Yep, the perfect place for it. Those rubes down there don't have a clue."

"And the hundred-dollar bills at Christmas time?"

"Same thing." Dexter hadn't been lying when he'd told me that.

"Well, wouldn't the banks know they were counterfeit?"

"No, them little banks around Middleberg dunno nuthin. A big outfit like the Bank of America might screen 'em more closely, but by then I'm long gone. A small amount of bills like the ones I passed at the Red Parrot won't even ripple the pond."

"Holy moly, Dex!"

He smiled at my amazement, but then his eyes narrowed, and he glared at me. "Before you start, lemme give you some advice. Keep your mouth shut and don't mention this to no one. Not your best girlfriend or your best boyfriend, our mom, or anyone, got that? Once they find out you're a counterfeiter, they'll want you to give them money, and they won't have any sense where to pass them bills. You're in the construction business, got that?" I'd never seen Dexter so serious.

"Got it, Dex. You can trust me."

"And one other thing. When Pinkie comes by, he might have a bosomy girlfriend or two with him. Don't talk to them or even look at them."

TWENTY-THREE

SHORTLY THEREAFTER, I began my new career as a counterfeiter. Dexter loaned me some money so I could buy a car and get to work, a 1975 Dodge Dart, a piece of shit if there ever was one. Dexter said to keep a low profile, but that didn't explain why he drove a Caddie. I guess he had different rules for himself. The work was easy, and this gave me lots of free time to roam around Chicago. For the first time in my life I had some real money, but I didn't save any of it, just spent it.

Dexter showed me around and introduced me to his friends as his little brother. I kinda liked that, him being my only close kin except for Mom and April. He palled around with men mostly older than himself with funny nicknames, Catnip, The Monk, The Plumber, and Grease Ball. He was particularly close with Big Buzzer who was like a mentor. They were all part of the Outfit, the gangsters that ran Chicago. When we went into certain establishments that Dexter said they *owned*, the manager would bust his ass to please us. Everything was on the house. The only money we spent was on tips, and we tipped big. That money was always legit. Of course, counterfeiting wasn't the only business that the Outfit ran. We were just a branch of a bigger organization that I knew nothing about.

On the days we didn't print, I could sleep to noon, then go in for a few hours to put away a shipment of paper or ink. Some days Sal told me not to show up at all. After two weeks, I was given thirty hundred-dollar bills, for mostly sitting on my ass. I'd never seen that much money in my life. I often wished that I could've sent some of it to April, but I couldn't figure how to do it without Connie findin' out where I lived.

Dexter had a fairly steady girlfriend. Sheila was a drop-dead number ten out of ten. She told me she was a secretary, but she never seemed to work. She mostly hung around with the other girlfriends of the Mob. I guess Dexter gave her money to live on. The Big Buzzer's girlfriend was named Toots, and he called all the other women broads. For some reason, you just don't hear those words any more, *Toots and broads*. I guess Big Buzzer was in his fifties, which seemed pretty old to a punk like me.

Toots introduced me to her niece, whose name I can't remember right now. We were in the sack after we'd known each other for about an hour. She was okay, but she wanted me to spend money on her, go to expensive restaurants like the Pump Room or Spiaggia's. She liked to wear them ultra-short miniskirts to the White Sox games. I had to get tickets right behind the dugout, so she could parade in view of the ballplayers. That showy stuff wasn't my style, and Dexter had told me to be careful. Before living in Chicago, I'd always figured out a way for the women to pay for me, partly because I never had any money, but I went along with it. Life was good.

One day, while we were cranking out the counterfeits, Pinky Pignatato and his party of lieutenants showed up in a big black limousine. He was fat, nowadays people call those folks obese. His head was huge and his cheeks were a bright red which turned purple when he laughed. His neck was squat, and it was hard to figure where his head ended and his shoulders began. Although he wore a tie, the top button of his shirt wasn't fastened, almost like he couldn't find a shirt collar big enough. He had a huge Cuban cigar in his mouth. He could talk and breathe with that thing between his teeth. There were a bunch of his lieutenants and two knockout babes trailing behind him. They looked young enough to be his daughters. One of them kept looking at me. In those days, that's all it took to give me a hard-on. She never said a word the whole time she was there. Afterwards, Sal told me that her name was Tiger and her sister was called Shark.

Pinky asked Sal to show him some of our bills. He made a whistling noise through his cigar and a big ash fell on the floor. "Looks like the real McCoy, Sal. Keep up the good work."

"Thank you sir, we do our best." Sal seemed to have trouble getting his words out, like he had no spit in his mouth. He had drops of sweat on his forehead which he kept wiping with a hankie.

"Who's your friend here?"

"This is Buddy, Dexter's brother. He replaced Joey."

"Oh, now I remember. Yeah, Joey's not with us no more. Good to meet you, Buddy." As he walked away, Tiger slipped a piece of paper in my hand. All it said was *call me* and a phone number which I reckoned was hers. I couldn't hardly wait to phone her, but I remembered what Dexter had said, so I asked him for advice when I got home.

"You've got to be kidding! You wanna call Pinky's girlfriend?"

"Well, she really looked like she had the hots for me and I sure do have the hots for her."

"She did the same thing with Joey."

"So what?"

"That's why he ain't comin' to work no more."

"He was fired?"

"No, Pinkie don't fire people, he kills 'em. He rubbed Joey out for just givin' her a call back." I had to give it to Dexter. He was looking out for me.

A few weeks later, we flew out to Vegas. I'd never been on an airplane before, and we flew first class. All the shrimp we could eat and all the Champagne we could drink. Dexter knew the stewardesses, too. You may or may not remember, but in those days the stews had to been good-looking gals before they got hired, and they wore them dumb little caps on their heads. We landed at night. I couldn't believe the lights on the strip, seemed like Satan himself was in charge of things. The Flamingo was some ritzy hotel. There was a football field of slot machines even before we got to the check-in counter. We took the elevator up to the top floor to the suite he'd reserved: two bedrooms, living room with a widescreen TV, pool table, and Jacuzzi. There was a wet bar and a refrigerator stocked with beer and sandwiches.

"Whaddya think?"

"I dunno if I can afford this. All I got is five hundred in cash."

"Don't worry, we're comped."

"Comped?" I'd never heard such a word.

"It's all complementary. The room, the restaurants, and all the booze we can drink. Only money we spend is to gamble.

And don't use no funny money. They're on the lookout for that."

"Fuck! That's amazin'! How'd you swing all that?"

"I didn't do nuthin. It's a perk for being in our business. This place is run by the *family* here in Vegas."

"Family?"

"Yeah, family," and Dexter gave me a wink. Then I figured it out.

That was one hell of a weekend. The stews came by that evening, and we all went skinny dipping in the Jacuzzi which was big enough for eight people. Then the four of us ate at the steak house on the ground floor. The maître d' came by with a wine list, and Dexter ordered a couple of bottles of French Bordeaux listed at one hundred and fifty smackers a bottle. He and I devoured some thick Delmonicos and the girls had filet mignon. We went to the casino and played blackjack. I turned my five hundred bucks into two thousand! I'm not shitting you. The stews went back to work the next day, but Dex and I found some babes around the pool that afternoon. We ate, drank, and screwed with them the rest of the day and most of the night. Forget Satan, this was paradise.

TWENTY-FOUR

LIKE I SAID, the five years in Chicago were the best of my life. Two or three years after I started, Sal retired to take care of his wife who had lung cancer, and I took over the printing operation. I moved out of Monty's place and found my own house a few blocks away. It was a small pile of bricks and the paint was peeling, but I wasn't to show any flash, like Dexter said. I even put on overalls and work boots when I left the house to make it look like I was going to a construction job. I sold the Dodge and bought a pale green Buick, but nothing as fancy as Dexter's cars. I hired a housekeeper to do the cleaning and cooking. I had all the babes I wanted, and even some I didn't want. I never planned to get married again, and I've stuck to that belief except for a few weak moments here and there.

One day, Pinkie dropped dead. He'd ate his dinner, then poof he was gone. He'd had high blood pressure and a bad heart for years. Dexter said he never took care of himself, but there was some in the Outfit who claimed that the ground beef in his lasagna had been laced with strychnine. Pinkie's death led to a bunch of gangland killings, as the rest of them fought to see who would take over the top job.

Dexter told me to close down the printing press until things sorted out. Eventually, Spiderlegs Spenilli became the don with Big Buzzer as one of the top lieutenants. This was good news for Dexter. He took over from Big Buzzer as head of the counterfeit operation and became a *made* man in the Mafia. That promotion kinda went to his head. He bought a condominium in one of the high rises on the Outer Drive with a great view of Lake Michigan.

Now that Pinkie was gone, Dexter dumped Sheila and took up with Tiger. I guess Tiger thought that someday Dexter would be the godfather of Chicago, like Pinkie. Nowadays, she'd be considered *high maintenance.* She demanded a lot of fancy clothes, necklaces, bracelets, and high-priced restaurants with an expensive wine list. Dexter started taking her to Vegas and leaving me at home which was okay. After my first success at the blackjack table, I was in the hole for about forty grand. I needed to pay off my debts before I could go back, and when you owed money in Vegas, it wasn't a debt that you could afford to ignore unless you wanted cement blocks tied to your shoes before you took a swim in Lake Michigan.

Even a made man like Dexter had trouble paying for all that high living. We'd always sold our fake bills out of the country, so that the Secret Service couldn't trace our tracks, but like I said before, after every run we'd take a few thousand counterfeit for ourselves. Dexter and me and even old Monty would drive to Oshkosh, Wisconsin or Terre Haute, Indiana. We'd buy TV's, or stereos, or jewelry, and sell them for a one hundred per cent profit. As Dexter needed more money, we started taking more trips round the country.

At some point, Dexter got tired of Tiger, maybe it was her spending habits. Shit, he could have had any piece of ass in Chicago or The Strip for that matter. As a consequence, Dexter did what most red-blooded American men come to do, and that was to cheat on her. He started going to Vegas by himself and told Tiger that it was business. He claimed he was fixing to set up a print shop to supply Nevada and southern California. Of course, this was just an excuse so he could visit the Gentlemen's clubs that were popular in Vegas. Dexter pretty much figured she'd be on to him soon, and I think he was hoping she'd pack up and leave. 'Course she went plumb bonkers when she found out about Dexter cheating, but instead of leaving him, she threatened to go to the govermint and squeal on him. After that, Dexter swore he wouldn't mess around any more. That's when things spiraled out of control.

Dexter broke an important rule. He started giving Tiger the fake money if she swore that she wouldn't tell anyone about it. Soon, there was nothing that gave her a greater thrill than going to a department store and passing the funny money, certainly a greater thrill than having sex with poor Dex, at least that's what he related to me.

Tiger was very close to her sister Shark, who had the same high-living habits as her sister. Shark was lonely because her boyfriend, Vito "The Monk" Moscone, was serving time in the Vienna Correctional Center in downstate Illinois. Despite Dexter's warning, Tiger told Shark about her shopping trips with the fake dough. Soon Shark wanted some for herself. Tiger pleaded with Dexter for more counterfeit, then she gave some of it to Shark.

Shark didn't like to travel, so without telling Dex, the girls started going to their favorite stores on the Magnificent Mile, right there in Chicago. Mostly they bought cheap stuff like underwear and stockings. They spent the legit cash that they got in change on fancier stuff like jewelry. One day, Shark spotted a fifteen-thousand-dollar emerald ring in the front window of Tiffany & Co. Goddamn Tiffany's for chrissakes! How dumb can you fucking be! She brought Tiger to see the ring, and she too loved it on her own finger. Of course, Dolly the saleslady loved it on both their fingers. She was an old friend from the Pinky Pignatato days. When they pooled their money together, the sisters had only 8,000 in cash, but they decided to throw in 4,000 of some of the best Ben Franklins that I'd ever made. They asked if they could have the ring if they paid 12,000 in cash. Dolly said she'd talk to her manager.

But Dolly just pretended to go to her manager for the discount. In fact, she knew there was something shady going down. I mean no one ever walked into Tiffany & Co. to pay for something that expensive in cash. That rang alarm bells for God's sake. Sure, they knew that Pinky had been a bigshot in the Mafia, but he always wrote a legitimate check or used his credit card, so they didn't give a shit what he did for a living. The manager came out and agreed to the sale just like everything was on the up and up. When they forked over the money, he right away figured out that some of the bills didn't look quite right, and fuck, he had the real bills in his hand to compare them to. Now is that stupid or what? As I've always said, *there's no brains in a pair of tits.*

It wasn't long before the Secret Service—the branch of govermint in charge of counterfeiting--came looking for Tiger and Shark. The girls were brought down to police headquarters, but Dex knew to call the Mafia lawyers before they confessed to anything. There were some pretty sharp shyster-type attorneys working for the Outfit, and they got the girls out on bail. The next day, Dexter was picked up in a car and taken to a hideaway in Waukegan, north of Chicago. Big Buzzer and Spiderlegs were waiting for him. According to Dexter, Spiderlegs yelled and cursed at him for giving the hot money to his girlfriend, and some of the goons roughed him up pretty good. But in the end, they tried to figure out how to get Dexter and the girls off. They feared Tiger and Shark would spill the beans on the higher ups.

Dexter, with his lawyer in attendance, talked to the Feds a few days later. The next day some cops come out to the print shop, hauled the equipment away, and arrested me. I spent the night at the Cook County jail. In the morning, a lawyer from the Mob, a Mr. Allen Richman, visited me. I knew I was in serious trouble, and I was happy knowing that Dexter had looked out for me and got me my own lawyer. I remember Mr. Richman wearing a fine-fitting dark suit with a red, white and blue tie. I told him my side of the story which was the truth. I had no idea that Dexter had told the feds a different tale. His half-brother, Buddy Jones, had given him the fake bills to pay off gambling debts that he owed to him. Dexter had no idea they were counterfeit. Mr. Richman made sure that Tiger and Shark backed up his story.

Mr. Richman looked me straight in the eye. He said I was in serious, serious trouble. He told me to plead guilty and keep quiet, otherwise the Feds would throw the book at me. He said that if I went to trial, I'd spend eight to ten years in jail, and when I got out, Mr. Buzzoni and Mr. Spenilli would come looking for me, and it wouldn't be to buy me a cup of coffee. The judge sentenced me to three years in the Federal Corrections Institution in Greenville, Illinois.

Dexter and the girls got off with suspended sentences. Mr. Richman made sure that the higher ups in the Outfit came out clean as a whistle. I don't know if he bribed some cops or the judge too.

A few months later, Dexter come out to visit me. He told me that everyone was just so grateful that *I'd taken one for the team*. He was terribly sorry for what had happened, and it was all Mr. Richman's idea. He said to call him when my time was up, and he'd find another job for me in the family. When I got out two years later, I called ol' Dex, but he couldn't help me right then. He was in trouble for loan sharking and breaking his probation. He let me know that Big Buzzer would get in touch with me just as soon as he could. The call from Big Buzzer never came. Dexter was sentenced to three years in prison. I had to find that out from Mom.

TWENTY-FIVE

WE GOT BACK IN the van after visiting Chickamauga. Floyd looked at me a little embarrassed. He snorted from the deep. "We won't have much daylight left this time of year, and I don't like driving at night. Doc says I'm getting some cataracts which puts a halo around all the lights."

"Yeah Floyd, that's what happens when you get old. Everything slowly falls apart."

"Let's spend another night at the Holiday Inn. We'll get an early start in the morning."

"That's okay with me." *Did I have a choice?* We started back on the winding country road toward Chattanooga. Floyd didn't say much for a while which was unlike him. Then he said, "Whaddya think of my family?" That caught me off guard.

"Different, I reckon."

"How so?"

"Oh, jes different. I mean I didn't expect 'em to be so…"

"So educated?"

"Yeah, except for Maurice."

"You won't believe this, but Maurice was the valedictorian of his high school. He went to Brown, majored in chemistry."

"A Negro college, I reckon."

"No, it's an Ivy League school."

"Never heard of it."

"Richard was planning for him to go to medical school. He dropped out his junior year."

"I guess I dunno black people like that, with money and them fancy clothes and all that."

"What black people do you know, Buddy?"

"Some of 'em come into MacConkey's Grocery to cash in their food stamps when they should be out workin'. I saw old Floyd's nostrils flare out and you could see the hair in them. I'd been with him long enough to know that he was holding back some anger when he held his face a certain way.

"You know any of their names or where they lived or where they worked?"

"Well not exactly. I mean some of 'em didn't live in our town so how would I know them?"

"If they didn't live in your town, why would they come to your grocery store?"

"Well a few did."

"Of all the people on food stamps, what percentage is black compared to say whites?"

I know that he was setting a trap for me, but I fall right in. "Oh, lots higher for the black race, but I wouldn't want to guess."

"Forty percent are white, twenty-five percent are black . A third of people on food stamps work for a living. They don't make enough to even feed themselves in this rich country. Over a billion dollars a year are paid out by the government to people who are working at places like McDonalds and Walmart and Amazon."

"I don't believe it. That's not what I've seen or what I hear from television. I dunno where you git that bullshit. You axed me, and I told you. Most of the blacks I know are livin' off the govermint."

"God damnit Buddy, that's the goddamned facts. It doesn't do no good to talk to yo about these things." When Floyd got mad he started falling into that po' black man accent of his. I shut up for a while. I still needed Floyd to get me where I was going.

After a while, I asked, "Well how about Maurice? You cain't be proud of him too much."

"It broke Olive's heart when he quit school and moved to New York. All that rapper jargon is a put on. He used to talk just like his parents."

"No shit."

"His music is being played on some stations, like he said. And that's even worse for Olive. She was hoping he'd be a failure and go back to college, but it doesn't look like that's going to happen. He's been out of school five years. You know, Olive used to be a lot of fun, but like I said, her heart's broken."

"I thought she was just stuck-up. Like she's too good for most people." I guess I'm not the greatest judge of character that ever was. But come to think of it, who is? "Why'd the kid show up at all? Who needed him there today?"

"That's a good question. Sometimes I think it's just to drive them nuts. He resents their lifestyle and all the material things they have, including sending him to a top university. I think the kid doesn't know who he is or what he wants to be. When he wakes up, I'm afraid it'll be too late."

"What does Richard say? He's the father ain't he?"

"That could be part of the problem. I know Richard's spent most of his life working those ten and twelve-hour days that doctors tend to work. I think he had to prove that a black man could be just as good a doctor as any white fella. He earns more than a half a million a year."

"That's a lot of money for lookin' at someone's pecker."

"He never spent much time with the kid, never made it to his clarinet concerts, or coached his T-ball team. He tells me he regrets all that now."

"And I guess Olive didn't have any trouble spending the money."

"I guess not."

We drove along in silence for a few miles. I was just settling into a restful nap when Floyd starts up again. "Maybe we could drive up to Lookout mountain tomorrow. How much do you know about the battle of Chattanooga?

"Just what you told me a few hours ago, that the Union won, and the Confederates lost." Christ, we just spent hours at Chickamauga and I didn't know nothing there, so why would I suddenly know anything about Chattanooga?

"They've got a nice movie about the battle at the top of the mountain. The view from up there is pretty spectacular."

"Floyd, I think I've seen enough Civil War shit for a while."

"After Chattanooga, Sherman chased the rebs towards Atlanta. He came across the Confederates again at Kennesaw Mountain, north of Atlanta. Sherman decided on a frontal attack. The rebels held their ground and beat his boys pretty badly. That was about the last battle that the South won. After that, the Union and the Confederates skirmished for weeks but the rebs were badly outnumbered. They were finally forced to evacuate Atlanta after Sherman cut the only remaining railroad into the city. That was a big enchilada for the North, just before the 1864 election. It helped Lincoln win a second term." Floyd was on a roll.

"Who'd he run against?"

"General George McClellan, the same guy who led the Union Army at the beginning of the war."

"Well, I wouldn't have figured that."

"If you remember, Lincoln fired him and replaced him with a bunch of other generals until he settled on Grant. As they say, truth can be stranger than fiction."

"Connie was always telling me to read this book or that book. She drove me plumb crazy. You kinda make things interesting, Floyd. I guess I never knowd anyone quite like you."

"You mean a black guy like me?"

"No, a black guy or a white guy." That surprised me coming out of my mouth.

"Speaking of Connie, where will you be meeting her and your daughter?"

"At the Hilton downtown. Connie said she had a special rate there. You know where that is?"

"It's not too far out of the way for me. I'll drop you off there."

"Thanks Floyd. That's mighty nice of you."

TWENTY-SIX

WE PULLED INTO THE Holiday Inn again and unloaded all our stuff. I went to the desk to check in. I'll be darned if there wasn't one of those scarfed up Muslim women at the desk. She was cuter than you'd think. Nice lipstick and makeup on. Now why take all the time to make your face attractive if you're going to wear a headdress like that? I gave her my credit card and she swiped it through. She looked at the machine and swiped it again, then I guess she frowned, but I couldn't see her forehead.

"I'm sorry sir, your credit card has been rejected."

"Well now, that cain't be. Could you try it again?" She tried it again.

"Sorry. No luck. Do you have another card sir?"

"No, I don't have another card, sir." I was getting angry. Just then Floyd come up to the desk with a Dunkin Donut bag from the store next door. He had some powdered sugar around his lips.

"Damn, my card's not working here."

"I'll pay for the two of us."

"Now, that's right kind of you Floyd. I'll pay you back."

"Sure."

After we took our bags up to the room, us two hungry men started looking to do some eating even though it was our third big meal of the day. We walked down Broad Street toward the Tennessee River. We passed by a vegetarian place. There was a chalk board outside with the special of the day written on it: tempura with quinoa and broccoli rabe. We don't break stride. We saw a sign up ahead, Eddie's Steaks and Beer. Our pace speeded up. The place was just starting to fill up when we walked in. The tables were covered with red and white checked tablecloths that you don't see much anymore. There was some country music playing. I think it was Garth Brooks. We sat down at a little table in the back.

"Mind if I light one up?" I pulled my Camels from my front pocket without waiting for his answer.

"Sure, go right ahead. I quit about three years ago after the stents. My doctor said it's a risk factor for heart attacks."

"Yeah, I got the same damn lecture."

"So why do you continue to smoke?"

"'Cuz I like to. Just like you eat all that bad food." For once Floyd didn't have no smart-assed answer.

The waitress come up and gave us menus. Floyd scanned it with a serious look, then he drummed his fingers on the checkerboard. The black bear was getting hungrier by the minute. About ten minutes later she returned.

"What do y'all have in mind for tonight?" She flashed me a smile with a sexy little wink. She had a little mileage on her but still pretty cute. All of a sudden, I reckoned I'm a single man again. Penny was gone and good riddance.

"Let's start with a big pitcher of Bud on draft," I said.

"That'll work for me," said Floyd. We both went for the twelve-ounce Porterhouse cuts. Floyd liked it broiled the same way I do: medium rare, with French fries and fried onions on the side. I was thirsty after all that walking around Chickamauga, and we drank that first pitcher pretty quick. We ordered another one while we waited for the steaks to come. I got to admit, I was feeling a little tipsy by the time the meat arrived. We wolfed them down. Then we ordered dessert. I asked for a few shots of Southern Comfort with the chocolate cake, while Floyd put down a slug of Baileys. We bought some cigars and just sat there smoking. I guess Floyd didn't count cigars as bad for you.

By this time, the Friday night crowd had arrived, and there were people in line waiting in line for a table. The waitress come up to us with our check. She stood right next to me.

"Hey honey, when do ya get off tonight?" I asked.

"It'll be way past your bedtime, old man." She said this with a friendly smile.

"How'd you know that? I can still show a woman a pretty good time." While I was still sitting, I put my arm on her tush and gave it a little squeeze. She swatted it away.

"I think you fellows need to pay your bill and move on." Suddenly, I don't cotton to the tone in her voice. I wasn't trying to cause trouble, just having a little fun.

"Buddy, we need to be on our way, I think this lady's upset," declared Floyd.

"Now you just hang on a minute Floyd. I don't need your goddamned advice." I tried to grab the waitress again, but she backed away. I fell off my chair lunging at her.

"I don't need you making an ass of yo'self." He raised his voice pretty loud as I wobbled back to my seat. "Haven't you made enough of an ass of yo'self already? Shit, you've messed up more things in one week than most people do in their whole life. Do I need to make a list of all your fuck-ups since I've known you?"

Floyd had done too much drinking, and I'll give him some excuse for it, but nobody talks to Buddy Jones like that.

"I don't need a fat man like you to tell me I've fucked up. You know there's a reason why the South didn't want any slaves fighting in their army. Just look at yourself in the mirror. You're an overweight, fuckin' *n*----!"

I guess my voice got too loud. Floyd stood up, his eyes narrowed, and his nostrils widened, like a bull ready to charge. I wasn't sure what he was going to do, but just then a burly brute came up to us. He musta been six foot six. He was wearing a name tag: *Hootie, Assistant Manager.*

"Is this boy here the troublemaker?" he asked. He came over to Floyd and got in his space. "You know we have to serve guys like you, but most of the time you're nuthin but trouble." Floyd was the only black guy in the place.

"We were just having a little argument, sir. We'll be happy to settle our bill and leave." Floyd had his radar antenna up. He musta smelled trouble with this bruiser.

"You goddamned right, you'll leave." The hulk walked away, leaving us with the waitress who had the check in her hand.

"I'll pick this up, Floyd," I gave her my VISA.

Soon she came back shaking her head. "It didn't go through. Do you have another one?" It's then that I knew that Penny had cancelled the card. I got twelve bucks in my wallet and fifty cents in my pocket. Floyd gave her his Mastercard and we left. He didn't say anything as we headed back to the hotel.

"Geez Floyd, I was way out of line, and I'm sorry for it. I guess I had too many beers. Dagnabit, you've really helped me out and you're right, I've made a mistake or two. But nobody tells Buddy Jones that he's fucked up."

"That's what you are, a fuckup and a bigot." That's all he said.

We went up to the room. I tried to make small talk after that, but it didn't do any good. Floyd kept silent. He went into the bathroom and I guess he got Helen on the phone. I couldn't hear what he said, but he wasn't laughing like he usually did. I heard the water running and a few loud farts. Then he came out. He'd got his pajama bottoms on. There were purple hippopotamuses on them that I hadn't noticed before. He got out the big Civil War book and buried his head in it. All them beers made me pretty sleepy, and I fell asleep with my clothes on.

It must've been about eight in the morning when I woke up. Floyd was gone. I could see his suitcase all packed and sitting by his bed. I went into the bathroom, took a shit, shower, and shampoo and put on a clean tee. If I was to meet my daughter today, I needed to look my best. There was a card in the lock and Floyd entered.

"Hey Floyd, I thought you'd walked out on me, just like Penny," I tried a chuckle. Floyd looked at me. His face would've made a stone look soft. "Just as soon as I get back and settle things with Penny, I'll send you a check for what I owe. I guess she cancelled the credit card on me. I should've known she'd pull a stunt like that." I went on, desperate for him to say something. "Okay, I was out of line, but when you rattle the chain of a lion you've got to accept a few growls." Nothing, not even a flicker of an eyebrow from big Floyd.

"When do you think we'll get into Atlanta?" I asked. I pulled out my phone. "Let me punch in the location of the Hilton on Google Maps." Floyd reached into his pocket and pulled out a wad of cash. He peeled off three twenties and threw them on the bed.

"This'll get you to where you want to go. There's a Greyhound bus station about ten minutes from here."

"I'll pay you back just as soon as I get back home and settle things with Penny," I repeated.

"You don't have to pay me back. I'll just chalk up our association to another stupid thing that I've done in my life." Floyd grabbed his suitcase and slammed the door behind him.

TWENTY-SEVEN

NOW THERE I WAS AGAIN, sitting in a hotel room, all alone. Sometimes things just go against you and there's nothing you can do about it. Okay, I'd made some mistakes, but if Penny had treated me with some respect, and Floyd hadn't dragged me through all that Civil War crap, I'd already be in Atlanta. I got a bus schedule from the lobby and went across the road to a coffee shop. I was sitting down to a meal of fried eggs and bacon when my cell phone went off. I thought it was Penny finally calling me back, but the caller ID said *A. Levine.* A woman came on the line. "Is this Buddy? Do I have the right number?"

"This is him, but I dunno anyone by the name of A. Levine."

"That's the name I go by now, April Levine. I'm your daughter."

"Is that you April? Well, I'll be darned. It's good to hear your voice after all them years."

"Where are you? Mom said you'd be in Atlanta by now."

"I've run into a few problems since leaving Middleberg."

"What happened?"

"My truck broke down in Paducah Kentucky. Then

Penny's aunt got deathly sick. After the truck got fixed, she took it back to Missourah."

"Penny? Is that your girlfriend?"

"Geez, how'd you know that?"

"Mom talked to Aunt Henrietta last month. She mentioned that you were living with a nice girl named Penny."

"Yeah, she feels bad that she won't be able to make it."

"Are you still in Paducah?"

"No, in Chattanooga."

"How'd you get there?"

"I hitched a ride with a trucker. He was sposed to take me to Atlanta, but when we got outside of Chattanooga, that black fucker stuck a gun in my ribs and took my wallet. Then he threw me out of the cab."

"Oh my God, that's terrible."

"All I got now is the seventy-two bucks that was in my suitcase."

"All that? Just because you wanted to see me?"

"Yep."

"So, you won't be coming then." She sounded disappointed.

"I got enough for bus fare to Atlanta, but I won't be able to pay for the hotel, and I got no way to get back to Middleberg until I get all my credit cards back. I guess I'll just go home from here."

"Well, I'm sure Bernie can take care of the bill at the Hilton and the airfare back to St. Louis."

"Who in the heck is Bernie?"

"Bernie Levine, my stepdad. I took the name *Levine* after he and Mom got married. He's a psychiatrist here in Atlanta"

"That would explain the *A. Levine* on your caller I.D." Sounded to me like Connie married a pinko Jew.

"Buddy, please come?"

"I'm lookin' at a bus schedule right now. There's one that'll get me in around twelve-thirty."

"That's terrific. You'll be able to make it to the party tonight."

"Party? What kinda party? I don't know 'bout any party."

"I'll tell you all about it when you get here."

"Good thing I brought my Sunday suit." There was a bit of a pause, then she said, "You know I think about you a lot these days."

"You do?"

"Well, sure. You're my only real dad, aren't you?"

"I guess so. And you know what? I think about you all the time, too." Penny was always nagging me to call April on her birthday, but like I said in the beginning, I didn't have her phone number.

"We're all staying at the Hilton this weekend. There's a Sunday brunch for the out-of-town guests tomorrow morning."

"Who's *all*?"

"A lot of Mom and Dad's friends from Los Angeles have come in for the party."

"L.A. huh?"

"As a matter of fact, they just got back from there. Bernie's pretty well known from the books he's written on psychiatry. Now he he's doing a pilot for a reality TV show. They tape it in Hollywood. Ten emotionally ill celebrities get analyzed by Bernie. Then he gives them insights into their problems. Each week they face a mock-up situation that tests their mental stability. The one that's judged to be the most neurotic gets kicked off the show. I think it's going to be called *The Great*

American Nut Show. Just kidding." Then she laughed like I'd always remembered. A person's laugh doesn't change.

"I'll be lookin' forward to meeting your step-dad, but I don't warn't any shrink gettin' into my head. I don't need that."

"No, he's very nice, not like that at all. Hey I gotta run."

"Bye, April."

"Bye, Buddy."

TWENTY-EIGHT

THE TICKET AGENT at the bus depot was a bald, beefy guy with dark-rimmed glasses. He was wearing a thin black tie with a wool sweater buttoned in the front.

"I wanna ticket to Atlanta," I said.

"That'll be thirty-seven fifty. Credit card or cash?"

"Cash. Is the bus on time?"

"I haven't heard that it wasn't."

I took a seat in the waiting room and picked up a *People Magazine*. The date on it was June 2014. There were only a few people waiting. No one who can afford to own a car or fly on a plane takes a bus, except if you're blind and have a fear of flying. A man in a rumpled suit came wandering by, mumbling to himself about losing his medicines on his bus that had come in from Cincinnati. He kept repeating the same story over and over. I buried my head in the magazine. That's the best way to avoid a psycho. I read something about Kim Kardashian's wedding to Kanye West. I thought of Floyd for a second. There were two older women sitting near me. I looked them over. You know someone's real poor when they don't have a suitcase, just a plastic garbage bag.

Five minutes before the bus was to get there, there's no bus in sight. I walked up to the ticket agent. "When's the bus gettin here?" I tried to be polite-like.

"Oh, it's goin' to be late." He didn't look up. I could see he was more interested in some computer printout that he had in his hands, probably his overtime hours.

"Well how late?"

"Oh, maybe another fifteen minutes, could be longer." If we were on some fancy flight to Vegas, there'd be an announcement every five minutes updating you because that's what most people demand. Folks on a bus don't get an answer unless they ask. Finally, the bus pulled up. A few people got off, then nothing. The bus just sat. The people on the bus sat and we sat. Soon, I'm back at the counter.

"Hey, when do we leave?"

"When the bus driver is off her break."

"So how long will that be?" I'm trying to control my temper.

"Depends on how long her break will be, wouldn't it?" How does a dipstick like that keep his job? A few minutes later the driver came out to the gate. She was a tall colored woman with an unhappy face. She was built like a Mack truck. She might've been a sergeant in the Marine Corps, recently retired. I went up to her and handed her my ticket.

"I can't take your ticket until you get in line."

"What line?"

"The three of you need to form a line."

The two women were standing off to the side. I got behind them. She took my ticket and we got on the bus. There was a vacant seat in the fourth row. Some Latino jerk, wearing ear phones and a cap on backwards, was sitting in the one next to it. He looked me up and down. I figured he didn't like what he saw.

"Sit over there." He pointed across the aisle. There was a big suitcase jammed in front of an unoccupied seat. Maybe the guy went in to take a leak. I kept going down the aisle. There was mostly blacks and immigrants all glued to their cell phones and a few white people, not many. Every seat was taken until I got to the third row from the end. There sat a big woman wearing a tank top, her naked arms hanging out like a pair of Smithfield hams. She must have been 350 pounds. She was next to the window, but half her butt was hanging over the empty seat where I'm gonna sit. She sneered at me as I squeezed in next to her, and if you remember, I'm not a small man.

The bus was pretty old. The seats were a dark blue corduroy with little pills of wool that clung to the cloth. The floor was a grey linoleum that Grandma Bess had in her kitchen when I was in kindergarten. As the bus pulled out, it made this rattling noise like the bolts holding it together were loose. Suddenly, there was a sharp sound that hurt my ears, like something was being torn apart, like maybe the roof. I realized it was feedback from the intercom system because the bus driver come on to tell us that the next stop was Dalton, Georgia.

I tried to shut my eyes. A ring tone went off across the aisle. The guy sitting there answered it. He was speaking English with an accent. He's talking in a loud voice. I could hear him over the noise of the bus. At first, he was calm, "You doin' okay. Dat's good. How's da baby doin'? Well good for him." This went on for a while until he got angry and started shouting. "Come on don shit me, don shit me.

You're shittin' me and I don like when someone's shittin' me. I talk real nice, I loan you money, then you piss me off. I don like that." He calmed down and listened for a while. Then he said. "Okay, pick me up at da bus station," and hung up. He looked over and saw me watching him. The woman next to me had fallen asleep. She was leaning toward me, and her body was pushing me into the aisle. "Hey mon, you got da worse seat on da bus," and he laughed.

I dozed until a baby started to wail in the very last row. It woke me up with a jolt. If it's one thing I can't stand, it's babies screaming. I looked at a road sign. It said Kennesaw, Georgia, population 29,700. I remembered Floyd telling me that Kennesaw Mountain was the last battle that the Confederates won. The kid kept wailing. I stood up in the aisle and looked back at the mother to give her a dirty look. Just then, she pulled out a breast and the kid started sucking on it. Jesus Christ! On a goddamn bus! I sat down and told the guy across the aisle. He said. "What's da big deal mon? She's got to feed da kid."

I slept again. I was woken up by the screech of the intercom. "We will be parking the bus in just a few minutes. Do not get up until the bus comes to a FULL STOP. I repeat a FULL STOP!" The announcement woke up Big Bertha sleeping next to me. She pulled away her sweaty arm that was stuck to my face.

TWENTY-NINE

I GOT TO THE LOBBY of the Hilton around two in the afternoon. By now I only had two dollars and fifty cents in my pocket. I'd spent most of the money on my breakfast, my bus fare, and a hot dog with a bag of Cheetos that I got when the bus stopped in Dalton. The Google Maps on my phone showed that the hotel was twenty minutes on foot from the bus station. After taking a few wrong turns, I made it there in thirty-five. It took that long to go from stinking poor to the filthy rich. The Hilton's one of those big high-rise hotels, almost as big as the Flamingo in Vegas.

I called April from the bus station and told her I'd made it in okay. She said that her and Connie would meet me at the coffee shop off the lobby. When I got there, the restaurant was empty except for an elderly woman seated at one of the tables. She was wearing a dress with a plunging neckline which did nothing to hide her tanned, wrinkled skin. She looked like a dried prune that had been sitting in the sun, or maybe a raisin. She stood up when I came in. She started to smile, then gave a little wave in my direction. Oh my God!

"Is that you, Connie?" I was kinda praying it wasn't.

"Buddy?" She come up to me and gave me a hug like all was forgiven, but I wasn't that stupid.

"Where's April?"

"She's a little late. Let's sit down and have a cup of coffee until she gets here." She walked ahead of me. I could see the varicose veins bulging in her legs where before there'd been muscles. We sat down, and she stared at me, almost like the old days in John Pudulsky's apartment.

"What's up with April and this party?"

"I'll let her tell you herself. What happened to Penny? April told me something about her mother."

I shook my head sadly. "It was her aunt. She suddenly took ill. Penny had to go back to Middleberg."

"Why didn't you go with her? You could have flown out here after you got back home."

"Yeah, I guess I coulda done that." *Yeah, I coulda done that if I'd found a goddamned pot of gold buried in the trailer park.* "But then I got robbed in Chattanooga and my wallet was stolen."

"Gee, you've had some unfortunate luck. Are the authorities looking for the perpetrator?" There she was using them big educated words again. Some people never change.

"Yeah, but you know they never find 'em. Two black dudes, you know with them long braids, held me up while I was takin' a piss at the bus station. Lucky, I had fifty bucks in my suitcase, enough for bus fare here."

"What does it matter if he was black?" *Goddamnit! I gotta listen to this?*

"Well them are the people that commit the crimes and I'm sick and tired of it. Thank God, we've got Trump in there. We need some law and order in this country." I said that just for the fun of it. I saw her face get red and she frowned, which made the lines in her forehead even deeper. I put this fake smile on my face which always got her mad. I knew she was about ready to give me a lecture on political correctness.

Just then a woman and a man came up to our table. The woman was about forty, ash blond, with the curves in the right places. She had those perfect white teeth, like it cost her a lot of money to get them in that condition. She's wearing a workout shirt and shorts that showed her muscular arms and legs. A woman I'd like to know a whole lot better. The man was older, maybe about my age, kinda stooped over. He had a pasty face with a hooked nose and thick lips, thinning curly hair and a short goatee. He looked a lot like old Horowitz from my childhood.

"Buddy, this is my good friend Hazel and my husband, Bernie."

"Hi Buddy." Hazel smiled. It seemed like she'd taken a fancy to me. I started to wonder if she needed a man to escort her around town.

"Good to meet you, I've heard tho much about you, Buddy," said Bernie. He spoke softly with a bit of a lisp. I shook his hand. His grip was weak like a woman's. I know this guy had heard a shitload about me from Connie, none of it good, but he pretended to be happy to see me.

"You fly in from L.A., too?" I'm looking at Hazel.

"Yes, we all flew together." I noticed she's got those blue eyes with a little twinkle that gives me a tingle down in my dingle. "We're in L.A. a lot because of Bernie's TV show."

"Yeah, April told me 'bout it. You live near them, Hazel?" I was thinkin' I gotta quit staring at her.

"Yes, we all live together along with the cat. His name is Bernie too. That was his name when we got him, and we didn't have the heart to change it. We call him Bernie the Cat."

"All together?"

"Let me explain, Buddy." Connie butted in. "Bernie and I have an open marriage. Hazel is my significant other. She's been living with us for ten months." I suddenly felt like a tire that's run over a broken beer bottle. Bernie just sat there, a half-smile on his face, like they're talking about the brand of kitty litter that the cat pisses in. Talk about pussy-whipped. Connie looked at me kinda serious-like.

"Buddy, at the time when you and I were married, I didn't comprehend that I was bisexual. I only came to that realization after many hours of psychotherapy with Bernie."

"The cat or the psychiatrist?' I asked. Bernie snickered.

"I guess my anxiety and my lack of sexual identification initiated my seducing you. And I wanted a baby so badly to confirm my gender association. I wasn't using birth control, but it had nothing to do with religion."

That was about all I could take from Connie.

"You gotta be kiddin'? You seduced me? And I thought it was my big dick all these years." Hazel giggled. Just then the waitress come over to take our order. Suddenly, I needed a drink. "Can I get a shot of whiskey here?"

"Sure honey, what'll you have?"

"A double Jack Daniels on the rocks." I always knew Connie was a little off, but this? I was waiting to hear about the goat in the barn wearing a garter belt.

"We'll just have coffee, but can we see your dessert menu?" Connie asked.

"I guess it all thounth a little complicated," added Bernie. His dried-up wife has left him for this beautiful creature and that was all he could say. I wondered if he was in the threesome, or out in the kitchen smearing some cream cheese on a bagel while they're tying each other to the bedposts.

"It might be rude of me, Bernie, but how to you fit into all this?"

"Oh, it's a long story. I'm happy that Connie has finally found fulfillment even though regrettably, I can't fill all her needs. As a matter of fact, this whole situation will be chronicled in my next book, *Confessions of a Lonely Lesbian.* I've written three books on the effect of modern culture on the human psyche. I have a girlfriend, too, but she couldn't make it. She's a top executive at Universal Studios. Her grandfather was a pioneer cartoonist. He created Woody Woodpecker."

"Oh Bernie, tell the truth," said Connie. "She never planned to come. You know that. She knows you're still in love with me." There was that *I-know-more-than-you* voice that she used to use on me.

"Connie has a penchant for being disingenuous from time to time, particularly when she's a little envious. She's going through a manic phase. She's up at three a.m. on the shopping network buying jewelry and makeup." Bernie talked like she was just another patient. He used a lot of big words that I didn't understand except for the part about spending money. Just then Hazel put her arm around Connie and gave her a kiss on the lips, then put her tongue in her ear. Holy fuck!

"Now that Hazel and I are a couple, we've found a new therapist," said Connie. "And guess what?"

"What?"

"She's says Bernie's full of shit and I never should have listened to him." Bernie never changed his expression. He kept the little smile on his face.

"I thought it was years of therapy with Bernie that straightened you out?" I asked.

"He only scratched the surface of my psyche, broke down my defense mechanisms. Melena's digging a lot deeper."

"Into *your* shit," I said. Bernie laughed.

"Buddy, you're still the same schmuck you always were."

"What did your therapist have to say about me, or didn't my name come up?"

"Oh, Melena has said a lot about you."

"Like what?"

"Like you're a stupid, mean, lying, cheating, misogynist human being who never got over his Daddy and Mommy rejecting him, which of course wasn't your fault, but your weak ego has you blaming everyone else for all the things that you've fucked up in your life including me, your daughter, probably your girlfriend and any other people in this world who've ever called you a buddy."

"Goddamnit, let me tell you sumpin Connie..." I felt the blood rushing to my face, and I got that twinge of discomfort in my chest. Then I heard a voice.

THIRTY

"BUDDY! BUDDY!" I looked around and there was a young woman running towards me. I reckoned it must be April. I stood up to greet her. She gave me a hug, then she started to sob. "I never thought I'd see you again." And she sobbed some more.

"Gosh, it's great to see you too. It's been a long time." She was tall and had that long graceful neck, just like my mother. I started to choke up. I couldn't believe Buddy Jones was almost crying. That's not supposed to happen. I let go and sat back down just as the waitress arrived with my drink. I threw half of it down in one gulp. April pulled up a chair and sat at one end of the table between Bernie and me.

"I'm sorry to keep you waiting. I just got off the phone with Douglas. He wanted to go over the menu with me for the party tonight."

"Who's Douglas?"

"Douglas is why you're here," said Connie.

Shit, can't my daughter do the talking without this buttinski interruptin' us?

"Douglas is my husband. I was hoping you could get here a few days early, so you could really get to know him. We were married by the justice of the peace four weeks ago. I thought no one needed to know about it, but Douglas convinced me that we should tell the world."

"Why couldn't you have told me over the phone?"

"I was afraid you wouldn't come, like you refused to come to my wedding with Jimmy. That's why I had Mom make the call, so the rejection wouldn't have been so painful. My therapist told me that I should have asked you myself, but I just couldn't have faced the disappointment if you'd turned me down." She put her arm around my shoulder.

"Therapist?" For Christ sakes, none of these people could take a crap without consulting a shrink.

"I've been going to Dr. Fennywort for about twelve years, right, Dad." Bernie nodded his head. It was then that I found out that she called *him* Dad.

"She was one of my distinguished colleagues at Emory University until she went into private practice."

"Anyone and anybody that we ever knew is coming to-night. It was Douglas who persuaded me to invite you, being that you're my real father, but not the father that brought me up." She took her hand off my shoulder and grabbed Bernie's hand that was on the table in front of her.

"Bernie's done so much for April," said Connie. "While I was in the depths of my depression—except for the three long manic episodes—Bernie was the rock that kept us going. April was thirteen when we got married."

"Dad woke up early every morning and prepared oatmeal and a soft-boiled egg. He said that a young woman needed glucose in her brain to learn. Didn't you, Dad?"

"I gueth tho." Bernie seemed a bit embarrassed and a bit overwhelmed.

"And it wasn't the instant stuff. It was the old-fashioned rolled oats that takes twenty minutes to prepare. Then he drove me to junior high school before he went to work, so I wouldn't have to walk the half mile to the bus stop," added April.

Connie went on. "When she was sixteen, Bernie bought April a car. A Volvo station wagon, something safe if she got in an accident. He flew to Alabama and bailed her out after her divorce from Jimmy Hotchkiss. He paid for the lawyer and brought her back to Atlanta. Bernie was the one who found April after her drug overdose. He sat at the bedside for three whole days until he knew she'd recover. She got well enough to go back to college and graduated summa cum laude from Georgia State University with a major in Chinese philosophy. Bernie paid for all of it."

I started to think that this Bernie must be a goddamned Jesus Christ. Well sure, Christ was a Jew, too. *And now you're blowing this guy off for a woman*? That made no sense, but Connie never did.

"So, are you working, April?" I asked.

"I found out that I couldn't do much with a degree in philosophy. I completed my MBA last year and started work at the Coca-Cola headquarters."

"Where'd you meet the young man?" I asked.

"At a restaurant in Buckhead. I was sitting at the bar one evening, and we started up a conversation. He was the bartender."

"Well that's a profession I know a lot about." That got a laugh from Hazel.

"He only does that part-time. He's a trader during the day."

"What's he trade?"

"He goes on the internet and trades stock futures. It's all very complicated. Douglas is a genius in math. His business is just getting off the ground, so we'll be living pretty much on my salary for now."

"Sound familiar, Buddy?" Connie added.

"When will I meet him?" I tried to ignore the bitch for April's sake.

"At the dinner tonight."

"Well, I'm really lookin' forward to it."

"I hope so." She looked down and I could see that something made her nervous. She started picking at her arms and the corner of one side of her mouth started to twitch. The waitress arrived with a big chocolate brownie and three forks. They all dug in. Nobody said much while they cleaned the plate.

"We have to go," Hazel said, wiping her beautiful mouth with a napkin. "We've got a little shopping to do. Connie's looking for a different pair of earrings and maybe a new belt. Are you staying here at the hotel Buddy?"

"Well, I was plannin' on…"

"Buddy has a problem, Hazel," answered Connie. "He was mugged by two men at the bus station in Chattanooga." April had a puzzled look on her face. I guess I'd told her a different story. Luckily, she didn't say anything.

"Yeah, this coon stuck a knife in my ribs just as I was zipping up my fly, and his partner pulled a Glock pistol on me. They took my wallet and all my credit cards." Connie glared at me, the other two stared down at the plate where the brownie had been. *I always tell it like it is, even if it's a lie.*

Finally, April piped up. "Guess what? Dad's going to pay for Buddy's room and his air fare back to St. Louis, right Dad?" April looked at Bernie. He nodded his head and kept the half-smile on his face.

THIRTY-ONE

BERNIE WENT WITH ME to book my room, after all, he was paying for it. He pulled out his credit card and gave it to the clerk. It's a big hotel and there were a lot of people working the reservation counter. Mostly black men and women, but they got on starched uniforms and act like white folk, none of that shuckin' and jivin' which I guess isn't permitted in a fancy place like that.

After finishing the paper work, our clerk told us, "Please don't hesitate to call the front desk if you have any questions. The concierge is available if you need any play or symphony tickets. The Bolshoi ballet is in town, and there's still some seats available. We're at your service 24 hours a day." She smiled that fake smile that only involved the lower half of her face. I smiled back like I was thinking that the ballet might just be perfect for this evening. As I headed to the elevator, Bernie was right behind me.

"Dadgumit Bernie, it's really great that you're helpin' me out. As soon as I get back to Middleberg, I'll cut you a check."

"Oh, that's okay, forget it. I can afford it, and I know April is gratified that you're here. Anything that makes her happy, makes me happy."

"I hope you don't mind me asking you this, but do you have your own room or do the three of you room together on the road?" Bernie laughed.

"No, I'm on my own. Actually, to make things less complicated, I sleep in Hazel's room and she stays in the room that Connie and I reserved. Even in this day and age, some things are hard to explain."

"Gee, I just never thought that about Connie."

"She's just going through a flare of her illness right now. When Connie takes her lithium, she gets jittery, but when she's not on it, she goes off the deep end. You might not believe it, but Hazel's transgender. She was a man up until a few years ago."

"You gotta be kidding? I noticed her arms were pretty muscular, but a man? Shit, I guess nuthin should surprise me by now."

"Yeah, it was a thurprise when Connie told me. Deep down, I don't think Connie's really a lesbian. That's why she likes the man aspect of Hazel. I have no idea how Hazel's plumbing is hooked up. Connie doesn't discuss that with me."

"I have to give you credit Bernie. How do you put up with all of this garbage?"

Bernie hung his head and his heavy eyelids closed, like a bloodhound too old to chase a squirrel. "Connie has had boyfriends in the past, but eventually she returns to me and begth me to forgive her. I try to look beyond the day to day and focus on the long term. I think over time Connie's mental health has improved greatly. Unfortunately, you've caught her during one of her setbacks."

"Is she in all them books you've written?"

"I guess she is, one way or another, except my best seller, *The Sexual Evolution of the Human Penis*."

"I'll have to buy it. See how my own pecker measures up."

Bernie laughed at that one. "It thold over a million copies. Do you know that the hominid penis is the only one in the mammalian order that doesn't contain a bone? Even the chimp has a bone. It's called a *bacula*."

"I never thought on it, but there's been more than a few times I wished the bone had been there. It could have saved me from buying all that Viagra." Bernie chuckled. I started to like this guy.

"April's new independence and us living part-time in L.A. has caught Connie off guard. When she feels insecure she thometimes does stupid things."

"What's your girlfriend think of all this?"

"Oh, I don't really have a girlfriend. I just made that up to help Connie cope with her infidelity."

"The part about Woody Woodpecker too?"

"Yeah, I thought that was a brilliant flourish."

It was my turn to laugh. "Does Connie like your humor?"

"Thometimes, I guess."

"She liked mine for a while, until the hots for me wore off."

"To be honest with you, I'm very embarrassed about all of this. Maybe I am sucker for sticking it out with Connie. But one thing I do know. I love April like she's my own daughter. I hope that doesn't offend you."

"No. I cain't make any claim to April. I feel bad that I never spent any time with her after we split, but with the lawyers and all—"

Bernie was thinking his own thoughts. "This just isn't a good time to leave Connie. And with the baby coming, I'm looking forward to becoming a step-grandfather. You must be excited too."

"What baby?"

"I thought you knew."

"Knew what?"

"That April's having a baby."

"No, she left that out."

"Well, that's why they wanted to get married. That might be a bit old fashioned nowadays."

"You mean it's old fashioned that two people are married when they start to have kids? That's old fashioned? Sounds like goddamned normal to me."

"I guess in some parts of the country it still is. But of course, it doesn't really matter to a child as long as somebody loves them."

"Maybe so." *Fuck, he's got all the money in the world, but he hangs in there with crazy Connie for the sake of April who's not even his real daughter.* I got to give him some credit. My brain doesn't work that way.

"We've got a few hours to kill," he said. "Let's take a walk."

"I'm not too keen on walking just to walk."

"I'd like to show you a little of Atlanta. You see a lot more on foot."

"Okay, let me unpack and I'll meet you in the lobby." What the hell, the guy's paying for my room.

THIRTY-TWO

BERNIE AND I SET OFF on our walk. The street was crowded with people enjoying the Saturday afternoon in Atlanta. Some of the men and women were gussied up with suits and ties and skirts. We got only a few people in Middleberg who dress like that, Mr. Frost, the head honcho at The Bank of America, and a couple of shyster lawyers. Most of the folk wear blue jeans and tee shirts that they bought at Walmart. XXL is the most popular size. They're three for eight dollars, made in Vietnam, same size for women too. The only difference is that they wear a brassiere underneath. There's a good many females in Middleberg that have a fat roll around their waist bigger than their tits, but with my belly, I guess I'm in no position to make a comment on that.

We turned onto Auburn Ave. We walked past some homeless folks who were sitting on the sidewalk. I don't know how we get those people to go to work. We went past a woman with a bunch of dirty plastic bags sitting on a little kid's wagon. She was missing all her teeth. Well at least she doesn't need money for a dentist. She's got a sign next to her, PLEASE HELP ME I'M HUNGRY, written on a piece of cardboard. She's talking out loud except there isn't anybody listening. Nowadays, lots of people do that when they're on their cell phones, but I knew this woman couldn't afford one.

Bernie reached into his pocket and got out some coins and a dollar bill. He threw the money into an old coffee can in front of the sign. She nodded her head and said "Thank you sir. May Jesus Christ bless you."

"You give all these bums money? They need to quit clutterin' our streets and panhandlin' hard-workin' people. That's the trouble these days, people always want sumpin' for nuthin. I include handouts from the govermint in that category, too."

"Maybe so, but I don't like carrying change in my pocket. It's a nuisance. Maybe she does need something to eat."

"Well, you just encourage 'em to keep beggin'." Bernie didn't say anything. We continued down the street.

"What's a messagenist?" I asked.

"A misogynist?"

"Yeah."

"Is that what Connie called you?"

"What does it mean?"

"A misogynist is someone who's dislikes women."

"I love women. I'm no gay man, goddamnit."

"No, not in that way. More like you don't have respect for women."

"Sure, I do. But I admit that in certain things in life, take for instance common sense, men have more common sense than women. That's what I mean."

"I imagine that your relationships with women might be a little strained if you feel that way."

"I dunno about that. I never really thought about it too much. It's just the way I am. I reckon it gets me into hot water from time to time."

"How do you get along with Penny?"

"Well, we have our ups and downs like most people."

"We're sorry she won't be here. Connie was looking forward to meeting her."

"Actually, we had an argument in Paducah after the truck broke down." I'm not sure why I said that.

"Is that the reason she's not coming, or is it the illness in the family?"

"No, not at all. Aunt Matilda had a humdinger of a stroke. She's in the hospital. Penny tells me she's comin' along."

"You know, we could fly her down tonight. She might miss the party, but there's a brunch for the out of town guests tomorrow."

"I don't think she'd want to be here with her aunt so sick." *Shit Bernie, I'm not sitting on your goddamned couch.* We kept walking. I noticed there's mostly black people on the street now. There were some nice restaurants, but also pawn shops, coin laundries, and liquor stores, stuff that you see where poor people live.

"Anywhere special we're goin'?"

"Let's just keep walking." Pretty soon we come to a church, Ebenezer Baptist Church. "This is where Martin Luther King preached and his father before him."

"No kiddin'." We walked in. The place looked like any other church except there was a recording of one of King's speeches on a speaker. A few people sat in the pews. We walked across the road and visited the gravesite of him and Mrs. King, then we toured the museum next door. We watched a movie about the police beating the Negroes as King and the marchers crossed the Edmund Pettus bridge in Selma, Alabama. I was only a kid when all that happened.

"So, you think he helped the country with all that preachin' about this civil rights stuff and all that?" I got to be careful, I could see Bernie here was a left winger. I don't want to get on his bad side if he's helping me out.

"Well, what do *you* think?" He asked.

"He kinda agitated things. He mighta done some good but I don't think a Communist is goin' to be much help to this country in the long run." I saw Bernie frown. It wasn't what he wanted to hear.

"Well, he was instrumental in giving black people the ability to vote in elections, and now they can eat in the restaurants where they want to eat, and sleep in the hotels where they want to sleep and marry the people they want to marry. You don't think this makes us a better country, if all races and religions and creeds can be equal?"

"Well maybe. But I still think white men made this country and that's why it's so great."

"There was a time when Jews couldn't be admitted to the best universities in the United States or stay at certain hotels, so I guess I'm sensitive about that."

"And guess what? The blacks get all the breaks, all that welfare and Medicaid. Under Obama they've moved up enough already. It's time for the govermint to stop discriminating against white people. That's why I like Trump. He'll keep out them immigrants who live offa the govermint and take our jobs. Let's open up the coal mines and maybe the lead smelter where my Daddy and Granddaddy worked. People need to earn a decent wage." We started walking back toward the hotel.

"You know we always lived in an integrated neighborhood. Some of April's best friends are black, boyfriends, too."

"Well, I guess Douglas'll put a stop to that." I chuckled.

"Buddy, there's something I should tell you."

"Yeah, yeah, I know you're a lefty Democrat, you don't need to tell me. Let's stop talkin' about black people and the govermint. You're a nice fella, but I don't think we're gonna see eye to eye on some things. I just want to enjoy my time here with April." Bernie was about to answer but then he stopped himself. We started down Irwin Street that ran in the same direction as Auburn. The houses needed paint and the sidewalks were crumbling. An old tennis shoe was lying on the road. Then we saw a whole block that was nothing but bushes and trees.

"What's all this?"

"It used to be a housing project. It was torn down years ago. I always thought that businesses or shopping centers or somebody would develop the land. It's so near where Martin Luther King, one of our nation's greatest heroes, is buried. Nothing has happened. It's as poor as ever."

"You're right. It ain't Disney World around here." Penny and I had been there last year.

We come across another beggar. He was holding a sign up, HELP FEED MY GRANDKID. The guy had a long grey straggly beard. He was wearing this big cross with Jesus on it. I kept walking, no way I'm going to mess with a weirdo liked that. I looked back. Bernie had stopped. He pulled a bill out of his wallet and gave it to the guy. The man hugged Bernie. The guy said in a real loud voice, "The Lord will bless you, you will walk in the footsteps of Jesus."

When Bernie caught up to me, I asked, "How much you give him?"

"Twenty bucks."

"Dang it, Bernie. You gave him twenty bucks to buy a couple of bottles of cheap whiskey."

"I'd feel terrible if he did have a grandchild who needed a meal." We didn't say much after that. About ten minutes later, the hotel came into view.

"Buddy, how many black people do you know?"

"That's funny. Floyd asked me the same question."

"Who's Floyd?"

"A black truck driver from Paducah, Kentucky. He gave me a lift when my vehicle broke down. He was sposed to take me all the way here, but we got into an argument in Chattanooga. He pulled a gun on me and took my wallet."

"I thought two men robbed you in the men's room while you were relieving yourself?"

"You know what Bernie? It's none of your business what the hell happened to me. I'm here now, ain't I?"

"Why did he ask you the same question?"

"About what?"

"About knowing black people?"

"Beats me."

Bernie started talking, almost like he was talking to himself. "Did you ever think, the more people you know of different religions and colors, the more you find out that they have more in common than not. We all struggle through life."

"Maybe so, I don't think too much about that. I guess I'm not much of a thinker. I only knowd what I know."

"Do you find that your interpersonal relationships often end because of arguments?"

"Waddya mean by interpersonal?"

"The people that you call your friends and lovers. Do you often have fights with them?"

"Sure, don't most everybody?"

"Well that's true, but there's fights and there's really big fights that cause you not to be friends with them anymore."

"I never thought of that, but you know I've seen nuthin but fightin' all my life. My parents fought like a pair of weasels over a dead rabbit, and when my Daddy got angry, he'd beat me with his belt. My Mom fought with her next husband and the next one. My brother fought, and my pals fought, and so did the inmates in prison. That's just the way it is where I come from. No fancy hotels or private airplanes or transgenders for us. Just simple folk." I could see the hotel in the distance.

"From what Connie's told me about you, some psychotherapy could really help you, and Penny could go too. When you get back to Missouri…"

"Did Connie and April put you up to this? To get me to see a shrink?"

"No, not at all. They never said anything. Sorry I brought it up."

"That's the last thing I need, a goddamned shrink. Maybe you think Connie's gotten better with your help, but to me, she's just as looney as ever." I thought that'd get him angry, but he didn't say anything, just kept moving. "Sorry I said that, Bernie. It's just that Connie puts me in an ornery mood. How dya ever get hooked up with her anyway?"

"I was a medical resident living near Atlanta Charity Hospital and Connie was living in the apartment below me. She was working as a social worker at the same hospital. She was clever and witty, and I found her very sexual. One thing led to another and soon I had moved into her apartment."

"When did you realize that she was a sick bitch?"

"We've been married for 22 years, and I guess she's had mental problems for all 22 of them, but we've had some good times along with the bad. I try to focus on the good times."

"Well, she did say you were the reason that April turned out as good as she did. She seemed to look up to you for it, but I don't figure that's love."

"Maybe after the baby comes, I should think of leaving, unless Hazel leaves first. I don't know. Maybe it's not in my DNA to abandon my wife."

As we entered the lobby of the Hilton, Bernie turned to me and the smile on his face was gone so I knew he was serious. "But aren't we all a little sick in the head? Maybe some more than others. I don't exempt myself from that." He wasn't a bad guy, real honest for a Jew.

"I guess I'm not perfect misself," I answered. Bernie nodded his head in agreement. When I got to the room, I got some burning in my chest. I laid down on the bed and took a nitro. The pain went away. The next thing I knew, the phone was ringing in my room.

THIRTY-THREE

AFTER I DID MY TIME in prison, I moved in with Mom into Grandma Bess' old house in Middleberg. By then, Grandma Bess had been dead a number of years, and Mom was between her fourth and fifth husbands. The house was completely paid up so it was a cheap place for the two of us to live. I was determined to go straight, no drinking, no drugs. Mom had quit the booze too. Our only vice was the two packs of unfiltered Camels that we each smoked in a day, the same brand that had caused Grandma Bess' lung cancer.

Billy MacConkey was nice enough to hire me back to his grocery store after I apologized for telling him to stick the job up his ass, but he demoted me to washing the floor and cleaning the toilet at night. He cut my salary by a third, but being an ex-con, I wasn't in a position to be too choosy.

Oh sure, I shacked up with some of my old high school girlfriends, even took a stab at my first throb, Norma Jean Fiddler. We went to bed a bunch of times even though she had four kids by then, but it wasn't anything serious. She'd come by after her shift at the lead smelter where she worked as a bookkeeper. She'd tell her husband that she had to work overtime. Mom didn't seem to care what I did by then, I was pushing forty. Shit, if someone wanted to commit adultery, she wouldn't stand in the way. Norma Jean soon was pregnant with her fifth child, and she went back to her husband full time. She was nice enough to tell me that I wasn't the father. I appreciated that, though how she really knew, I never bothered to think on it.

I started going with a gal that I met at church. Yes, old Buddy attended the Baptist church with his Mom in those days. Doris Nooter sat over in the next pew. She was with a man who I figured was her husband, but one Sunday he wasn't there, and he never came back. Poor Doris just sat there singing and praying all by herself. I admit she was no bombshell, but Mom whispered in my ear at church that she was supposed to have a lot of money.

One Sunday, Mom was up visitin' Aunt Henrietta in St. Louis, so I took the occasion to sit beside Doris. I started up a little chit chat like I know how to do. In between praising the Almighty and his son Jesus Christ, I found out that the man that had sat next to her was her brother. He was supposed to go back to the Ozarks for only a few days, but he'd never returned. She guessed he was cooking meth again.

That afternoon over coffee at the Steak n' Shake, Doris told me that she'd been married to an older man, a postman from Batwing Creek just a few miles up the road from Middleberg. He'd dropped dead of a brain hemorrhage eight years before. She never planned to marry again because she'd never find another man like Glen Nooter. She'd find peace for her soul in the blessings of Jesus Christ. I let her know that I'd been to bed with only one woman in my life, my ex-wife Connie, who'd left me for a rich man and moved to Atlanta. I agreed that we'd just be friends. In the women business, you've got to learn to improvise and tell the right story at the right time.

I don't need to go into all the details of the courtship, but you get the picture. It wasn't long after we met that the chastity thing went out the window. Shit, she was forty-five and she made up for the eight years of being without a man. She'd drive in from Batwing Creek and stay with me on weekends. She even helped with the electric and grocery bills when we got short. For those reasons, Mom liked her quite a bit. She thought that Doris would be good for me, seeing that she didn't drink, smoke or use drugs.

It turned out that Mom was also right about her money. Glen Nooter had delivered mail in Batwing Creek for his entire adult life, but he'd gone to high school with Sam Walton's cousin—yes that Sam Walton—and they'd kept in touch. In the 1970's, the man gave them one hundred shares of Walmart stock as a wedding present, and Glen had bought more shares over the years. When Glen died, the shares were worth 1.5 million dollars. Now how could old Buddy take a pass on a woman like that? And even though she wasn't gorgeous, she wasn't that ugly, and all that money made her even prettier.

Murray Bumb was a farmer that Mom had known as far back as grade school. He started courting Mom soon after his wife died, about a year after I moved back to Middleberg. Murray and Mom were in their mid-sixties by then. Believe it or not, there's a large clan of Bumbs in that part of Missouri. Murray told me that his ancestors came from Germany in the 1850's, just before the Civil War. I regret to say that Murray really liked his German lager. It wasn't long before Mom fell off the wagon, and she fell pretty hard. Murray would drop her back at the house plastered, and that led Doris to do some scolding of the both of them. Mom moved to Murray's farmhouse on the outskirts of town to get away from Doris. Not long after, Murray became Mom's fifth and final husband.

I got to admit, Doris and I had some real good times together during them years. She kept me on the straight and narrow, and we had Doris' money to go on trips. I introduced her to Las Vegas where she'd never been. Gambling wasn't anything that she'd ever done before. We'd go out to The Strip about six times a year. I never mentioned that I'd been connected with the mob at one time, and that they skimmed money off the rubes of the world which included her. For all she knew, I'd been in the grocery business all my life except when I'd been in jail which of course warn't my fault. That was the truth. I took her to see all the entertainers, Glen Campbell, Pat Boone and Wayne Newton.

It turned out that Doris took a liking to poker. At first, she just played the poker machines, but then she started playing in some real games. She and I would sit at a small stakes table playing one-dollar Texas Hold'em. Sometimes we'd win and sometimes we'd lose. Even if we lost a few hundred dollars in an evening, it didn't make a dent in Doris' fortune. I started a model train collection and soon I had three of four lines running through the basement of the house. A few years later, I bought a used Cadillac Deville, and after that, a $70,000 power boat that we'd take to the Lake of the Ozarks. I mortgaged the house to buy the boat, and Doris helped me with the monthly payments. Those were good years and I kept off the booze for the most part.

Mom and Murray had been hitched five years when the farmhouse burned to the ground with both of them inside of it. The fire marshal checked it out, and blamed Murray for falling asleep with a lit cigarette. There were three gin bottles scattered around the living room floor, and the coroner figured they'd been drinkin' pretty heavy. I guess Murray had dropped his beer for Mom's Beefeater that she liked so much.

THIRTY-FOUR

DEXTER CAME DOWN from Chicago for Mom's funeral. After he'd gotten out of jail, he went back to the mob. They gave him a job running a front business. It was a cigar place that sold Cubans under the counter and laundered drug money. Otherwise, it was pretty legit. Big Buzzer and Greaseball had recently gone to prison, and some of the other associates, as he called them, had been killed in a fly-by shooting. Dexter said he needed a place to live until things cooled off. He was short on cash and asked if he could stay with me in the old house. Tiger had found another boyfriend while he'd been in prison. Dexter called himself a *free agent.*

He took a job in Middleberg, at an auto repair. Dexter really had a knack for fixing cars: brakes, air conditioning, electrical systems. You name it, he could fix it. And he could steal them too. Like I often said, he was good at most things. He knew how to break into a vehicle, hotwire it, then drive off. He had a buyer for the cars out of state, in Southern Illinois. Pretty soon he had scraped together enough money to purchase a brand-new Ford Mustang and a bunch of custom-made suits.

Dexter and I started going to the Red Parrot for beer and whiskey, just like old times. One evening, after a few bubblies for us, and a few rounds for the locals—Dexter always liked to look more prosperous that he was—he asked me, "Buddy, when you goin' to ask Doris to marry you?"

"I dunno, Dex. I told you before. I never planned to get hitched again after Connie, and I'm pretty much gonna stick to that. Plus, Doris don't ever wanna get married."

"Why dya think that is?"

"Sumpin to do with her dead husband. Says she really loved him."

"Maybe it's got sumpin to do with all her money."

"How'd you know about that?"

"Most everyone in town knows how Glen Nooter bought all that stock. How much does she exactly have?"

"One and a half million." Ol' Dex whistled through his teeth when he heard that.

"Maybe it'd be worth our while."

"Whaddya mean by that?"

"Well, don't you wanna come into possession of that kinda money?"

"I already am. I mean she's pretty generous paying for them trips to Vegas, and she pitched in to help me with my model trains and the boat and the car and all."

"No, I mean like come into possession, like it'd be your own. You wouldn't even have to marry her which she don't want you to do anyway."

"Oh, I see your point. And how'd we do that?"

"She got any vices other than going to church?" Dexter laughed at his own joke.

"Well she likes to play small stakes poker."

"We could try the old poker scam, couldn't we?"

"You mean like take all her money and leave her broke?"

"Sumpin like that."

"Jeez, I like Doris. I'd be plumb sorry if we cleaned her out."

"Yeah, but just think about this. You and I could split the money. You could quit that stinkin' grocery job and we'd move to Las Vegas or Hawaii. We'd have all the women that we'd ever want, like the old days with the stewardesses. Remember that?"

"Yeah, I remember that real well," I said.

The next day Dexter told me his plan. The three of us would plan a trip to Vegas, but I'd hurt my back at the last moment, and they'd go by themselves. Dex promised he wouldn't mess around with her when they were there, the two of them would sleep in separate rooms. They'd start playing Texas Hold'em in a small casino off the strip that Dexter knew from the Mafia. The other guys in the game would be in on the scam. They'd pay off the dealer to signal the cards to everyone before they turned over, everyone but Doris. On the first night, it would just be a fun game. On the second night, the stakes would slowly increase, and by the third night, Doris would win a ton a money. On the fourth night, the stakes would be even higher. Doris would lose a small amount, but she'd play a fifth night hoping to win it back. That's when they'd take all her moolah.

After they'd get back to Middleberg, Dexter would break the news to me. I'd pretend to get angry with him for letting her play in a game like that. We'd put the old house up for sale and give Doris the proceeds so she could have some money to live on. She'd thank us for being so generous. Then we'd claim that we were going to Vegas to strong arm the gamblers into giving back her money. Instead, we'd fly to Hawaii and divvy up the proceeds with the other guys in the game. Of course, Dexter and I would get the lion's share of the cash because we'd thought it up. I admired at how smart ol' Dex was. Like I said before, he could have been a doctor or a lawyer.

The day before we were to leave, I faked a terrible pain in my back after lifting a case of toilet paper at MacConkey's. I came home early from work and took to my bed. Doris wanted to cancel the trip, but we'd already paid for the rooms. Dexter and Doris flew to Vegas just as we'd planned.

Five days passed, and I didn't hear anything from Dexter. I began worrying that maybe Doris had caught on to our scheme, or maybe she never wanted to play poker for that much money, or maybe she quit the game after she won all that cash on the third night, and now they were just going to the shows. All of a sudden, Dexter's plan didn't seem so hot. There were too many ways it could go wrong. On the sixth day, I got a telegram from Dexter.

TERRIBLEY SORRY BUDDY **STOP** *PLANS HAVE CHANGED* **STOP** *DORIS AND I GOT MARRIED LAST NIGHT* **STOP** *LEAVING FOR HAWAII TOMORROW* **STOP.**

A few months later, I declared bankruptcy.

THIRTY-FIVE

THE PHONE WOKE ME up, and I answered it. It was Connie's angry voice. "Where are you? We're down in the lobby waiting for you."

I looked at the clock, one of those digital ones with the red numbers. It was six-thirty. "I guess I overslept."

"Meet us there. The party's at Ali's, a Lebanese restaurant just down the street. The bell hop will give you directions."

"Okay," and I hung up. It figured. Let's go eat some *Ayrab* food. I guess no one asked me if I liked it. I shaved the four-day growth off my face and tried to take a shower with the dinky bar of soap they supplied. A hotel this nice should have something bigger to wash your body with. I put on my suit and tried to straighten the wrinkles. It'd been sitting in my suitcase all them days. I hadn't worn the pants for a long while, and they were too tight on me even then. I sucked in the gut just to get the outside button buttoned, so I could zip up the fly. I fastened the clip-on red and purple tie over the one dress shirt that I owned. I looked in the mirror, not bad for a man my age. I took a Zantac as a precaution, just in case the Muslim food gave me heartburn.

The restaurant was real big and busy. I went up to the woman at the reservation desk. "I'm here for a party."

"And what's the name sir?" She smiled at me and I smiled back. I could see on her face she thought I was someone important with my suit and tie on.

"It's a party for April and Doug, maybe under Levine."

"We have no one by that name. The only private party we have is Washington. It's down the hall to the right."

"That don't sound right." I said.

"Sometimes people use names like Washington or Lincoln or Lee if they have a hard to spell last name."

"I'll check it out." I headed down the hall and found the banquet room. There musta been a hundred people in there. Some of them were standing around with wine glasses in their hands and some were already sitting at tables. The men wore suits, but a few had on sweaters and blue jeans. Seemed like most of them had short whiskery beards. I could've showed up without bothering to shave. The women wore fancy dresses, and I took notice of the ones wearing low cut tops. About half the people in there was uppity black. No poor folk or rednecks like myself to be seen. There was a table with some women wearing head scarfs and long gowns. I guess they must've recommended the place to April. There was a platform near the back with a microphone on it.

I have to admit, all those people laughing and talking made me nervous. At that moment, I wished Penny had come. I stopped by the bar to get a drink. Then I remembered that I'd left my last two dollars and fifty cents back at the room. I was plumb surprised when the bartender told me that the liquor was free. I asked for a double Jack Daniels. Bernie was paying a pretty sum for this party.

Suddenly, I saw April. She waved. They were at a table near the microphone: April, Bernie, Connie, Hazel, and some black man. There was a sign on the table: RESERVED FOR THE BRIDAL FAMILY. They'd already sat down and started to eat. As I got nearer, I saw the black dude put his arm around April, and they kissed. Then it dawned on old Buddy. Well fuck me. She'd married a black guy. I felt a tight feeling in my chest again.

When I got to the table, April gave me a long hug. I just stared straight ahead and didn't put my arms around her. I saw Connie and Bernie behind April with fixed smiles on their faces. Hazel was wearing a sleeveless gown, showing off her muscular arms again. Maybe she'd been a hockey player when she was a man. The black fella was just behind April. He was tall, and I have to say good-looking for a man of that race. He had a short haircut and a goatee, none of that Afro crap.

"Buddy, this is Doug Washington, my husband. Doug, this is Buddy, my real father." She seemed nervous after she saw the look on my face, like I'd seen a black ghost. I was trying to keep it together, but the thought of a Jones from Middleberg marrying a—

"Good to meet you." I shook his hand. His palm was cold and sweaty. I guess April must have filled him in on my preferences in regard to a husband, and he knew it didn't include him.

"Washington eh? You related to a Floyd Washington?" I asked.

"No, I don't think so. Washington's a common name with us. You ever met a Washington who was white other than George?" I'd heard that one before.

I sat down at the only empty chair, between Connie and Bernie. On the plate in front of me, there was something that looked like an enchilada with some pasty greyish goo and some little green suckers mixed in. I took one bite and put it down. I finished the double bourbon in one gulp.

"What's this crap?" I asked. Connie gave me a dirty look. She was wearing a tight-fitting black dress which would've looked good on her twenty years ago or maybe thirty. She had on her new pair of earrings and a matching belt. Little jade bunny rabbits carved on each earring and a larger cottontail on the buckle. If I'd had my AR-15, I would have put those suckers to sleep and taken Connie's body parts with them.

"It's a falafel wrap with baba ganoush," said Connie in her *you're-a-stupid-man* voice.

"What the fuck is that?"

"It's eggplant mixed with tahini paste wrapped in dough."

"Are these here peas?"

"There called lentils." Hazel had to chip in her two cents.

"You've never had them before, Buddy?" asked Connie.

"No, we don't have many Lebanese restaurants in Middleberg. I dunno if you knowd that."

"I guess I didn't *knowd* that," she said. I felt my face turning red.

"I need another drink." I could feel my heart skipping beats.

"I'll have one, too," piped up Connie.

"Are you sure that's a good idea?" Bernie said. "You've already had two, dear." He'd seen her tanked up like I had, and he knew it wasn't a pretty picture.

"I'll get them for you two," April said. "Doug and I have to get up and circulate anyway." I waited till they were gone.

"Jesus Christ. Why didn't she tell me she was married to a Negro?"

"She was afraid," Bernie said.

"Afraid of what?"

"Afraid that you'd disapprove, and dethide not to come. She tho much wanted you to be here." Bernie lisped more when he was agitated. We sat in silence for a while as the rest of them ate their *Bobby Goulash.*

"Well, she's probably right. I wouldn't have come. I don't see her for years and then the one time I show up, I've got to accept this shit sandwich. Why didn't she talk to me before she made her choice? She's cute and perky. She could've had any white fella over there at Coca-Cola. At least *you* could have told me before I met him."

"Bernie was supposed to tell you. That's why he took you to the Martin Luther King grave," said Hazel.

"Was he sposed to talk up black people before he told me? Give me a locker room pep talk before the big game?" I guessed everyone was in on it but me.

"My wonderful husband got cold feet," said Connie. I could see she'd saved a mean voice for him too.

I looked over at Bernie. His eyes were fixed down on his plate and he kept eating. He must have been worried about twenty lashes from Connie's new belt. April returned without Doug. She put the drink in front of me and I chugged it down. Connie did the same with hers. Now I've had two belts of whiskey on an empty stomach, not counting one bite of the appetizer. That's never been good for me, and it wasn't good this time.

"Well, what do you think of Doug?" April asked.

"I hain't said two words to him so how would I know?"

I guess my voice was a bit edgy. I could see April's eyes, those beautiful blue eyes, fill with tears, but I was just so goddamned mad that nobody told me. Like I was some goddamned race bigot. And sitting next to Connie brought back nothing but bad memories.

"Oh, let's all have a good time, shall we?" At that moment, I didn't need to hear from Hazel.

"So, tell me, when did you become a woman?" I asked.

"Oh, it's a long story Buddy. Maybe another time."

"No, I'd like to hear it now. Do you two use your own equipment for screwin' or do ya'll need a steely Dan."

"Buddy! That's enough," Connie snapped. Doug sat down again as they brought the main course, rosemary chicken and potatoes. I have to admit, Rosemary did a pretty good job on the chicken.

"So, Doug whaddya you do for a living? I mean do you work?" I asked.

'Remember Buddy, I told you he was a day trader," April said.

"What the fuck is that, Doug?" I wanted to hear it from him.

"I place puts and calls on various trading vehicles according to a mathematical system which I developed during my MBA at Emory."

"I hope you can make a living doing that. My daughter here, needs the best." I forced a smile at April, and she smiled back.

"Just like the life you gave her, Buddy." Connie snarled.

"Connie, I'd have hung around and been a decent father if you hadn't been such a goddamned bitch. It's amazin' you didn't give birth to a litter of mongrels."

"Please, just for once, can't you all shut the fuck up." April started to cry after she said that. Doug put his arm around her and gave her a Kleenex. She pushed him away and got up to go to the ladies' room.

"What's wrong with you two? Jethus, the one night in your life where you need to be thivil to each other and you can't." Even Bernie was losing it.

"I've never seen you like this Connie," added Hazel.

"Well Hazel, you ain't knowd her long enough." I felt a sharp sting on my face. Jeez, Connie still had some zip in her right hand. It temporarily sobered me up. Now I had a choice. Take it like a man or strangle her and be done with it.

"I'm sorry Buddy. That was fucking stupid." Connie was completely looped, but even she was ashamed at the she-devil that lived inside her.

"This is supposed to be the happiest day of our lives," Doug said. "And you're ruining it, God damnit." Now everyone at the table had cursed at least once.

"You're right Doug, I'm sorry too," I said.

Connie kept quiet for once. Bernie went back to eating his chicken, and Hazel went out for a smoke. I got an urge to piss and went looking for a toilet. On the way back to the table, I asked the bartender for another Jack Daniels. He said they were out of it, so I got a straight vodka instead. I staggered back to my seat and drained the glass. When Hazel sat down a few minutes later, I could smell that she'd just smoked a joint. She had a silly smile on her once-hairy face.

"I'll check on April." Doug got up and went looking for her.

"He mus' be wondern whad he's getting' into, Bernie boy." My speech was starting to slur.

"I think he already knows. The good news is that he's marrying April, not one of us."

THIRTY-SIX

WHEN APRIL SAT DOWN again, she wasn't teary-eyed anymore. I don't know what Doug said, maybe he told her that after the evening was over she'd never have to see me again. They served baklava for dessert. I'd never eaten it before, but I found it really tasty, like a cinnamon roll but sweeter. After our tussle, Connie and I kept our distance, like two boxers between rounds. The rest of them engaged in bullshit about the weather, the Atlanta Falcons, and the shopping malls in Buckhead. Suddenly, Douglas shouted out, "There's Booker from Paducah." I looked up and there was Floyd coming towards us.

"Hey thas Floyd Washington, Doug. Guy I tol' you about." I was drunk as a coot.

"I only know him as Booker. I think they call him that because he went to Tuskegee University that Booker T. Washington founded." Then I recalled that his brother had called him Booker, too. Floyd went up to Doug and gave him a hug and a few pats on the back.

"Good to see you DeWayne, sorry I'm so late. The clutch on my van went kaput just outside Kennesaw. I had to get a tow to the nearest service station." Now it all came back.

Doug was the DeWayne that Richard and Olive had talked about. Shit, couldn't they have just kept the names they were borned with?

"This is my wife, April."

"Good to meet you, April." He gave her a hug.

"This is my mother-in-law Connie, and my father-in-law Bernie, and their friend Hazel. Buddy here tells me he knows you."

"Yeah we do." He's as cold as an ice cube when he said that. I got up and offered my hand. He shook it, but I could see that he was still mad as hell. He wouldn't look me in the eye. Dang it, you can't hold a grudge forever. I said some stupid things, but I didn't mean most of them.

"Let's see if we can get you some dinner before the speeches," said Doug.

"Yeah, I'd like to say a few words if I could," answered Floyd. He walked off to a table at the end of the room. For the first time, I noticed Richard and Olive sitting there. I wondered if they'd seen me before when I got up to pee. I guess I couldn't blame them for not coming up and giving me a hug and a kiss. Floyd had most likely filled them in on our dust-up.

"How do you know this guy?" asked Connie.

"Oh, he's a frien' of mine from St Louis. Went to high school with me. I guess it's a small world." I hee-hawed even though it wasn't funny.

"That's strange, I never remember you saying anything about him. I don't ever remember you having a black person as a friend."

"Well I did, Goddamnit. You didn't knowd everythin' 'bout my business."

"No, you're right on that. I certainly didn't know all the women that you fucked while we were married. So how would I know Floyd?" She even had a nasty remark about my lies.

"I hope you get up and say a few words," said April. At first, I figured she was talking to Bernie, but when I looked up, she was looking my way.

"I dunno what to say. I hardly knowd you and I ain't proud of it."

"Well just say you're happy to be here and then sit down."

"I guess I can do that. I think I need nuther libation." I never liked talking in front of people. In fact, it scared the shit out of me. I got another vodka at the bar and gulped it down right there. I asked for another and brought it to the table.

Soon the speeches got going, the usual bullshit. Their best friends got up to tell us what a happy couple they were, just *made* for each other. Then we heard the corny little stories about how they met at the singles bar. How Doug called her ten times before she'd go out with him, the fight on the first date, and then he doesn't call her. And then she thought about how cute he was, and then she called him, and he was really hoping that she'd call, and then she did, and then one thing led to another, and now they're just so happy to be hitched together. Like two chocolate bunnies in an Easter basket, only one of them's white chocolate. And how Doug likes goddamned stuffed pandas and she does too, and they got twelve of 'em. And they have the same favorite food, egg foo young. And can you believe they didn't know it until Doug moved in with her? Everyone laughed even though the mike wasn't working quite right, and nobody could hear half of what they were saying, but it must be funny or why would they say it? The black and white races just as happy as could be, all mixed together in a chocolate sundae without the cherry. Well fuck, I thought. Things never work out. At least they never worked out for me. I'm starting to feel sorry for myself which I do when I'm drunk. I sat there waiting my turn, getting more stewed.

Then Bernie got up with his stories about April, what an intelligent, beautiful girl she was, and what a fine woman she'd turned into, and how proud he was that she was marrying Doug. Doug's family does the same thing. His dad and mom have both passed, but his mom's sister got up. She had a pretty face and probably was quite a looker at one time but now she's the size of a refrigerator. She talked with an accent and threw in a few Spanish words that I didn't understand. That didn't surprise me. By this time, I figured there must be an Eskimo in the crowd. A few more aunties got up and some cousins. It seemed like the whole family had something to say. They googooed and gagaed over April. You'd think Doug was marrying Aunt Jemima, and she'd flip pancakes every morning for breakfast. I'm getting meaner and meaner.

I started to lose track of time. I vaguely remembered Connie talking. Something about how hard it had been to be a single mom, and how she scrimped and saved to bring up April on a social worker's salary. And how things changed after she met Bernie, and how he'd been to April like the father that she'd never known. It shouldn't've, but it made me mad.

April got up and thanked everyone. She thanked her friends for their speeches. She thanked Bernie and Connie.

Even transgender Hazel came in for thanks, I'm not sure why. Then she thanked me. Buddy's car broke down. Then the aunt got sick and he hitched a ride from Paducah. He was robbed by the driver just outside of Chattanooga and had to take a bus to Atlanta. She teared up as she told them that I arrived with only two dollars and fifty cents in my pocket. Just so I could meet her husband Doug. Then she asked me to come up and say a few words.

I'm afraid my words were a bit scrambled. I don't doubt that some of the people there probably knew I was drunk. I hope they don't still think I'm a bad guy, but I'm sure some of them still do.

"It's so grea' to be with ya'll tonight. I'm a littl' drun' and I hope you'll bear with me. First off, what's the difference between a black man and a bike? None aya know that huh? The bike don' sing *Old Man River* when you put a chain on it." I heard a few hisses, but I'm too drunk to care. I recall looking over at April. She'd hung her head in the plate of half-eaten wedding cake. I felt a tug on my arm, maybe it was Bernie, but I had to keep going.

"I've never seen as many beautifu' brown people in one place. You know, I've never liked the wor' black. Some of you are dark chocolate, some of ya are mocha and a few of ya are like the lattes they serve at Starbucks where mos' of you hangout. We don't have rich people like you where I come from. In my neck of the woods, most of the blacks are on food stamps." The room was spinning by this time, and I felt like I wasn't going to be able to stay on my feet.

"I'd like to talk 'bout April. As I look at her, I caint believe she's my daughter, so beautiful and all grown up. I never spent the time I shoulda with her. I was too busy tryin' to make a livin', or goin' to the bar to drink. That shouldn' come as a surprise to y'all, considerin' the state I'm in at this momen'. But seein' as I only had a tenth-grade education, I couldn't really get a real good job like mos' of you here. I cain't read real well, and don't have no pieces of paper behind my name. It's not like the old days where you could get a good job workin' with your hands. Now you need your brain, and unfortunately God gave me one that didn' work jes' right. Some of my relatives worked in the lead smelter in Middleberg, Missourah. It's closed down now thanks to Obama and his buddies, but they say that lead can cause your brain to go haywire. Them good jobs are gone for people like me, and with my bad back I caint work no how, but even if I were fit to work, some immigrant would probably get hired 'stead of me."

"I'm sorra to say, April's mother and I didn't get along. I knowd some of it might have been my fault, but we warn't meant for eesh other. You see Connie here is sick in the head, *very very sick* in the head." I made circles around my ear with my finger and then pointed it at Connie. Connie sat there looking like she just chewed on a porcupine. I don't know why I said that about her, but I was still mad from before. That's what alcohol does to you, makes you say things that you think, but shouldn't say. I recall hearing some boos from the crowd. A bunch of people got up and left the room.

I started to feel a twinge of pain in my chest and the room started to go hazy. Somehow, I kept on my feet. I remember Bernie had his mouth open. He'd turned red and I thought he'd choked on something. He told me later that I said some of the dumbest things that he ever heard anyone say, and he's a shrink. But I wasn't done, no sirree.

"I'm sorry that my girlfrien' Penny couldn' be here. She found out that her aunt had taken sick after we got to Paducah. If any you ever been there, you'll know that you ain't never wanna go back unless you really like blue grass, or bourbon, or pure-bred horse shit. A big man, dark as the ace of spades, stuck a gun in my ribs. He took five hunner bucks from my wallet and all my credit cards while I was takin' a piss in the men's room at McDonald's." God knows why I brought up that mixed-up story again, but April had felt so sorry for me when I'd told it before.

"I wanna thank Bernie here, for helping me out and payin' for my hotel room and my airfare back to St. Louis. For a tight-fisted Jew-boy, he's been pretta generous..."

Suddenly I heard some noises, the scraping of a chair and the rattle of knives and forks as if some dude had got up real suddenly. Sure enough, I saw big Floyd rise up and come running toward the stage. I'd never knew old Floyd could run like that, like he was on a mission, like when someone kills a bear with his bare hands out of rage, or a soldier charging up a hill knowing he's going to die in about five seconds. He grabbed the mike from me and pushed me away.

"This man is a liar, a goddamned liar!" He bellowed into the microphone. "I met this man, Buddy Jones, in Paducah Kentucky where you all know I live. His girlfriend left him there because he's a misogynist, bigoted, lying bastard! And a drunk! There is no sick aunt. I was generous enough to offer him a ride to Chattanooga. I even took his dirty underwear to my house and washed it for him. He's gone bankrupt twice and has no credit cards. He sponges off his girlfriend, that's how he lives. We stayed in a hotel room in Chattanooga and had breakfast, lunch, and dinner together.

I paid for it all. Little did I know we'd be celebrating the same marriage of these two wonderful people. We got into a fight in Chattanooga and he called me the "n" word. This man in front of you called me that. Then I gave him sixty bucks so he could take a bus here. Despite how he abused me, I gave him more money. And now this man stands before you and makes more racial slurs and tells you this pack of lies--"

That was all I could take. I charged him with my head low and butted into that big stomach of his.

THIRTY-SEVEN

THE NEXT THING I KNEW, I was in a big room, so big that I can't see any walls, but I wasn't outdoors. There was a *being* present. I could feel that it was alive, but it didn't have the shape of a man or a woman. There was no long beard, or pearly gates, nobody singing the psalms. Just a feeling that there's something there. I guessed that I passed out at the restaurant and I figured this was one of those bad dreams that you have just before you wake up and the hangover hits. I can feel this *thing* starting to talk to me but not with any words, nothing like that. I understand what he's thinking, but for the sake of this book, let's pretend that he's talking.

"Buddy Jones, huh?"

"Yes sir." I figured that if it wasn't a dream, I should act like this guy's in charge of the place.

"Buddy Jones, what are we going to do with you?"

"Do with me, sir?"

"Yeah, do with you. I got a soul here named Buddy Jones, and it's my job to evaluate you for further placement."

"Evaluate me?" Those are bigger words than I usually mess with. "Like a judgement?"

"Well, I don't particularly like that word. I'm looking for something, and I can't seem to find it."

"Like what?"

"Well, it's somewhat like a ledger, but not exactly. It's the best word I can find that you might know. I get to see all the *good things* you've done and of course all the bad things, to put it simply. Not that it's the final determination or anything, but I like to look at the raw data so to speak."

"Raw data?"

"You see, your whole life comes in a printout. Again, it's not really a printout but I try to use concepts that you might understand. With your lack of education, I have to bring it down to a certain level, if you know what I mean."

"I follow you. The good deeds and the bad deeds, the kindness and the meanness, the helpin' people, and the hurtin' people."

"Yeah, something like that. But we don't call balls and strikes here, just a reckoning, as you might say in Missouri."

"Missourah."

"Sorry, Missourah."

"So, what's the problem?"

"Well, like I said, we usually receive all the positives and all the negatives. All I got here is the negatives which goes on for several pages as you might expect, but of course, there are no real pages. The problem is that the list of good things is missing. I've made some calls, okay, they aren't really calls, they're more like communications to see if I can locate the missing data. This occurs only once in about two billion people. About one hundred billion people have ever lived on earth, so this has only happened to around fifty people since Moses brought the tablets down from Mt Sinai. Okay, he didn't physically bring down those tablets, but it makes for a great metaphor, if you know what a metaphor is. That's why no one can find Mt. Sinai to this day, because it never really existed." He continued on.

"You know, even Saddam Hussein and Gaddafi kissed a baby at a campaign rally, and Hitler once bought his girlfriend, Eva Braun, a pair of silk pajamas on Valentine's Day. So, you must have what we call a good list, but it's not really a list if you get the gist."

"I reckon I get the picture."

"Then let me briefly sum up the bad side of the ledger for you. Of course, this is just a superficial interpretation until I have time to give it more study. The long and the short of it indicates that you're an intolerant, small-minded, deceitful, son-of-a-bitch."

"What's intolerant mean?"

"A bigot."

"I think I could explain some of that. I jes don't like people who aren't like me, but the word *bigot* I think is jes a little too strong."

"You don't like anyone that doesn't look like you, or think like you, or eat what you like to eat. That's the definition of a bigot. Do you think they're evil people or do they frighten you, like your way of life or your race might not exist anymore?"

"Maybe sumpin like that. Maybe they scare me. I don't plumb know. I never gave it much thought. What about deceitful?"

"What about it?"

"I don't think I know that word."

"It means you're dishonest, a liar."

"Okay, no argument there. But you know, I've done a lot of good in my life, yessiree I have." This was the time to present my side of the things.

"Like what?"

"I often pat my dog, Pepper, and I give her treats, slices of cheddar cheese. I can list more than one old lady that I've helped across the street. Mrs. Clara Bottomley comes to mind right off the bat."

"I'll mark that down. Is that 'ey' in Bottomley?"

"Yes sir, I think so."

"Let me ask you something else?"

"Shoot."

"Do you know what a misogynist is?

"I sure do sir. It's a man who sorta puts women down. (I didn't want him to know that I just learnt the word.) But you know, I used to praise Penny a fair bit. There's lots of good things I said about her iffen I was horny and wanted to have sex with her."

"Can't that be said for every red-blooded American male?"

"Even Connie, early on, had her good points. I'd say good things about her pretty damn often. You know, she's not a bad cook. I mean if you like tofu and asparagus and parsnips, she's not a bad cook. If celery tastes better to you than salty French fries from McDonald's smothered in Heinz ketchup, she's a downright good cook. I bet her lefty transgender friend just loves the rabbit food she serves. Maybe you can tell me why Bernie puts up with her? He's a saint, but the last I heard, they don't have no saints. You know, the Jews. But who am I to tell you anything?" There was a silence. I wasn't sure if The Being had listened to me.

"I had the good fortune to see Mother Teresa when she came through," he finally said. "She had the opposite problem. There were no bad things to speak of. I had a record of a spider that she stepped on as a kid. Once, she rapped the knuckles of one of the children at her school when it was actually another kid who shot a spit ball at her, but at least the page wasn't blank. We expect people to have some good things and bad things. But you must understand, we're not here to judge you, we just like to see how things are going with the human race. Let's just say that an experiment in human behavior might describe our interest."

"The human race is a fuckin' experiment?"

"Well maybe *experiment* is too strong a word, but it's something that no human can even remotely comprehend. Your brain is just too small for the task, just like your dog Pepper. Does she know where her dog food comes from, or who pays the bills? You know, I'm just so perplexed that I can't' find your *good* page. You certainly can't be worse than some of the gentlemen that I've mentioned. I'd like to know more about you. Do you have a passion for anything or anyone? Some days, I can take the time to fill in some of the blank pages, but not today. Things are really hectic. There was an earthquake in Turkey yesterday and a hurricane in Haiti tomorrow."

"Before we go into all that sir, can I ask a question that's been eatin' at me?"

"Go right ahead, I'm listening."

"Am I dead?"

"That *is* a great question, and it's a difficult one to answer. I prefer to think of it as existence in World A, World B, or World C. Of course, those aren't their real names, but it'll suffice for our purposes. You've been living in World A. And let me put it this way, there's a good chance you'll be in World B or C before *Jack can jump over the candlestick,* if you know what I mean. But I need to find the dossier with the good things in it."

"So, is World A being alive?"

"Yes."

"And World B is *heaven*?"

"To be honest, I don't like to use a strong word like that. Some of my colleagues might, but I don't. It's not a useful term for us up here. Maybe for the human race, yes, but not for me. It's a little unrealistic, if I can just speak for myself."

"So now I'm kinda in limbo until you weigh everything and find out if the good outweighs the bad."

"Not exactly."

"I mean isn't that the point of religion, to git us sinners into heaven?" Isn't that what prayin' is for? I mean there's no point botherin' to pray if there ain't no heaven is there?"

"Well, maybe yes, and maybe no. Praying can make you feel good inside without necessarily affecting the ledger. As I told you, you humans want to put things in terms of black and white when actually it's not the way we work up here. We like grey."

"So, you don't weigh the bad with the good?"

"Well, someone's *bad* might be someone else's *good* and vice versa. Think of your Civil War that you're just learning about. Many charitable people fought for the South and some not-so- good people fought to abolish slavery. Almost everyone has a little of the good in them. That's why very few of you end up in World C."

"Would World C be like *hell*?"

"World C is currently on a planet near the star Enif. Its atmosphere is comparable to that of Uranus. The human concept of hell is completely erroneous to my way of thinking. Believe me, a lot of people would rather have their tootsies toasted than put up with the boredom of World B. Actually a few souls have…

"Have what?"

"I'm getting ahead of myself. There's no point going into a lot of detail until we're sure where you're heading. However, looking at the database that I have here of your transgressions, your chance of ending up in World C is a little worrisome."

"Just wait one second, you hain't heard the whole story." I heard a wailing ambulance sound. There were some muffled noises like he was talking to someone else.

"That tragedy in Turkey has all of us working overtime. I mean when you've got a billion galaxies to worry about, things are always hectic. Why don't you take a nap or look at the heavens, and I'll get back to you. I'm going to put you in the holding area for now. Well it's not really--"

"I know, it's not really a holding area."

I'm not sure how long I was there. I ran into a few stranded souls from galaxy MACS0647. They were hung up on their journey for one thing or another. One guy told me that he'd had forty-two previous lives. I met a female soul trying to find her way back to earth. She claimed she'd been one of Solomon's 1,000 wives and was still a virgin. I found that hard to believe.

I'll be honest. I was very, very scared. For the first time in my life, I prayed. They say every man in a foxhole gets religion. I can understand those sentiments. I prayed that if I could just come back for a little while, maybe I could get something on the *good* page. I knew it was empty. That's why it wasn't there. I felt ashamed and being ashamed is what I never was.

Eventually, The Being got back to me. He told me that I couldn't get to World B or C without a complete record. He was sending me back to World A and there'd be a thorough reckoning of the snafu. He wished me luck, although he said it wasn't really luck that decides what happens to us.

THIRTY-EIGHT

THE NEXT THING I knew, I was in the Intensive Care Unit of Atlanta Charity Hospital. There was a lot of beeping going on. I had a bunch of needles in my arm and there were tubes in my mouth and nose. I had no idea how I got there. Only later did I find out that my heart had stopped. According to the doctors, it started to fibrillate—a fancy word for quit beating. Instead of pumping, the old ticker just giggled like a bowl of jelly. Luckily, Richard and another doctor in the crowd beat on my chest until the paramedics showed up, and I'm thankful for that. They could have let me die after the speech I gave. Someone was bending over me, checking the connections on my heart monitor. The person squeezed my hand and I squeezed it back. Then I started to feel the pain of that tube in my throat. I felt like I couldn't breathe, like a hot poker was put down there to stir up a fire in my lungs.

"Just stay calm, Buddy," I heard the nurse telling me. Her voice was soft and gentle-like, almost like an angel's, but I wasn't with The Being any more. "You have a breathing tube going down into your lungs." I blinked my eyes and she came into focus. I wanted to ask her name, but of course I couldn't, on account of the hose in my throat. I tried to mouth some words, but this just made my coughing worse.

"My name is Suzy," the nurse said, like she'd read my mind. She brought over a white board with one of them grease pens. I wrote, HOW LONG HAVE I BEEN HERE?

"Three days," she answered. "That first night, your heart stopped beating five or six times and we had to perform electric shock each time to keep it going. We thought you might be brain dead, but yesterday you started waking up. Do you understand anything I've just said? Nod your head if you know what I'm talking about. I nodded my head.

I asked for the white board again and printed, WHY ARE YOU TAKING CARE OF AN SOB LIKE ME?

"Buddy, we don't get to choose who we care for. We take of all comers, even a son of a bitch like you." She laughed. Even in the Intensive Care Unit, they laugh.

That night, they took out the breathing tube and the next day Suzy and I started to talk. She'd been a nurse for 25 years, all of it working in Intensive Care, or the Unit, as I heard it called. It's then that I noticed that she was kinda cute, maybe more funny than cute. She was way out of my league as far as brains and stuff, but taking that out of the picture actually made it easier to talk to her. For the first time in my life, other than my mother, and this might be hard for someone to believe, she wasn't a sex object to be accepted or rejected based on the way she looked.

I talked about where I grew up and shit like that. I tried to put on the best face that I could about my life. I rambled on about my Grandma Bess and her chocolate cake and all. You can figure I left out my time with the mob, and Dexter, and jail. I told her that I'd been at a party to celebrate my daughter's marriage, and that I hadn't seen her for almost thirty years. I didn't mention the asshole speech that I'd made, or my fight with Floyd, or the fact that I was homeless and didn't have a pot to piss in except for the pee jug that was hanging on the rails of the bed. I talked to her about the grocery store in Middleberg, and that I'd been the manager there for ten years. What was I going to tell her? That I cleaned the toilet and washed the floors?

Bernie stopped in once or twice when I was in the Unit. I thought that was pretty nice of him. He didn't have to do it after all the shit I did, and the lies I told. April never came. I can't blame her for that. I asked about Hazel, not because I cared to see her, but just cause I wanted to know if she was still a couple with Connie. Bernie said she was, but it was only a week since my heart attack so I wasn't surprised. He had a pained look on his face, and I knew it was a stupid thing to say.

The doctors came in every day. The name on my hospital wrist band was *Dr. David Goldstein*. The resident doctors did most of the work, checking your progress and whatnot, but the head guy made the decisions, and this was the guy you needed to talk to before he flew out of your room. I asked him one day if he was related to Jeremy Goldstein who did my colonoscopy in St. Louis, but he said no. He said Goldstein's were to doctors, like Smith's were to plumbers. He snickered, and I could see that he'd told that one before. One day he came in with a smile on his face.

"Buddy, you've made good progress. We're moving you upstairs to the cardiology unit."

"What kinda card games do they play up there?" Goldstein ignored my half-assed joke. I guess if it wasn't his joke, it wasn't funny.

"Do you drink much, Buddy?"

"Whaddya mean drink?"

"I mean like alcohol. Your liver tests are a little off."

"Naw, not much. In fact, I've really cut back except for the night I was brought in." *I'm not going to tell this joker 'bout all my business.*

"I'm going to perform a cardiac catheterization on you tomorrow now that you're stronger. If there's further blockage, I'll put in some more stents. There's always a risk of the heart fibrillating again, or a clot could be thrown off and cause a stroke which could paralyze you. There's a small chance you could die during the procedure. Fortunately, that's pretty rare." *Nowadays doctors need to cover their ass with a very large beach towel.*

"So, I can say no. And just go home." I saw Suzy standing behind him shaking her head like that's a bad choice.

"Yes, you can, but there's a risk of another attack and the next one could be fatal. If we can unblock some of the vessels, you've got a much better chance of living a while longer."

"Well, let's give it a shot. I wanna be in World A a little bit longer. I've got some things to attend to before I die." Goldstein had a puzzled look on his face.

The next day they wheeled me into the procedure room. Everyone was wearing those heavy lead aprons to keep the radiation off them, but not off me. They gave me some sedation and the next thing I knew, I was back in my room. I could move all my arms and legs, so I figured it went okay. Goldstein came back around five o'clock.

"Well Buddy, the news isn't too good. The major artery leading to your heart is partially clogged and you've got blockages in four of the smaller arteries including the stents that they put in a few years ago. One of your heart valves is leaking, and the heart muscle's been damaged. All those years of smoking, drinking and eating bad foods have taken their toll. You'll need an operation, a quadruple bypass and a valve replacement. That's your only chance of living longer than six months. Actually, you're damn lucky to be alive." I thought of The Being looking for my paper work.

"I'll have Dr. Simpson come by and talk to you tomorrow."

"Who's Dr. Simpson?"

"He's a cardiac surgeon. You could also go back to St. Louis and have it done there. It might be helpful to have some family around when you're recuperating." *What family?* "There's some fine surgeons at Washington University."

"Mind as well send Dr. Simpson up to see me. I've got as many close relatives here as in St. Louis." *Zero here and zero there.* Just then Bernie stopped by.

"Goldstein told me I'll need heart surgery," I said. "The ticker's in shit shape. He said I could go back to St. Louis, but I'm better off havin' it done here. If I go back, I might lose my nerve. He says I've got six months tops if they don't cut on me."

"I ran into him in the hallway just now. He told me the news," Bernie had that half- smile on his face that he probably used with his patients. "Mickey'th an excellent surgeon," he lisped. *How the fuck did he know? He's a goddamned psychiatrist.*

"Have you told April that I'm still here?"

"Yes, she knows."

"How's she doin'?"

"She's doing okay. They've moved into a starter home way out in the suburbs."

"So maybe that's why she ain't visited with me?"

"No, that isn't it."

"I didn't think so."

"She's very angry with you, and for good reason."

"Bernie, I was dead drunk. I'm ashamed at what I did. Tell her I wanna see her real bad and that I love her." *I can't believe I said that.*

"Did you ever think of calling her and telling her that?"

"I guess I'm afraid of her answer."

"What have you got to lose?"

"I guess I never thought of it that way. I was just thinkin' how disappointed I'd be if she told me to jump in the lake."

"You never know 'till you try."

"How's the pregnancy? She feelin' all right?"

"Yeah, it's going fine, Buddy. Well, I gotta be running, I still have a few consultations to see."

"Why waste your time with them crazy patients when you can make all that money on TV and writing books?"

"You know, I still enjoy talking to folks that need my help." That sounded real corny but coming from Bernie I could sort of believe it.

Just then there was a knock on the door. It was Suzy. "Whaddya doing here?" I asked.

"Oh, I like to visit my old patients. I kinda got attached to your redneck jokes." Some color creeped into her cheeks when she said that.

THIRTY-NINE

THE NEXT MORNING, Dr. Michael Simpson came by. He was wearing scrubs and a disposable paper hat with matching paper booties. He was dressed like a clown, but he had this stern look on his face, not someone who'd tell you a knock-knock joke or make a dog from a balloon. But who's in the mood for a laugh? I'm on my deathbed or sitting right next to it.

"Mr. Jones, I reviewed everything with Dr. Goldstein. I think we're set to go. I've got you on the schedule the day after tomorrow. It's a big operation and there's risks because of your weak heart, but I think you've got a better than 70-30 chance of pulling through."

Let's just wait one cotton picking minute here. I haven't said anything about consenting to this. Those odds mighta looked good to him, but not so hot to me. I'd lost many a Blackjack hand with odds better than that. But what real choice did I have? When faced with death, most of us choose life, the hell with World B and World C. "This is pretty risky, huh?"

"Of course, there's risks. I've put them all on the consent form that you'll be signing." Dagnabit, I don't really wanna know all the bad things that could happen to me. What could I do about it anyhow? I looked it over, something about cardiac arrest, cardiopulmonary failure, excessive hemorrhaging, cerebrovascular accident. I couldn't hardly read the words, never mind knowing what all that doctor mumbo jumbo meant.

That afternoon, I finally got the nerve to call April.

"Hello. Is that you Buddy?" Nowadays, you don't have to introduce yourself on the phone. Your number just comes up.

"Yes, honey it's me."

"Bernie told me that you'll need surgery."

"Yep. The old ticker needs an overhaul. It's kinda worn out. All them years of rotten livin' are catchin' up with me."

"I guess."

"Hey, congratulations to you. I hear you're going to be a mom."

"We're pretty excited about it."

"How's Doug?"

"Doug? You really want to know about Doug?" I could hear an edge in her voice. "Doug's a black man and my baby's going to be black too."

"Oh jeez, I'd like to forget about the party. I had too much to drink."

"You know I agonized for weeks before I invited you. I spoke to my psychologist six times before I had Mom make the call."

"Yeah, I remember you told me."

"I've cried every day since you've been in the hospital but not for you, for me. I'm just so ashamed that I had you come. Do you know how many people you insulted that night?"

"I just want you to know something if I don't make it through."

"What Buddy, what? Make it quick. I've got to go. I'm at work."

"I love you." I couldn't hold back a little sob, but I wasn't sure if she heard it.

"Well Buddy, thanks for saying that. That's nice of you," and she hung up. That's April for you. As much as I've been a fuckup, she still said thanks. That was enough for me. I thought I still might have a chance.

The rest of the day was spent with all sorts of junior and senior doctors poking and prodding and listening to my heart, what little there was left of it. The nurses hung up a bunch of antibiotics to prevent an infection. That night, they gave me a sleeping pill. It was still dark the next morning when they hauled me up to the operating room. I felt like a prisoner about to be executed. I guess the feeling isn't all that different, except I had a chance of coming out alive. I joked with the nurse attendant if I could get my favorite meal before I went up. He said I was NPO which meant I couldn't eat or drink anything. He didn't get the joke. The last I remember was Dr. Simpson's ice-blue eyes staring out from his mask.

FORTY

I WAS BACK in the room. The Being was close by, I could feel him. He seemed less in a hurry than before. I heard him humming. I knew it was Bach even though I couldn't tell you a damn thing that he wrote. Maybe I heard the tune in church.

"I see you're back, Buddy."

"Yes sir, I guess I am. I dunno why."

"You know when your full report didn't arrive, I presented your case to The Big Daddy."

"The Big Daddy? You never talked about him before."

"The early Greeks called him Chaos, and the Hindus called him Brahman. The Jews called him Yahweh. They weren't even close to describing the primordial presence except possibly Buddha who taught that a creator God didn't exist. He leaves most of the decisions to us, but he's available for consultations."

"How about Jesus, is he still around?"

"Fine young man, nothing against him. He came through here not long ago."

"Not long ago?"

"Well, two thousand years isn't much when we've been

around for infinity. He did a lot of good work for you fellows, if only you'd followed what he said instead of making up your own rules."

"So, what did he say?"

"Who, Jesus?"

"No, The Big Daddy." *Goddamnit my life's on the line here, or is it my death?*

"As I told you, I reviewed your circumstances with him. He told me to check for the paperwork again, still nothing. Then he suggested that maybe you'd never done anything good in your life and that's why the page was blank. I'd never thought of that before."

"That's hard to believe, sir. Didn't I tell you that I'd scratch my little mongrel under her chin from time to time, and I fed Cecil, my pet turtle pretty regularly when I was a kid and once Mrs. Bottomley..."

"Wait, something did come in this morning, something about your daughter. It says here that you told her you *loved* her yesterday. So now we have one thing to go on. It's not much, but like I said, I'm pretty lenient."

"So, World B is still a possibility?"

"I think it's fair to say it's still in the picture. Like I told you, it's a little more complicated than plusses and minuses. I'll know more after I get back from vacation. Even us supernatural fellows need a break from time to time."

When I woke up, I was back in the Unit. Suzy was tending to all my tubes, just as before, except I'd gained another one, a big sucker coming out of my chest. It was attached to a plastic can on the floor. That thing hurt like hell. I found my white board and started asking questions.

"HOW AM I DOING?"

"Okay, Buddy." I could see that smile on her lips, but no twinkle of the eyes. After that I went back to sleep and didn't wake up for a long while, like Rip Van Winkle. They told me it was a few weeks before I opened my eyes again. The breathing tube was now connected to a hole that they'd made in my windpipe. I had a tube to feed me going right into my stomach. Some white liquid goo was being pumped into it. Suzy wasn't there, so I figured it was the night nurse. They dim the lights in there after 9 p.m., but it's never completely dark. An intensive care unit is a lot like Vegas. It never closes down. There's green and red colors flashing and stuff beeping, but no slot machines. *There's bigger bets going on, bets on life and death.* I don't think the nurse knew I had woken up. I didn't ask any questions.

The Being was back in the room. "How's everything going?"

"Now that's a strange question. You're sposed to know everything."

"I was just trying to be nice, that's part of my job."

"How was the vacation?"

"Oh, pretty good. I needed a rest, well not really a rest as you might think of it." I was tired of those fucking *not reallys.*

"Where'd you go?"

"I found a wormhole and took a cruise of what you might call the *heavens.*"

"A wormhole?"

"What do you know about physics?"

"My mother would give me a physic when I was constipated. You ever try Castor oil?" He didn't laugh.

"A wormhole is a structure that connects two points in space-time, like a tunnel. It's consistent with Einstein's general theory of relativity. I thought they taught that in the high schools of America."

"I dunno, maybe the eleventh or twelfth grade or college. I never got that far."

"The Big Daddy was on the ship. He updated us on the latest developments in existentialism."

"You mean like an extension cord?" *What a cocksucker, throwing around them big words. If there's anything in the world worse than a bullshitter, it's a bullshitter from heaven.*

"Maybe," and he laughed.

"Did my name come up on this cruise you took?"

"As a matter of fact, it did. The Big Daddy made a remark, but maybe he was just kidding. I'm sorry to say I don't have a very good sense of humor, so it's hard for me to know when he's serious. All he said was four words in regard to you."

"And?" I was getting anxious. This was life or death.

"And what?"

"What were them four words for Chrissakes?"

"Excuse me Buddy, we'll have no blasphemy here."

"What were the words?" I yelled.

"He threw up his hands, okay, he doesn't really have hands, but then he said Buddy's *too mean to die*. Now I don't know how to take that, but I'm sending you back for now. Once all your paperwork comes in, I'll take it up to The Big Daddy, but you're safe in World A for now.

FORTY-ONE

I WAS BACK IN THE UNIT. All the lights were on, so it must have been daytime. Suzy was back. All the tubes were still in me. I took that as a bad sign. I'd got more hoses in me than a goddamned fire truck. Some were putting stuff in and some were taking stuff out. You've got to admire the human body, that it needs this many tubes to keep it going when it's on the blink. I mean when things are good, you eat, drink, breathe, piss, and crap, and the average dick, of which I include myself, doesn't ever think too much about it. I guess I was barely alive. Suzy could see my eyes were open.

"Buddy, do you know where you are?" I nodded my head. "You've been here three weeks. You've been very sick." I nodded my head again.

"After the operation you had a lot of bleeding from the heart. Just when we thought we had that under control, your blood stopped clotting, then you started hemorrhaging from everywhere else. You've turned a bright yellow. Look at your hands." I looked at my hands. She wasn't kidding. I had bananas for arms and my clenched fists looked like lemons.

"Your liver failed after the surgery. You went into a coma because it wasn't clearing the impurities in your blood. Dr.

Mukhopadhyay, the liver specialist, said that the stress of the major surgery was too much for your liver to handle, and it shut down." I shrugged my shoulders. "Only a few days ago, the doctors talked about pulling the plug." When the nurses and doctors talk about pulling the plug, that's not a joke. That means your life goes down the drain, just like dirty water in a bathtub.

"We needed April's permission because she's the next of kin. She told us to keep going a little while longer." I raised my eyebrows. "She's been here a few times," Suzy said. I raised my eyebrows higher. *Wow, what did I do to deserve that?*

I don't want to dwell on all the details, but it took another three weeks before I was out of the Unit. There were some setbacks which I'm not going to bore anyone with, because I couldn't really understand most of what was going on. My mind is pretty hazy for the whole thing. That's what Suzy said happens, that you forget a lot of it, and it's probably for the good. All I remember was Suzy taking care of me, Suzy changing my bedpan, Suzy fixing my IV, and Suzy giving me a back rub. Without the tubes and Suzy, I would have been dead, no matter how fucking mean or not mean I was.

I started to get well enough so I could sit in a chair, and I began telling Suzy and the others all my redneck jokes. They even laughed at some of them. I had names for all the doctors, like Porky and Hairy and Stinky and Roseanne. Suzy always showed up for work with a positive attitude, as if that was the day I was going to get out of there. One day I asked her, "Are you that cheerful with your husband *before* you leave for work?"

"I don't have a husband anymore."

"That must be some kinda louse that would walk out on someone like you?" I joked.

"He didn't walk out. He died."

"Jeez, that was stupid of me. I'm sorry."

"That's okay. You didn't know. He was a cop. He was shot during a robbery, but I'm lucky enough to have two wonderful daughters. One is a medical student in Nashville, and the other one's an accountant. She's got a two-year-old, a little girl."

Before they shipped me out of intensive care, Dr. Mukhopadhyay came by with the interns. "Buddy, you're one lucky guy to have pulled through this."

"I gotta thank you and all the other docs and nurses."

"Your liver was severely damaged by all that alcohol. You must have been drinking pretty heavily before you got here." Of course he was right about all that drinking before I got sick, and if you've paid attention while reading this book, you'll know that I did a shitload of boozing before that, probably enough beer and whiskey bottles to circle the earth more than once. I forgot to mention the gin that I drank every night so I could sleep. I kidded myself that it was only one glass, but I filled an eight-ounce sucker to the brim. I never really counted that as drinking. I chalked it up as medicine to help me sleep.

"We gave you a drug called prednisolone which has been around for over 60 years. Maybe it helped in your case or maybe the liver just got better on its own. There's not much we can do if your liver gives up the ghost. We just hope you don't become one." He let out with this big belly laugh, this guy that they all called Dr. Muko. He thought he was pretty funny. Some of the interns snickered, I guess they had to.

They moved me to what they called a *step-down unit*, only it was five floors higher. Suzy wasn't my nurse any more, but she came by to say hello every few days. I was thankful for that. Coming from me, you might think that was my usual bullshit, but it wasn't. Slowly, they took out all the tubes except the one that was feeding me. It took me another three or four weeks before they took that one out. By then, I was at the nursing home.

FORTY-TWO

SO, WHAT IN DAMNATION (or out of damnation) was I going to do with the rest of my life? If there was to be much of the rest of my life? I'd almost died twice in the space of six weeks. My heart was stronger, and my liver had got back some of its mojo, but Dr. Muko warned me that any more boozing, and it would check out for good. I was still weaker than a flea without a dog when they shipped me to the Peach Valley Extended Care Facility. I soon found out that *extended care facility* was another name for a nursing home. Before that it was called an *old folks home*, but in the politically correct world it's got this new name. Shit, if you made it to old, you shouldn't be upset that you're in a home.

One day, Penny called and the operator connected her to the phone in my room.

"Buddy, is that you? It's Penny."

"Hi there. How ya doin'?"

"Just fine. When you didn't show up at the trailer, I began to worry and I called Connie. She told me about your heart surgery and your liver failing."

"Yep. All that drinkin' finally caught up with me. You were right. My liver specialist told me that beer was just as bad as the hard stuff."

"I tried to tell you, Buddy."

"Yes, you did. I'm sorry I was so bone-headed not to listen to you. And I'm sorry about a lot of other things too."

"That sounds strange coming from you. You know, you're just about the stubbornest man I ever met."

"And the meanest."

"Well you said it, I didn't."

"Hey, why don't you drive down and pick me up? Maybe we could find a new place before the trailer completely falls apart."

"Sorry Buddy, I can't do that. You see ... Gloria and I are..." there was a little pause on the other end, "a couple."

"Like lesbians?" Jiminy, there's nothing that surprises me anymore.

"Something like that."

"And to think, all this time, I thought it was just me that was looking at her tits." No laughter on her end.

"I called to tell you that if you give me your mailing address, I'll send along your Social Security money that's built up since you've been gone. I'll ship your clothes and your fishing gear and your model trains too."

"Okay, send the clothes, but sell the rest of that crap or give it away. I'll connect you back to the operator. She can give you my address here at the home."

"Thanks Buddy. And get well, you hear."

"I'll do my best and take care of yerself."

I guess I can't blame her for finding someone else, even if it was a woman. I'd always felt that men could be stupid about a few things, like washing clothes and eating right, but not most things. Now I've come to find that I don't know much about a lot of stuff. Even the stuff I should know, I don't no. But what the heck, Penny just wasn't my type.

A few days later April stopped by. This was the first time she'd been there since I'd been out of the coma. She'd called the day before and asked if she could come. Of course, I said yes. She looked very pregnant in the tight jersey that the new mothers wear nowadays.

"Hi, Buddy."

"Hi, sweetheart." I could tell she was a little edgy to be there.

"How're you feeling? You look so much better." She got up close to me and looked into my eyes. "You're not yellow anymore."

"You know, I've been thinking about us a lot."

"Us?"

"Yeah, like when I took you to the park and pushed you on the swing. It seemed like I could push you forever. You never got tired of it."

"You always bought me an ice cream before we went home. Mom wondered why I didn't want my dinner. You said it was our little secret."

"You remembered that? I'd plumb forgot."

"Oh, there's so much that a kid remembers. I bet it's the same way with your childhood."

"Yeah, I guess so, but I also remember some of the bad things."

"So do I. Like when you left."

I wish I hadn't said anything about the bad things.

"Buddy, I need to ask you a question."

"What's that, sweetheart?"

That's the second time I called her that. I kinda liked the

sound of it.

"Why do you tell lies?"

"Lies? Like what?"

"Like why'd you say you were robbed by a black man?"

"That was stupid. I was drunk."

"You told me that before you got drunk."

"I did? I don't remember it."

"And why'd you tell me you'd visit me in Atlanta and you never came?" Her eyes filled with tears.

"I can explain that."

"What explanation could possibly make sense to an eight-year-old?" I'm sorry to say, that triggered my anger zone, not at April, but at Connie.

"Cuz your mother was a piece of shit that's why. She had lawyers and a sheriff after me, tryin' to take all my money away. That's why Goddamnit!"

"That's *not* good enough, Buddy. It's always someone else's fault, isn't it?"

"Well, when it comes to me and your mother, it is her fault. I'da come if she'd let me." April got up to leave. "I'm sorry. I've fucked up your life and I'm sorry!" I was yelling as she slammed the door behind her.

FORTY-THREE

AFTER SIX WEEKS, I'd had all the rehab I could stand. In fact, not only could I stand, I could walk almost half a mile. Bernie visited me a few times. It turned out that he'd been right about Hazel and Connie. Hazel moved in with the producer of Bernie's TV show in L.A. The show got cancelled before it made it on the air, so he and Connie weren't flying out there anymore. Connie was back on her bipolar meds. Bernie said she was behaving herself, whatever that meant. I asked if she minded him coming to see me. He said she didn't care as long as she didn't have to come. It sounded like they were just sticking it out, like some people do. I always wondered why he visited at all, after the ass I'd made of myself. He told me a few times that I needed some counselling for my alcoholism and my anger problem. I think he wanted me to see a therapist for April's sake. Maybe he wanted to be my psychiatrist or maybe deep down he had a bond with me, our hatred of Connie, but I don't know that for sure.

One real nice evening in early May, Bernie and I were sitting outside in the courtyard drinking diet Cokes when this guy, Ike Wilson, came up to us. He had an artificial leg and was getting rehab so he could walk again. We'd had breakfast together a few times since I'd been there. I told him about my liver and how they thought I wouldn't pull through. He liked my joke about it not being called a *dier.* I thought the guy looked familiar, but hey, who would I know in Atlanta? He kinda squinted at Bernie. Then he limped up closer with his walker, about six inches from his face.

"You the man. You the man, ain't you?" He grabbed Bernie's hand and kept shaking it. Then he started to lose his balance. Bernie stood up and grabbed him so he wouldn't fall. "I'll never forget you, as long as I live, never!"

"You're mithtaken. We've never met. My name is Levine, Dr. Bernard Levine."

"I don't know your name nosiree, but you saved my life and my granddaughter's life that day."

"What day?"

"That day I was beggin' on Irwin Ave. You gave me a twenty-dollar bill. I had that real long white beard, kinda looked like Santa Claus." Bernie and I realized that he's the guy.

"We were so hungry. You know my daughter had been arrested for heroin trafficking and left me with a three-year-old grandkid. That twenty bought us a hot meal that day and the next. I'll never forget that."

"I'm glad I could help out, but to be truthful, I didn't have a smaller bill in my wallet to give you." Good old honest Bernie.

"We didn't get much food after that. I neglected my diabetes, and they had to amputate my leg last month."

"What happened to your granddaughter?" Bernie asked.

"She's in a foster home. I'm hoping when I can walk again, I can get a place for us to stay." Then he looked at me. "Shit, now I remember. You were there, too. You made a face at me and walked away. They were right about you." He laughed.

FORTY-FOUR

SUZY PHONED ME about two weeks after I'd been at Peach Valley. She asked if she could stop by. My heart started to race, and I said okay. In fact, it was a damn sight better than okay. The next morning, the van at the home drove me to a barbershop. I got a nice haircut and a close shave. With my Social Security money, I went to Walmart and bought a new pair of blue jeans and a couple of them soft tee shirts. I sprung for the five-dollar ones made in Mexico over the two-dollars tees from Vietnam.

When Suzy arrived, I could see she had spruced herself up. She looked different from what I remembered in the hospital. She had a little more makeup on, some of that glossy lipstick, and mascara around the eyelids.

"Thanks for letting me come, Buddy."

"Letting you come? Why I plumb wanted you to come. I sure did."

"Well, it's something I seldom do."

"Seldom do what?"

"Visit my patients from the Unit, but I kept thinking about you and wondering how you were doing with your rehab."

"I guess you don't often get the chance to visit someone who was in there as long as me. Most of 'em don't make it."

"No, that's not it. I just don't let myself get emotionally attached to patients. It interferes with me doing my job."

"So what made me different?"

"I'm not sure. You know you're just about the funniest patient we've ever had with all you went through. The other nurses said the same thing, about how brave you were." Her face turned red and I thought she might cry.

"Was I cracking jokes when I was in a coma?" She laughed. I could always make her laugh.

"Yes, even then Buddy." And I laughed too. I asked about all the other people that worked with her, the nurses, the techs, the interns and the top brass. She said they all missed me, and she missed me too, then she looked down at her lap embarrassed-like and the blush returned to her face. Jeez, all those people missing fucked-up Buddy Jones? Before she left, she gave me a hug. God damnit, I don't know why, but I started to sob. I didn't want to let her go.

Just before I was released from the nursing home, she invited me for dinner at her house. She told me her family would be there. I could tell it was a big deal for her, introducing them to her new friend, maybe future boyfriend. When she picked me up that day, she was real serious. I could see she something was bothering her.

"Buddy, I need to fill you in on a few things."

"Shoot."

"My daughter's husband is of mixed-race heritage. He's part black and part Latino."

"So what?"

"Well, I just thought you should know."

"Why, cuz I'm a bigoted redneck?"

"Well, no, I don't believe you're like that, but I thought you should know. He's light-skinned and..."

"So, I cain't be myself. Is that it?"

"Well, I don't mean that, but the jokes and all..."

"I'm just tryin' to be funny. Why the fuck is everyone's so sensitive to a few hillbilly stories? I was drunk at April's party and I'm ashamed of it, but I didn't mean nothing by it."

"I believe you and don't be offended but—"

"But what?"

"My daughters and my son-in-law really don't like that kind of stuff."

"Okay, I got it. Don't tell any of my jokes in front of them."

"Thanks Buddy."

The dinner that night went pretty well. I kept my mouth shut for the most part which you can appreciate is kinda hard for me to do. No opinions and no jokes. It helped that I was no longer on the hooch. Her daughter, the doctor, hardly talked. I could see she didn't approve of me. The accountant looked a lot like Suzy, same eyes, same smile. Her husband was one of those left-wing liberals. He wanted more immigrants to pour into this country. That's didn't surprise me. They had a little girl named Rosalina, who I got to admit was as cute as a button. She called me *Bubby.*

The social worker came by to see me a few weeks before my discharge. She let me know that I could qualify for a low-rent apartment not far from where Peach Valley was located. She asked me if I knew anything about cooking, cleaning, grocery shopping or washing clothes. I told her no, that was woman's work, and I wasn't much good at any of it. But guess what? It turned out that I didn't need to learn about those things if I didn't want to. Suzy invited me to stay in the vacant basement room where her daughter had lived before she left for medical school. So you see, I wasn't kidding when I said that I had a certain way with women, even a brilliant gal like Suzy.

FORTY-FIVE

A FEW MONTHS went by and I sort of settled into a routine. I guess you must've already figured that I didn't stay in that basement room for long. Pretty soon, Suzy invited me into bed with her and that's where I stayed. I got to admit, them first few months we were really in love, helped by some generous doses of Viagra.

I hit it off real good with little Rosalina, too. Suzie's daughter would bring her over on Wednesdays when the nanny was off, and I'd babysit her. We'd go to the park near the house where she'd swing or play on the jungle gym. It reminded me of my time with April. She liked strawberry ice cream just like April did. The rest of the days, I tried to help out around the house if Suzy was at work. I got to admit, I did learn to vacuum and empty the dishwasher. Once in a while, I even washed some clothes.

Suzy was nice enough to put my name on her credit card and I appreciated that. I was still locked out of them on account of my poor credit. Ike Wilson rented a place not far from us. He was getting around pretty good on his artificial limb. He would come to the park with his granddaughter, who was about the same age as Rosalina. It turned out that he'd done some time as well, so we had lots to talk about. Sometimes, he'd come over to the house with his grandkid, and we'd play checkers while they played with Rosalina's toys. I never touched any alcohol, but I gotta admit I did bum a few cigarettes from Ike who had started smoking again despite having his leg amputated.

I mailed Floyd a check for the money that he'd loaned me on our trip. Suzy helped me write him a note telling him how bad I felt about what happened. He cashed the check, but he never got back to me. Some people don't forget, and I hold it against him to this day.

April gave birth to a little girl that they named Beatrice after good old Bernie. Suzy and I went over to their house a few weeks after she got home from the hospital. Doug was a good host, better than he needed to be. He offered me an alcohol-free beer, but I asked for a Diet Coke. I got to admit, he's not a bad guy. I just wish I'd gotten to meet him before the night of the party. Things might have turned out different. April let me hold little Beatrice, but I could see in her eyes that she was uncomfortable with me being there. I told her I'd come over and babysit when she was a little older, and Suzy offered that I did a real good job with Rosalina. April said she'd think about it, but she didn't say definitely yes.

I decided to go back to work. Dr. Muko told me that my liver was working pretty close to normal but it was permanently scarred—he called it cirrhosis. He warned that it'd go haywire again if I started back on the booze. I got a part-time job at Kroger's working mostly weekends. Suzy took out a second car loan to buy me a used Toyota Corolla, so I could get to work. I enjoyed talking it up with the customers, and helping the seniors out to their cars, just like I'd done in Middleberg.

The only problem was that at ten dollars an hour, it didn't do that much to help with paying the bills, but Suzy was cheerful about it. My Social Security money went to pay down my hospital and doctor bills which were considerable, even with my Medicare. I was only able to work a few months. I was carrying a carton of eggplants when I slipped on a wet floor in the produce aisle. I felt a terrible jolt in my back. They helped me into my car and I never went back. I slept in a recliner for three months.

When I started feeling better, Ike and I got the idea to drive to a Harrah's in North Carolina to do a little gambling, just to have some fun. I never knew until then that there weren't casinos in Georgia. I brought along five hundred bucks that I took out of my checking account. I only planned to play with a hundred, and we'd be back before Suzy got home from the evening shift. Things didn't go well right off the bat, and I lost the whole five hundred plus three hundred more that I borrowed from Ike who had struck it rich at the slots. When we rolled back in about 3 a.m., Suzy had a fit. I told her we'd gone fishing and that when we tried to start the car to come home, the battery was dead, and we had to wait several hours for a tow truck. That was a good old-fashioned humdinger of a falsehood that I never should have told.

By then, the football season was in full swing. Ike got me in touch with a local bookie, and I started going to bars and watching the games on TV while Suzy was at work or visiting her daughters. Pretty soon, I was about one or two grand in the hole from my football wagering. I told Suzie that I couldn't pitch in any more money for the house expenses, because I'd loaned Ike some cash to help get his daughter into a drug rehab. Ike was good enough to go along with my story although Suzy didn't speak to me for a few weeks. I took that as a sign that she didn't really believe me.

FORTY-SIX

ONE DAY, DEXTER ARRIVED in town. I never thought I'd hear from him again. He was staying at the Atlanta Hilton of all places. Against my better judgement, I told him to come on over, but I made sure that Suzy was at work before he showed his face at her house. I'd never told her much about Dexter, and I figured maybe leave it that way.

Ol' Dex hadn't changed much except his hair was thinner on top and had turned pretty much all white. He had on a dark suit and tie with them fancy shoes that he liked to wear.

"Good to see you, Buddy boy."

"Good to see you, Dex." We hugged like long lost brothers, which we were.

"How ya feelin'?" he asked.

"The doctors are surprised at how well I'm doin'. Been off the booze for six months."

"That's gotta be a record for you."

"Yeah probably, since I was seventeen."

"I just came from Middleberg. I stopped by to see you there. I didn't realize that you warn't livin' there no more. I had no idea you'd been sick. If I had, I would've stopped by a lot sooner. As soon as Penny told me where you were, I just had to see you." Knowing Dexter like I did, I had no idea if any of that was true.

"Well that's plumb nice of you, Dex."

"I met Gloria over at Penny's. She got one big set of knockers, ain't she? I'm fixin' to call her when I get back there."

"I wouldn't move too fast on her."

"Why's that?"

"Cuz she's got a girlfriend."

"Penny and Gloria?"

"No shit, Sherlock. You were always pretty dumb about them things. You still in Hawaii?"

"Nope. I moved to New Mexico 'bout six months ago. Couldn't stand livin' there after Doris passed on."

"Uncle Waldo told me sumpin 'bout a car accident a few years back. I guess I didn't feel that bad to hear it after she dumped me for you. I always wondered if you told her that it was all my idea to take her money."

"That's complete bullshit Buddy and you know it. When we got to Vegas she just threw herself at me. What could I do?" *Dexter could lie better than anyone I ever met, including myself.*

"So, how'd it happen?"

"How'd what happen?"

"How'd she die?" I asked.

"We were living on the Big Island in Hawaii. Our home was on top of a mountain with a beautiful view of the ocean. She was on the way to the hairdresser when she went off the road and down an embankment. Broke her neck."

"I always remember Doris as a pretty careful driver. I'm real surprised she'd run herself off the road."

"The car burned up pretty bad. The cops couldn't be sure what caused it."

"Maybe the brakes failed."

"Who knows?'

"Where were you at the time?" I asked.

"At home. I was waiting for her to get back, so we could go out for dinner. It was our fifth wedding anniversary."

"So, I guess you had nuthin to do with the accident?"

"Buddy, you're a son of a bitch to ask a question like that."

"And her money?"

"Oh, we'd spent most of it by then."

"Was there was an insurance policy?"

"Sure there was."

"I'm guessin' you've run through all that money too." Dexter didn't answer. He didn't want to talk about it anymore.

"So, are you living by yourself in New Mexico?"

"Guess what? I've hooked back up with Tiger."

"Shit Dex, she's trouble, always was and always will be."

"So whadda *you* doin' with yourself, other than mooching off other women?"

"Now don't go there with that. Suzy was my nurse in intensive care when I was in a coma. She saved my life."

"You've moved in with her, and now you're going to spoil that by taking all her money."

"God damnit Dexter, why are you such an ass?"

"Are you workin'?" he asked.

"Until I hurt my back."

"Still betting on football?"

"Oh, some."

"I bet you could use some cash." Dexter always knew more about me that I knew about myself.

"No, I don't. I've been hittin' it pretty big on Sundays this year."

"You know, things've never gone better than down in New Mexico. We own a real nice house in Las Cruces, right on the border."

"And whaddya doin' there? Volunteer work for the local Red Cross?" Dexter laughed. He liked that one.

"Smugglin'."

"Whaddya smugglin'?"

"Mostly heroin and fentanyl, some pills."

"The Outfit involved?"

"Nope. This is our own operation. Ziggy Zignorelli and me are partners. We set this thing up far away from the mob. The money's fantastic for just a little bit of work. You know, we could use some help."

"How much you pay?" I got no intention of working with Dexter again, but hey, he's my brother, and he's come all the way from New Mexico to see me.

"Ten thousand cash for each run over the border. Three runs a week is thirty grand. In six months that's over a half a million smackeroos. We've set up a legit business in Phoenix selling imported beef. We bring in cattle from Mexico on eighteen-wheelers and hide the dope in the animal feed. What border guard's gonna enter one of them pens with twenty steers weighing over a thousand pounds each? You don't even need to drive the truck all the way to Phoenix. Just pick up the animals in Juarez and drop 'em off in Las Cruces. You work for six months then you can quit. You can fly back here every other weekend if you want. We'll even pay for that."

"So just temporary. No long-term commitment."

"No, nuthin like that. I've done four runs myself. I've got forty grand in a bank account in Panama."

"Why me? Just to screw me again?"

"Cause you're my brother and I owe you. You know what they say, *blood is thicker than water.* I'll be busy setting up our slaughter house on this side of the border."

"You know Dex, as much as I need the money, I don't think I can do that to Penny."

"Penny?"

"I meant Suzy. Fuck, she saved my life. I'da been dead without her."

"I'll tell you what. I'm flying back to Las Cruces first thing in the mornin'. I'll call you tomorrow or the next day, after I talk to Ziggy and firm everything up."

FORTY-SEVEN

AS I WAITED for Dexter's call, I pondered on what I should do. I was at a crossroad in my life and as Yogi Berra once said, *when you come to a fork in the road, take it.* I knew that breaking the law could get me in jail again and that no matter how good the deal seemed, it might not be so good after I got there. And why would my half-brother want *me* to do it? Why wouldn't he keep doing it himself if the money was so good? I thought about Penny and Floyd and Bernie and all the other people that had helped me on my journey. I thought about April, and how it felt to hold my grandchild. I thought about how Suzy had fought to save my life. But God damnit, a half a million bucks in six months! Can you blame me? More money than I ever made in my entire life.

Three days later was a Saturday, and I hadn't heard from Dexter. I sat on the front porch waiting for the call, Ike was sitting next to me. I'd invited him over because he knew a lot about smuggling. His first jail term was related to that. He just closed his eyes and kept quiet as I told him about Dexter's fantastic offer. Then he spoke.

"Buddy, the money might be just too good to pass up, but is Dexter a liar and a conniver like you is?"

"At times, I guess. But I won't know until I take the job, will I?"

"No, I guess you won't." Then we sat silent again.

"Buddy, can I tell you something?"

"Shoot."

"You know the twenty dollars that Bernie gave me when I was begging? You were right about it."

"Right?"

"I spent ten dollars on food for the granddaughter and me that day, but I spent the other ten on a bottle of rotgut whiskey."

"No, shit."

"I guess once a drunk always a drunk. That's why I'll probably end up in World C with you."

"I figured you'd been up there."

"Yep, same time you were there, right after I had my leg removed. The Being told me about your missing sheet. He wanted me to keep an eye on you, so he could make a final decision, but I guess The Big Daddy had it right all along."

"Right about what?"

"About you being *too mean to die.*"

My cell rung. It was Dexter's number. I hung up without answering it, because just then I saw Suzy driving up the street. I helped her carry the groceries into the house. She said thank you, but she didn't talk too much to me anymore, and she'd quit laughing at my jokes awhile back. She said she had a headache and went upstairs to the bedroom and closed the door. I told Ike goodbye and went down to the room in the basement. I locked the door. Then I called back. Dexter didn't answer. Tiger did.

"Who's this?" she said in a sobbing voice.

"It's me, Buddy, Buddy Jones, Dexter's brother. Remember? Can you go get Dexter and put him on the line? I got sumpin to tell him."

"I can't."

"It's pretty important Tiger. I got to talk to him about the job he offered me. I wanna know when I can start."

"He can't, Buddy. He's dead. Dexter's dead."

"Dead? I just saw him a few days ago here in Atlanta. He looked just fine."

"He was taking out the garbage last night when a car came by and filled his innards with ten bullets. Ziggy's not answering his cell phone, so I'm dialing Dexter's recent phone calls to see if I can find out what happened." She broke down bawling.

"I can't help you there Tiger, I'm sorry."

"Dex and Ziggy were trying to start their own operation without the Mob. I knew it was risky, and they'd never get away with it. Dex told me that they were hiring more people for the dangerous border work, then we'd move to Phoenix to count our money."

I hung up. As it turned out, *the fork in the road that I wanted to take wasn't no fork at all.*

EPILOGUE

WELL, I'VE BEEN BACK in Middleberg about six months. As you probably might have figured, Suzy and I split not long after the phone call. A few weeks after Dex passed away, one of the goons from the gambling operation came to the door while I was at the park with Ike and the kids. He filled in Suzy about how much money I owed, and what would happen to me and her, if it didn't get paid. She wrote the man a check for $10,000. She told him that was all that was left in her savings account, and he agreed to forget the rest of the $15,000 that was due. I thought of calling April, and Bernie too, before I left. But you know what? I didn't need their lecturing how I messed things up with Suzy. Hey, I wanted to stay. She kicked me out.

I took a bus back to St. Louis. Good old Stu Lumpkin was nice enough to pick me up at the station and drive me back to the trailer which had been vacant since Penny and Gloria had found a better place to live.

Nowadays, I just sit outside on a lawn chair and play with my little dog Salty, a runt that Stu gave me from a litter off his bitch. I do my own cooking, cleaning and washing that I learnt from Suzy. I got to admit that I drink some beer once in a while, even though it might be the end of me. *But shit, I gotta have some fun before I leave this world, don't I?* I still like my Fox News, but now, instead of the big forty-eight incher, I only got a crummy little Motorola that I bought second hand from the junk dealer. Trump's still the president and trying to drain the swamp, only his hose isn't big enough. When he gives a speech, I can just feel that he's talking to me, like he's one of us, only he ain't. He's a bullshitter. But maybe that's what I like about him. He's a bullshitter like me.

Penny and Gloria opened a diner serving breakfast and lunch and it's pretty popular. Every Sunday, I go over there and get some waffles and eggs and them plump pork sausages that I'm partial to, smothered in ketchup. They make me pay with cash in advance, and I can't say I blame them. I noticed that Penny's removed the *Trump-Pence* and the *Nobama* bumper stickers from her truck. She's replaced it with one that got all the religious symbols that spell COEXIST. She doesn't know anything about any of those other religions, take it from me. Pepper hangs out at the restaurant and barks at the customers, but she doesn't seem to remember me.

I met the new cashier at the grocery store the other day. She just settled here from Oklahoma. Her name is Frieda, she's divorced with a seventeen-year-old son. I asked her if she knew her multiplication tables because her boss, Billy MacConkey, might spring a surprise quiz on her. She just giggled. She's dark and fat but kinda pretty. I can't tell if she's Indian or a Mexican, but who gives a damn. This is a white man's country and we started it, but I've learned that some immigrants can be pretty decent people as long as there aren't too many of them, and that goes for the blacks, too. Like I said in the beginning, deep down there's no prejudice in old Buddy Jones' bones. Maybe I'll call April on her birthday next year.

ABOUT THE AUTHOR

David Margolis MD retired from the practice of gastroenterology in 2013 to become a full time writer. His stories have appeared in *The Canadian Medical Association Journal*, *JAMA: Internal Medicine*, *Missouri Medicine*, *HumorPress.com*, *Long Story Short*, *Still Crazy*, and *The Jewish Light of St. Louis*. A book of humorous poems and short stories, *Looking Behind: The Gaseous Life of a Gastroenterologist* was published in 2013. A recent poem "What's a Filibuster" recently appeared in the publication of the *Society of Classical Poets*. He's published two previous novels, *The Myth of Dr. Kugelman* and *The Plumber's Wrench*. He resides in St. Louis, MO with his wife Laura, two rescue kids, three small rescue dogs, and a set of golf clubs.

CPSIA information can be obtained
at www.ICGtesting.com
Printed in the USA
FSHW011401160319
56320FS